THE
FIREMAN'S
FAIR

THE FIREMAN'S FAIR

JOSEPHINE HUMPHREYS

VIKING

VIKING
Published by the Penguin Group
Viking Penguin, a division of Penguin Books USA Inc.,
375 Hudson Street, New York, New York 10014, U.S.A.
Penguin Books Ltd, 27 Wrights Lane, London W8 5TZ, England
Penguin Books Australia Ltd, Ringwood, Victoria, Australia
Penguin Books Canada Ltd, 2801 John Street, Markham, Ontario,
Canada L3R 1B4
Penguin Books (N.Z.) Ltd, 182–190 Wairau Road, Auckland 10, New Zealand

Penguin Books Ltd, Registered Offices: Harmondsworth, Middlesex, England

First published in 1991 by Viking Penguin, a division of Penguin Books USA Inc.

10 9 8 7 6 5 4 3 2 1

PUBLISHER'S NOTE
This is a work of fiction. Names, characters, places, and incidents
either are the product of the author's imagination or are used
fictitiously, and any resemblance to actual persons, living or
dead, events, or locales is entirely coincidental.

Grateful acknowledgment is made for permission to reprint
excerpts from the following copyrighted works:
"The Best Things in Life are Free" by Lew Brown, Ray
Henderson and B. G. DeSylva. © 1927 Chappell & Co.
(Renewed), Ray Henderson Music & Stephen Ballentine
Music. All rights reserved. Used by permission.
"You Were Only Fooling," words by Billy Faber and
Fred Meadows and music by Larry Fotina. © 1948
Shapiro, Bernstein & Co., Inc., New York, renewed.
Used by permission.
"With My Eyes Wide Open, I'm Dreaming" by
Mack Gordon and Harry Revel. © 1934 WB Music Corp.
(Renewed). All rights reserved. Used by permission.

LIBRARY OF CONGRESS CATALOGING IN PUBLICATION DATA
Humphreys, Josephine.
The fireman's fair / Josephine Humphreys.
p.   cm.
ISBN 0–670–83907–8
I. Title.
PS3558.U4656F57   1991
813'.54—dc20   90–50575

Printed in the United States of America
Set in Granjon
Designed by Ann Gold

FOR REYNOLDS PRICE

THE
FIREMAN'S
FAIR

CHAPTER 1

In his lawn chair under the Carolina sun, Rob Wyatt sat recuperating, keeping an eye on what was out there—his ruined island town, the blue yonder—as if recovery could be gained by the old southern method of sitting, mulling one's fate, watching things that don't move much. Over the deserted houses, the water tower loomed. Air stirred in the oleander. Sunk in the mud marsh across the street, listing but upright, was a white piano, by now not a strange sight among the herons and the barn swallows—for now, and here, one saw extraordinary things. Past the piano was a stairway leading to nowhere, and then a four-poster bed, forlorn but inviting. Rob believed in salvage. He could have retrieved some good things; but instead he let them be, as reminders.

It was only by chance that the general ruin, the wreckage of the mainland city and its islands, coincided with the specific ruin of himself. The two things simply happened together: the place ravaged by hurricane, the man by something more complicated. One was sudden, night before last, and was not something he could profitably mull, having no cause beyond weather; and what can be learned by mulling weather? The other had been years brewing, maybe all the thirty-two since his birth, its cause and course obscure but not accidental. He couldn't be sure how bad it was. Ruin, when you are in its midst, is hard to gauge.

The day of the storm, he hadn't left the island as ordered because he couldn't find his dog. The police kept driving by to call out warnings, and the town's old fire alarm rang wild, seven blasts at a time. By night, when Speedo finally showed up, the causeway to Charleston was closed and the oleanders were whipping like grasses. Rob called Louise, hoping she and Hank had evacuated, but she was still there in that beachfront house.

"Hank says we're safe," she said. "He says tell you there's no need to panic."

And what could he say to that? He hung up and stared at the phone. Then he picked it up again to call her back, to deny panic, to tell her to tell Hank it wasn't Rob but the mayor himself saying on the radio this could be the storm of the century—but the line was dead, and then his lights flickered and died, and the mayor's voice on the radio was cut off in mid-sentence. Rob dropped the phone and kicked it. He'd wanted to call his parents again, and Albert. This wasn't panic, this was concern for the safety of others. He groped in the refrigerator for a beer, and roamed the house, checking his doors and windows. He found the candles Louise had nagged him to buy, and regretted not buying the radio batteries she had also suggested. His house looked mysterious by candlelight, as if small votive fires had been lit for some ritual. The candles were Jewish; he didn't know their religious purpose but he assumed they had one. The light they gave seemed solemn, and made him feel lonely.

Speedo had slunk into a corner, where he cringed at every new howl of the wind; he must have thought it was an enemy, the way it roared with the rhythm of a breathing thing. Rob tried to coax him out with a bowl of cat food (Speedo loved fish, could catch them in the surf), but without success. Rob wasn't hungry either. For three hours he sat in the kitchen, discovering how boredom may alternate with terror, trying to stay bored. He talked to the dog.

"It will be over by morning," he said. "All we have to do is wait."

He had been through other hurricanes but none this loud, none this long. And none this *invisible;* he couldn't see it happening.

He tried to remember what the mayor had said about the speed and the diameter, in order to figure how much longer it would last, but the wind interfered with his ability to calculate. Hard to divide 53 by 13½ when the wind is doing over 100. He was distracted by what sounded like the roof blowing off. But then the wind slowed and died, and the still, blind eye of the storm opened.

"The worst is over!" he said. "Let's have a look." He couldn't risk letting Speedo out, although the dog clambered behind him when he opened the door. There were a few stars overhead. The mayor had said the wind would be weaker in the back half of the storm. There was water in the yard, and some trees were down, but he could see no more than that. He hollered into the night: "Is anyone out there?" No one answered. He felt better—almost cheerful—as he closed the door. Maybe it was true that the worst was over.

But it wasn't. The wind came back stronger, from the south now, as if it had reconnoitered only to attack on a new flank. Something slammed against the roof. Speedo shivered and jumped, planting his forelegs on Rob's chest for the dance they sometimes did. "No dancing," Rob said, taking Speedo's wet feet in his hands. Wet feet?

There was a puddle under Speedo. But it wasn't Speedo's doing; it was the Atlantic Ocean. How the hell had it got in? Rob lifted the candle and could make out a sheet of water, spreading. Wavelets worked across the linoleum. It was coming in from all sides, along the baseboards, rising faster than he would have thought possible. The chairs began to move, and the table. When the room was knee-deep, Rob lugged Speedo to the counter and boosted him onto the refrigerator, then climbed up next to him. Speedo appeared to be moribund. Rob had seen captured birds go into that state, uninjured but death-bound by fear. Speedo's big body leaned limp against Rob's side; he was hardly breathing. Rob tried to think. The house stood on a ridge of ancient dune, far from the front beach in a neighborhood of tiny old bungalows. Seawater in this house meant the whole island had gone under.

The thought occurred to him, at first only curiously, as if it were a coincidence or a joke, that he could die here, trapped in his own kitchen, squatting on the refrigerator with an incapacitated dog. He did not panic until, thinking out the ramifications, he came to the one that said he might never again watch Louise tee off at the Sewee Club in her sporty outfits. He didn't want death if that was what it meant. In his panic he became as slack-limbed and dull as the dog, and fell into a torpor that was something like sleep but deeper; he was out cold, propped between the dog and the wall, until dawn.

He woke when Speedo leapt: a thump to the counter, a splash to the floor, where there was still an inch or two of water. Following the dog down, he caught a glimpse through the window, in the gray light, of something bad out there. But he wasn't ready, when he opened the door, for what he saw.

At first he thought his house had moved. Nothing looked right. But it was the house next door that had moved, rotated a quarter-turn and gone twenty yards toward the creek. Water was still flowing across the island, carrying along a matted raft of vegetation and small household items. He saw the piano—had it floated in? or flown?—and in the yard something that looked like a satellite dish but wasn't, it was snaky and black. . . . "Oh no," he said to Speedo. "Goddamnit, my *oak*!" That dish thing was the root system, ripped whole from the earth and lifted vertically. Past it, the trunk lay horizontal in a tangle of its own crushed branches.

Ruin stuns the senses. Rob couldn't take it all in at once. His tree, his enormous, leafy, bird-filled tree . . . and what about the birds? He was mourning the tree, looking for surviving birds, when suddenly his knees went weak. Then he ran for the car.

"Let's do it, let's go," he said to the Toyota, hoping it had not drowned. When it started, he promised to reward it later. He let the motor run while he hooked up the boat and trailer, then drove, dodging parts of houses and searching out the shallowest course, cutting through yards until he was on Palm Avenue, the long straightaway paralleling the beach. "Jesus," he said out loud. Houses were missing their fronts; houses had moved into the road. He saw a drowned dog. There was no living soul in sight.

He found himself bargaining as he drove, for the lives of his four people. "Only four," he said to God. "Give me them, take everything else, the oak, the island, whatever you want." Even in normal times, he was in the habit of checking on those four, making sure they were all right. And now—he cursed himself for failing them, for not collecting them all and getting them to a place of safety, for *falling asleep*! "Let them be okay, and I'll—" What? Make a cash donation? Join back up? He had little in the way of an offering. The steering wheel slipped in the sudden sweat of his hands. "I'll change," he said. "I'll be a new man."

Those four were his mainstays, unlikely as they were. In Charleston a man of his age and station would ordinarily have as mainstays a wife and a dog, some children, and two or three lawyer hunting-buddies. Of those, all he had was the dog. His others were someone else's wife, a reclusive black man, and his own two parents. Without them he would be lost. He had not really known that until now, but it was true. The thought of dying had not been half so terrifying as the thought of living without them.

Then he saw Louise's house, still there. He had never seen it from this angle before, but it was visible now because the adjacent lot was newly vacant, sparkling with a fresh layer of white sand. In the dark night, a house had gone intact to sea. When he saw that white gap, his jaw shook.

He stopped in the middle of the road and honked the horn, got out and walked through standing water toward Louise's porch. But there were no steps. He yelled for her. He pounded on the concrete pier with a piece of banister.

"Hey, Rob, I'm here," she said, leaning out over the railing in a faded bathing suit and white shirt, holding a mop, reaching

5

down to him with her free arm but still twelve feet up. If there had been steps, if he could have gotten to her, he'd have grabbed her. She had never looked better. He could hardly speak. He steadied himself against the pier.

"You're okay," he said.

"Hell, no. Part of the roof blew off. Can you come up? You'll have to shinny up the pier. Hank says our steps are wrapped around a phone pole two blocks down the beach. Can you believe this? Are your parents all right?"

"I don't know. I'm going in by boat. I can't stay, I need to get in there."

"Go. Hank went. He's at the office."

"You promise you're okay?"

She promised. He took off again, drove to the inlet, where the swing bridge hung broken, one end dipping into the waterway. The doors of the Conch Café were wide open with no sign of Huong or Anna; they had probably evacuated. Huong's ducks, four of them anyway, were wandering out front. Rob went in, closed the doors and tied their knobs together with marine rope, found the duck food and a beer, and climbed through a back window. The ducks seemed dazed, and wouldn't eat the meal he tossed them. On a whim he tried the pay phone in the parking lot. It worked.

His mother's voice was breathless with energy. She was fine, she said, "but Daddy isn't doing too well."

"Put him on."

In his old age, his father had come to depend on Rob for encouragement, but didn't like to ask for it. Rob could tell when it was needed. He was flattered, and embarrassed, that his father thought of him as wise.

"The bridge is out," Jack said. "I heard it on the radio. Don't try to come into town. Don't come over in the boat. It's too dangerous." His voice faltered. "I don't think you could make it across the harbor, Robby. Do you?"

"I can make it," Rob said. "I'm on my way."

He couldn't get through to Albert. He would have to stop there on the way back.

It was slow going, down the waterway in the johnboat. The water was rough, the Evinrude old and feeble. He puttered along close to the marsh, lined with shattered boats, and then across the open harbor to the yacht club, where the dock was missing. Hank's big Boston Whaler was tied between two broken pilings. Just under the bow Rob could see some yellow patio furniture, a chaise and a chair and a striped umbrella, from the yacht club porch. How could a man leave his wife in a roofless house at a time like this—everything out of its place, houses in the road, furniture under water—and go to the office? Hank was an admirable man, but sometimes Rob didn't admire him. He sometimes did not admire the people who were universally considered admirable. He often admired the others.

Walking the three blocks to his parents' house, he stuffed his hands in his pockets in order to keep them steady. St. Mark's, his own small church on the bay (though he hadn't been inside it in five years), had lost the point of its steeple. Fallen trees and roof tin blocked parts of East Bay Street, and mud covered the pavement. For a minute he stood on the corner, watching the palmettos blow and the water still flowing in rivulets down the edge of the street and the shutters hanging loose from the old big houses. He was struck by a certain beauty in the scene, the beauty that comes in any aftermath and is difficult to pin down. Was it really there, in the objects themselves? The houses, pink and cream and gold, looked brighter than normal, sparkling in the swept air. The bricks of St. Mark's had darkened with moisture, to a deep rust, and the tree trunks to black. The harbor glistened. Or was all that shine and tone in the eyes of the beholder? The beholder's eyes had been known to read beauty where no one else could see it. The beholder's eyes, at any rate, were dazzled.

2.

Jack was sitting befuddled in the courtyard, and his eyes were dull. "I didn't know it would be this bad," he said. He shook his small head. Jack was at that point in life (the winding down of it) when a man can see the drama of himself, and is hoping for a denouement, an outcome that will cast light on all that's gone before. A reward, preferably; lacking that, a penalty—as in a play, when the last events reveal a secret justice: the marriage of the lonely king, the blinding of the unseeing son . . .

As denouement a hurricane is worthless, unless you care to think a whole innocent town deserves annihilation, along with animals and plants. The only other possible conclusion would be that life may end in freak coincidence, and therefore has meant nothing all along. A seventy-year-old man, especially one on the lookout for signs and portents, can be baffled by a storm.

"I don't know what to make of it," Jack said, hands clasped tight in his lap.

Rob tried to lift his spirits. "Make nothing of it," he said. "Look, Doc, this is not the finale. Any lawyer will tell you" (and Rob was at that moment still a lawyer), "it's nothing but an act of God." Jack frowned. Rob had chosen the wrong term, one lawyers understood as meaning something accidental, but which Jack took literally. Rob searched for other words. "*Force majeure,*" he said. "Out of our hands and beyond our ken. It has no connection to us. Can't be blamed on anyone." He made a pretty good speech, saying things he wasn't sure were true, concluding with "It's just an accident, Doc."

"Signifying nothing?" his mother said, backing through the French doors to drag out a waterlogged rug. "Full of you-know-what?"

Jack frowned again.

"Sound and fury," she said, with a tilt and wag of the head. "That's all I meant."

She, unlike Jack, was in fine spirits. Wearing his old khaki pants and his undershirt, her hair pinned up, she had already spread two rugs on the flagstones, and now draped the third over a pile of bricks knocked like bad teeth from the cap of the garden wall. The wall, except for those holes in the cap, still stood, held by the century's worth of fig vine matted across it. He knew she was all right, because of her hair. When she was not all right, she let her hair fall to her shoulders.

"Have you heard from Ernie?" she said. His adopted brother, true apple of Maude's eye, was at eighteen roaming Florida on a Harley FXRS.

"My phone's out. He'll call," Rob said.

"Oh, I know," she said. "I'm not worried."

Around the courtyard rippled a fringe of shredded banana trees. Fast clouds blew in the sky, churned by leftover winds. Everything was wet.

Maude put her hands on her hips and grinned at Rob.

"*You* look good," she said. "I'm glad to see you all in one piece." She hugged him, then held him at arm's length, her eyes shiny with excitement. "Rob, weren't you scared to death? I'll tell you, I was. There was something *thrilling* about it." Maude thrived on thrill. That was why she had once loved acting: "The stage is the love of my life," she used to say, before she took up genealogy instead. Lately she'd been spending her time mapping her ancestors, eleven generations' worth of Huguenots, the Bonnettes, spread out on the dining table. Genealogy, Rob thought, was the last resort of a disappointed life.

"But we came through," she said. "The thrill of being scared to death is even better if you don't have to die. Don't you think, Jack?"

"I see nothing thrilling in tragedy," Jack said. He was still shaky; his skin was gray.

"It's not all bad," she said, looking out into the street. "Not the ill wind that blows no man to good. Who said that—I can't remember—one of Falstaff's cronies. Anyway. We needed a kick in the behind, some of us."

"Lives have been lost, Maude," Jack said.

"I know that. I'm not saying it's not sad. But lives weren't lost because a god snatched them away. Lives were lost because of substandard housing. Now we'll just clean up and get on with things, and maybe learn a thing or two from all this. Get a new lease on life." Jack was a regular churchgoer. Maude spoke of "a god" to imply that the Episcopalian deity was on a par with Neptune and Loki.

"I don't know," Jack said. "There were signs. We should have been ready, we should have known."

"He's talking about something he saw written on a wall," she said. "Just some graffiti."

" 'Behold God Army,' " Jack said. "I didn't know what it meant at the time, but now . . . it's all too much to be coincidence. It adds up to something. I don't think we'll recover. I don't see how we can." He looked beyond the gate to the street, where three cars had floated into a heap under a swinging power line. The wind, still gusty but warm as a Caribbean breeze, fluttered the loose tin of the roofs that were still on houses. Over that metallic rumble came the chop of helicopters, television crews out for an aerial shot. "It looks like Armageddon," he said. "It looks like the Last Days."

"Oh, for goodness' sake, Jack." Maude glanced at Rob for help. "His study group's on Revelation now." She rolled her eyes. But Rob had nothing else to contribute. In fact, he didn't entirely disagree with either of them, then or in the days to come.

3.

In some ways, she was right. There was a chance for a new lease on life. Even before the storm, Rob had taken steps in what he thought was the new-life direction. He didn't know exactly where they were leading, but he'd taken them. Moved out of his fancy apartment downtown, into the beach bungalow; sold his Alfa. But the idea of quitting his job was only a vaguely formed thought until now, something he'd talked over with Albert as if it were the kind of thing every man wants to do and none actually does, like taking a solo sailing trip around the world. Suddenly, as he watched his father fret, worrying about a life maybe misspent, the idea of quitting crystallized into a possibility, and then a great idea, and then the only thing to do.

Now was the time to do it. With the whole place thrown into confusion, one man's leap into a small personal chaos would be less noticeable. He knew that if he waited, and everything returned to normal, he wouldn't do it.

He walked up Broad Street to his office, past television trucks from Florida and Massachusetts, cameramen and anchorgirls in safari suits, who must have been on their way here even before the storm made landfall. Rob was about to cross the street at the point where the water was only an inch deep, when a camouflaged jeep pulled up in front of him, sending a small wave over the tops of his shoes. A National Guardsman, a black kid, swung out of the jeep and took up his post under the spot where the traffic light had been. Rob wondered if the rifle slung over the guardsman's shoulder was loaded. These guys were trained at a secret base camp in Honduras, and were ready for anything. He hesitated. He could not, without veering from his path, avoid passing within speaking distance of the guardsman, and he needed a couple of seconds to choose his words.

He often had trouble speaking to black people: not because he had nothing to say but because what he wanted to say was impossible ("I am with you; I am on your side"). So he would mumble something meant to convey fellow feeling without going overboard, usually failing.

"Man, this is something, isn't it?" he said. The guardsman moved his head—maybe it was a nod—then stared toward the end of the street. The failure was dismal—more dismal than usual, not even a word of response. He gave up; he would stick to Albert, he could talk fine to Albert, they understood each other. He sloshed onward, to the other side of the street.

11

At the entrance to his office he had to step through a foyer several inches deep in crushed glass; the doors had blown in. And yet inside, despite the saturated carpet and water still dripping from the ceiling, business was proceeding. In the reception room, Laura the faithful paralegal stopped sorting wet files to greet him. "Oh Rob, thank God. This place is a mess. What are we going to do? Mr. Camden needs the Weber file, but the documents are ruined and I can't get them off the diskette until the power—"

"Laura, how long have you been here?"

"I spent the night upstairs in the ladies' room. I was here until ten moving the computer, and then it was too late to leave."

"Go home."

"There's too much to do, everything's soaking wet, and Mr. Camden wants me to try to dry it all out before it starts to mildew." She glanced toward Hank's closed door.

"He's in there?"

She nodded. Rob took a breath, rehearsed his first line, and went in. Hank was behind his big desk, in coat and tie.

Rob meant to be quick and clean. But later he couldn't remember exactly what he said. Stormtalk first, then something about how this might seem like the wrong moment but actually he'd been thinking about it for some time, it wasn't a snap decision, and Hank couldn't be too surprised anyway the way things had been going, and he would leave the important files on Laura's desk.

"Hold on," Hank said. "What are you talking about?"

"I'm quitting."

Hank was surprised; his face showed it.

Rob said again, "I've thought it through, and it seems like the best step to take."

"Look," Hank said. "Maybe you need some time off. Everybody's shook up right now."

"I'm not shook up. I'm perfectly okay."

"You have any damage to your house?"

"Minimal."

"Take a week and get things straightened out. We aren't going to be doing much good around here for a while. Everything's on hold. The courthouse was flooded, nobody's got power. All we have is the phone."

"Hank, I wasn't doing much good here anyway. I haven't been doing much good for a year. You know that." Rob's billable hours had been steadily falling, to a low of twenty-eight the whole month of July. Hank sometimes billed twenty-eight hours in one day, a feat that he explained was completely ethical because you could have clients with common interests and charge your time on one case to additional similar cases, plus you could count the hours of your paralegal, and your commuting time, and even the hours you lay in bed at night pondering. Rob never pondered his cases at night. He hardly pondered them during the day. Some days he hadn't even gone in to the office.

"I've pretty well decided, definitely," Rob said.

Hank eyed him. "Has another firm made you an offer?"

"Of course not," Rob said.

"Then what can I say to talk you out of this? Is it a question of money? What would it take to make you happy?"

(Your wife. It would take your wife, Louise. May I have her?)

"There's nothing," Rob said. "It's not money."

Hank turned paternal. "Now, Rob, I know you take things seriously, you're an idealist, and that's admirable. But you have to be realistic. For instance, what about insurance? What about your retirement plan? If you're not leaving to go to another firm, then why don't you stay on here until you figure out what you're going to do?"

"I haven't been pulling my weight," Rob said. He congratulated himself on the choice of phrase. If you can couch yourself in the right words—familiar and casual—you're safe. The couching is the thing. Hank couched himself well, always.

"A temporary slowdown," Hank said. "Everyone has one, sometime. You're a damn good lawyer, and you know it."

Rob didn't speak. The fact was, he knew he was no lawyer at

all. But he knew that people thought otherwise, and that their false impression was his own fault. You create an image of yourself, and convince others of its truth, and it goes along with you, mocking your own mediocre self.

"Take a week," Hank said. "Pull yourself together. We can talk about it Sunday night. You got your invitation?"

"I figured you might postpone it. Louise said you lost the roof."

"She exaggerated. Only a corner. We'll be in good shape by Sunday. You take it easy for a few days, and we'll talk then." He sat back down behind his desk, as if the matter were settled.

But Rob didn't yield. He was no match for Hank, but he had momentum on his side. He was quitting and could not be stopped; the ball was rolling.

"I'll put my files on Laura's desk," he said. "There aren't many of them."

Hank started to speak, but then stopped. "You've made up your mind," he said. He looked at Rob with a mixture of curiosity and maybe some vague sort of understanding. "Well," he said, "at least check on your insurance. Leonard's in his office. Let me get him on the phone."

Rob agreed. All he wanted to do was make his exit. As it turned out, a premium was due, and he wrote a check, considering it not insurance but the cost of escape, and when it was done he began moving toward the door.

"I'll be there Sunday night," he called from the hallway. "We'll talk then." Another payment for escape, the implication that he would soon explain himself. But he had no intention of doing so. How could he? He didn't *know* the explanation.

But out on the street, his heart zoomed. It was a moment of triumph, walking out into the wet and the wind, a man without a profession. He saw things anew, yet in an old familiar way: he saw with the eyes of a boy again. There were possibilities afoot, even in the midst of ruin.

Take it easy, Hank had said. That was exactly what he did not want to do.

4.

On the island, he turned at the corner before his own and pulled up in Albert's yard. Albert was on the roof with a chain saw.

"How'd you do?" Rob said.

"Not bad, compared. How about you?"

"Better than you. Nothing came through my roof. Plus, I'm now a free man."

Albert squinted. "Meaning what?" he said.

"Quit my job."

Albert stared, shook his head, and revved up the saw. Rob found the ladder against the back of the house and climbed it. He steadied the tree while Albert sawed; wet sawdust flew in the air. When it was cut through, nothing happened. The top was still lodged in the attic. The trunk hung on the roof ridge, unmoving.

"You didn't think I had it in me, did you?" Rob said.

"I knew you had it in you. A screw loose, is what it is." He cranked the saw again and went after the pine. This time the amputated midsection rolled free, down the shingles to the ground; the trunk teetered and dropped off, leaving only the leafy top inside the house. Together they managed to pull it out by cracking the branches that had opened like a parasol under the rafters.

"I don't know about you," Albert said.

"You know everything there is to know."

He and Albert had several contexts. By day Albert functioned as sexton at St. Mark's. Rob was still fond of the church, the small brick portico with brick floor and rounded brick columns, so much warm brown brick as to make the church seem *earthen;* from the portico, an airy view of Charleston harbor and Fort Sumter; and inside, along the cornice, a flock of plaster cherubim molded by the hands of Barbadian slaves. Rob as a boy liked the old hymns, such as "Eternal Father, Strong to Save." He had never minded singing, "O, hear us when we cry to Thee/ For those in peril on the sea," while simultaneously gazing through the tall windows toward the perilous sea itself. And he had liked Albert from the beginning, when Albert first arrived at age fourteen to work for the church. But a grown man can't go to church for the view, for the music, for the sake of sitting around with the sexton on the gravestones at the edge of the sea, shooting bull. Eventually he quit going. Maude, whose attendance had always been sporadic, had dropped out two years ago when St. Mark's went charismatic.

But Jack and Albert hung in. Albert had no choice. He had worked for the church more than half his life, living in an apartment over the parish house until last year, when he moved into the little enclave of island houses surrounded by upscale development. He had told Rob there was a nearby house for rent; Rob had taken it. They joined the Isle of Palms Volunteer Fire Department. They commuted to town in Rob's car when it worked or Albert's when it worked. By night Albert moonlighted as bartender to the parishioners, who needed bartenders with some frequency, though Rob didn't like to take a drink from Albert unless it was Albert's liquor or his on Albert's porch or his—or when they met for a beer at the Conch.

So Albert was his ex-sexton, neighbor, fellow firefighter—and confessor. He knew Rob's secret discontents (Louise, the law, his balding head) as well as his secret loves (Louise, the birds, his old fine boat). Sometimes when Rob realized how much he had told Albert, he felt uncomfortable. Taken together, it added up to a picture of failed dreams and petty pleasures and lack of action.

But Albert never said so. Albert was an observer. From his spot in the back of the church, from behind his linen-covered table at the cocktail parties, Albert watched. Sometimes Rob got the feeling that Albert was studying him. He also studied books and had earned a correspondence degree from a Bible college. But what Rob admired most was that Albert was outside the official world. He had never paid taxes, didn't have a Social

Security number or a driver's license. The government had no record of Albert Swan. His face was wide and high-boned, the color of metal, and you could not tell from it what was going on inside.

He and Rob had known each other for almost twenty years but still might not have described themselves as friends. They were something different. More, and less, than friends.

"It was a great idea," Rob said. "It came to me out of the blue. You'll see."

"I don't know," Albert said.

"How about a beer at the Conch? Huong's cooler still has ice. The back window's open."

"I'm busy. I have a job, remember? Giving out emergency supplies today. The rector came over with a boatload and asked me to handle this area."

"You could use some supplies yourself."

"Got this saw. He's bringing back another boatload. Food, saws, generators. It's coming in from Pennsylvania. Including a thousand boxes of pencils and a truck of Kool-Aid. The church don't know what to do with it all."

"I could use a generator."

"These are meant for the needy. But I guess you qualify now."

Rob climbed down and watched Albert kick small branches from the gutter. He had a feeling that he had lived thirty-two years under a veil, and now it was lifting, and nothing was what he had thought it was (permanent and dense). Everything may fall; everything is therefore spectacular, a wonder to behold. Buzzards wavered in a rising cone, spiraling up. The air was piney, sharp and green and ceremonial.

5.

Back home, he sat in the sun and savored his liberty awhile. Maybe a ruined man is the only free man. But he had no time to waste; he had plans, at least for the time being.

He gathered all his food—canned beans, rice, beer; hoarded

not against disaster but against supermarket trips, which he disliked—and put it in the trunk of the Toyota. For two days he drove the back roads of the island, giving beans and rice to people who had run out of food and couldn't get to the mainland, giving beer to folks who were trying to cover their roofs with scraps of other people's roofs. He checked in with the Volunteer Fire Department. The island had a regular professional crew now; the Volunteers were more or less obsolete, a bunch of grizzled, chain-smoking islanders who'd been around since the days when the place was a real town, before it fell into the hands of the leisure class. But some of them were town men like Rob's father, who by virtue of his having rented various shabby island cottages over the years had come to be accepted by the Volunteers; and some were newcomers like Rob and Albert, who joined but were considered hangers-on. Nevertheless, he was proud to be among the Volunteers; he'd wanted to be one of them since his young summers on the island.

Most of his official duties had entailed preparations for the annual fish fry. But now, with the storm, the Volunteers were in demand. That first week they nailed "No Burning" signs along the highway and rounded up a lot of sorrowful, displaced dogs (found two Labradors in a rowboat, caught in the upper branches of a small mimosa tree). They righted an overturned mobile home, in which a family had been living for three days, climbing in and out of the door like a hatch on top.

One night he woke to the sound of the fire alarm whooping. Groggy, he thought first of another hurricane. Some noises were forever linked in his mind to the storm: that alarm, the sound of rumbling tin, helicopters, chain saws. But this was fire, four blasts. He jumped out of bed and called Albert, who was supposed to get the location on his CB. "End of the avenue, across from Huong's," Albert said. Rob grabbed his boots and the protective vest he'd been issued, and his fire-swatter, a hoe handle with a wide flap of rubber at the end. He and Albert got to the fire before the engine, found someone's illegal burnpile smouldering.

They swatted out the small flame and raked the charred debris—
lumber, shingles, a melted doll, a clock—till no light came from
it, only the sharp smoky smell. A minor job but satisfying, an
accomplishment. Across the street they found Huong's back window still open. Huong was a friend; if he'd been there, he'd have
offered them the warm beer they lifted from his cooler. They
meant to drink the sun up, but fell asleep after only a couple of
cans each. In the morning, looking up from the pine boards of
Huong's deck into the sky, Rob felt temporarily useful and good.

Ravage, because there was so much of it, became a familiar sight,
almost comfortable. And after a week, people no longer needed
supplies. Power and phone service were being restored; daily life
was resuming. Daily life, it seemed, was hard to keep down, once
people had food and television. Albert left a small generator on
Rob's porch, only 600 watts but enough to run the television and
two light bulbs, all he needed. The Clemson-Carolina game was
played. Stores opened up behind plywood-covered windows. The
Army Corps of Engineers lifted the bridge out of the waterway
and bolted it back in place. The Corps was a know-how, can-do
outfit, possibly the best of all the outfits that came to town. The
place was crawling with Red Cross, FEMA, National Guard,
linesmen and adjusters and contractors. Also an influx of the
nation's unemployed, in search of work. Times must be especially
hard in Alabama; Alabamans were everywhere, driving dusty
pickups or just standing on the highway holding signs: "Roof
Man," "Tree Man." They were big and sunburned and amiable,
ready with roofing tar and chain saws and stump-grinders to set
things right again. O Alabamans, welcome, he thought as he
drove by; if we have said unkind things about you in the past,
forgive us.
    It would not, he thought, be unpleasant to stand on the highway
and offer yourself in that manner, saying to the world: *I am
available.* But what would his sign say? Till now he had been a
divorce man, and he supposed it was an honorable enough oc-

cupation, but not so honorable, not so straight and clear, as roof
man or tree man. His sign might say "Bird Man"—and he could
go around teaching what he knew of raptors and waterfowl and
passerines. . . . That was the only service he could have rendered,
and it would have been a valuable one, but there was not much
call for it. In fact, most people thought it was an oddball sort of
thing, his interest in birds. A man may lie low in the cattails
waiting for blue-winged teal, but he is supposed to shoot them
when they come. He is not supposed to be *seized,* stricken by the
flash of color and beat of wing, in transport suspiciously similar
to religious trance or brain-wave malfunction.

So he had no sign to raise, no service to advertise. The work
of roof men and tree men proceeded apace. Machines with jaws
began clearing the roadways. The mayor, a kind and wise man
no older than Rob, assured citizens (as Rob had assured his father)
that everything was going to be all right. Rob liked the mayor
very much. Sometimes, when he saw him on Broad Street, he
felt inclined to stop and speak his admiration. "Hey, Joe," he
might say, in the breezy shirtsleeve manner of lawyers these days,
"good job." However, he had never done it. In fact, when he did
pass the mayor on the sidewalk, he looked the other way and
pretended to be lost in thought, for he was not a breezy shirtsleeve
sort and could not get the style right.

Coming from the mayor, the reassurance was convincing.
Maybe everything would indeed be all right.

But he was still worried about his father. He went by the house
again to deliver ice and batteries, his real purpose to study Jack's
face for despair. It was there. Rob tried to get them both to go
out for a ride, but Maude was busy replacing panes in the French
doors; Jack sat in his deep old leather chair, the week's newspapers
piled around him. "He won't let me clean up around him, so
I'm just letting him have that little corner," she said. "He reads
the hurricane stories over and over again, especially the ones about
old men who lost everything."

"What can I do for you, Dad?" Rob said. "You've got to snap
out of this."

"He's all right," Maude said. "He just needs some time. You don't have to worry about us. Go on now, if we need anything else I'll call you. The power is coming back downtown sometime in the next two days, they say. Don't you have to go to your office?"

"Ah . . . no," he said. "I quit the firm."

"You what?" his father said, letting the paper fall.

"It's been coming for a long time," Rob said. "I'm sorting things out."

His father's head went back, eyes closed. "I knew it, I knew something like this—"

Maude interrupted. "You mean you're planning to quit, you haven't actually done it yet."

"Well, no, I've done it."

"But Rob," she said, "that's . . . that's *exciting*. You mean really, honestly? It's . . ." Her eyes roamed the room, then came back to him. She leaned toward him and lowered her voice. "Was it hard?"

"I don't remember."

"But now—oh, Rob, you have the chance of a lifetime. I'm so happy for you."

And probably she was, but he also knew that when people say they are happy for you it may mean they are sad for themselves.

When Rob left, she was busy again with the new panes, spreading glazing compound with a kitchen knife; maybe all this work would keep her away from the family tree. In his corner Jack was slumped behind his newspaper, still trying to decipher the message of the hurricane.

At the end of the week, Hank and Louise went ahead with their annual lawyer party. Guests climbed a ladder to the porch, from which the screens hung in ripped flaps. The laughter and the ice in glasses and the background songs sounded happy.

And yet, even as Rob came up over the rim of the porch into festivity, into music and well-being, he understood his father's uneasiness. Not that he thought there was any secret message to be found in the direct hit of the storm; he didn't go that far. But it did seem that something in the order of things had been altered. If this was not a finale, maybe it was a setting of the stage, and ought not to be ignored. Maybe people should not rush back into daily life quite so fast, quite so eagerly. Maybe there was need for caution.

CHAPTER 2

In his usual fashion he lurked on the sidelines of the party, appreciating. The women were lovely and chattery, still in summer costume, sunburnt on the shoulders. The exhilaration of survival made them even more lovely, as their voices rose in the telling of hurricane stories: where they had been when it hit, how much damage their houses had suffered, what their children said in the middle of the storm. The men talked about insurance coverage and then moved on to business as usual, keeping an eye out for judges. That's why all the lawyers were here, to see a judge or two.

Except for Rob. He was here to see Louise.

She greeted him at the top of the ladder, in her hostess skirt and a low-necked T-shirt; then she disappeared into the throng. Albert was tending bar, but the thirsty were three-deep in front of him. Rob slipped behind the table and poured himself a gin and tonic.

"Thanks for the generator. Runs good," he said.

Albert was in bartender mode, head down, slinging ice and limes. He raised his head an inch. "Is that right," he said. Then the head went down.

Rob knew that in some contexts his presence made Albert jumpy. In this one—Albert pouring and Rob drinking—Rob was just another white boozer. To speak with familiarity was not allowed. He'd crossed the line. Albert turned his attention to the next customer, who was Hank.

"What can I give you this evening, sir?"

"Quite a storm, wasn't it, Albert?" Hank said.

"That's right."

"I hope your home wasn't damaged."

"No, sir, everything fine. Just fine."

"Except for a pine tree piercing the roof and nine inches of mud on the floor," Rob said. He moved away from the bar. He didn't want to talk to Albert when he was like that, sloughing verbs deliberately. Albert was multilingual; he could speak the language that his listener wanted to hear.

Rob didn't want to talk to Hank either, or to anyone else. So he found his place in a corner and settled in to watch the women. Sometimes when he saw a new one, he could be filled with longing, but he didn't mind. The ache wasn't unpleasant, if it didn't get out of hand, if he kept his distance.

But he was unprepared for the one that caught his eye. Across the porch, standing in a shaft of sunset. He knew he could be in for trouble if he wasn't careful. He tried to maintain his safe position, with a barrier of two dozen cocktail drinkers between him and her. But the crowd parted in order to tempt him. He had a clear view of her face and her extraordinary posture— knees cocked, chest high, hips tilted.

He admired the tilt. The pelvic confidence.

And yet there was also a certain contrasting timidity of gesture. The napkin around her glass was shredded. Her hair was in some disarray, and was an odd peach color, matching her dress. She didn't look like a lawyer or a lawyer's wife, certainly not a judge's wife. She looked like a waitress. He was a great fan of waitresses. His heart ached.

All he could do was hold his ground, drink his gin, and watch her arms. They were bare and, unlike the arms of the other women on the porch, untanned. He watched her eat a shrimp, her wide-set eyes glancing around first to see if someone was watching before she downed the pink curl of meat.

Physically, he was not a noticeable man. He had a degree of

social camouflage that enabled him to move on peripheries, and to observe without being observed. Surreptitious observation had been a habit of his since boyhood, practiced first on wildlife and then on women. There were some similarities.

The birds most worth seeing, for example, were those that were secretive and skittish, and wouldn't show themselves unless he waited hours in the woods without moving and without making a sound. He could do it. Even in boyhood, his desire was that great. A small desire demands culmination, but a great desire is self-sustaining and will wait despite heartache, despite the solitary woods of the Francis Marion National Forest, and a boy's impatience, his legs asleep, and the gnats abuzz. He'd spent whole days there—and some nights, in an old abandoned shack known only to him—waiting. Culmination, the longed-for moment when a wild bird would eat from his hand or perch on his shoulder, never occurred. It hardly mattered. Desire and imagination and observation were nearly enough.

At any party, the old heart could ache "real bad," as Louise, always careless of her adverbs, would have said. It ached real bad now, not only for the lonesome-looking girl but for everything in sight. The setting was one that always dazed him: Louise's house, with Louise in it, the ocean in front of it. And tonight, feeling the exhilaration of survival himself, he was even more susceptible. Through the strips of waving screen he could see sunset in the palmettos, sunset on the flat sand. It was all very slow, very lovely, the glow burning and the darkness coming and the water moving. And the water moved in its rightful place, looking convincingly innocent. That look can be achieved only by the most deranged of culprits, those who have no motive and may not even remember their crime. A string of pelicans passed, inches over the swells.

Like those pelicans, he had always been respectful and half afraid of the ocean but liked to come near it. In boats he always felt a thrill, safe but close to a danger so great it was more than a danger, more than an enemy. It was a void.

Louise's house seemed charmed, having survived in spite of its perch on the edge of the void. Her neighbor's house to the south had crumpled, its foundation washed out. And on the other side, to the north, there was that shallow depression, the empty lot. When Rob saw it again, he stared. How can an entire house vanish without a trace? There was not a splinter of wood in the white sand, not a nail.

And what must it have looked like, the house bobbing away in the tempest, complete with food, china, furniture, mementos? Its occupants, the Heffrons, had evacuated, but Louise had been right there next door all night; she might have gone to sea herself. Hank was supposed to be responsible and competent, but he hadn't even taken her to a shelter. His negligence enraged Rob, who had not evacuated either, but then he wasn't officially responsible for Louise, or for anyone else except his dog. The image of the house launched seaward horrified him.

But here was the odd thing: his horror was accompanied by fascination. He imagined the reeling, swirling house; recoiled; and was drawn back to it. Saw Louise and himself in it, provisioned for long voyage, sailing for the horizon; sitting down to dinner at the table set for two, while the cups jiggled in their saucers and the known world receded behind them.

Mad voyage has its appeal. The more ill-considered the better, judging from the examples he could think of: Ishmael's, Huck's. Even the illest-considered have nobility. The now-extinct Sewee Indians had once left this very shore in a last-ditch effort to escape the misery of life in white Carolina; set out for England in canoes, aiming themselves in the direction they'd seen ships come from, hoping to trade their deerskins direct instead of through Charlestonians (who were of a stock brilliantly mercantile). And who knows, maybe some of those Sewees got to England. Maybe the Heffrons' house was even now heaving into sight off Weymouth.

Louise had known the risks. People choose to live in danger zones—on the slopes of volcanoes, atop fault lines, on barrier islands—even when there's no doubt that catastrophe will occur sooner or later. Later, they assume. Louise loved the house. Sometimes Rob thought she had married Hank for it; it had been the Camden family's summer place. Hank offered to buy her a downtown house—Hank was a great buyer and seller, a brilliant mercantile mind himself—but she refused. She wanted to live here, out of sight of downtown.

Rob had mixed feelings about the house.

It was built of concrete blocks, in the solid, stubborn architecture of the fifties, and furnished casually, Louise-style. The porch had the look of a room, with grass rugs worn to soft turf underfoot, and some wide slipcovered sofas, and tarnished brass lamps with big shades. The lights were on, despite the loss of power. Hank had hooked up three enormous generators. Under the house they reverberated like an inboard engine, powering up all the appliances, including the freezer, where Hank had two deer carcasses stowed. The storm of the century had hardly slowed the Camdens down. A cowboy crew out of Birmingham had chain-sawed the fallen trees, cleaned the yard, blanketed the roof with a gigantic blue tarpaulin. Hank dickered with his claims adjuster, a hurricane expert from the Texas Gulf Coast, whose job it was to declare a minimum of wind damage (covered) and a maximum of flood damage (not covered); but Hank had let the fellow know he was a lawyer, and collected a fat check. Louise rearranged her furniture and covered some of the mildewed chairs with green Indian bedspreads. Unable to locate a functioning florist, she made a centerpiece of palmetto salvaged from the yard.

Rob liked the look of it, the big fans of split fronds bending out over the shrimp and the pepper jelly. He imagined her hands adjusting the stalks, turning the vase.

Her interest in decor always surprised him. It seemed almost too feminine for Louise. Not that she wasn't feminine; she was, in all the good aspects, but she had a brain worthy of better projects. Also, of course, the house was Hank's. Rob didn't like to see her energy go into it. Once, when he suggested that there were bigger things in life than one's household, she agreed: "Yeah, but I don't want to think about them. I need distraction from them. The house occupies me." That made sense. He avoided thoughts of some big things himself.

But tonight, in Louise's household, he was assaulted by an awareness of them. Death by drowning, for instance, because it had been escaped, and, as a corollary, the beauty of women's arms. He was spying on the arms and listening to the combined hum of generators and ocean and music (Ink Spots, a secret between him and Louise) when she bumped his arm with a tray of pickled shrimp.

"Eat up, Wyatt," she said. "Free food."

He stabbed three shrimp with one toothpick and ate them.

"You're pitiful," she said. "You're starving. I'm going to have to bring casseroles to your house."

"You said you didn't like my house, that time you came over."

"I didn't. I thought it was pitiful and depressing." She had stopped by one morning before the storm to pick him up for golf, because his Toyota sometimes didn't work until midday. He knew she wouldn't like the house. There was his scavenged sofa, the model (wooden arms and back) that you sometimes see at the Goodwill bin, which is where he'd found it; his big television in the middle of the floor, revealing by its prominence the role it played in his life; Jack's old vinyl recliner, from the back room of the drugstore, a recliner with quite a history, upon which had reclined more than a few Charleston ladies; and a pole lamp, circa 1976, relic of Rob's days at Calhoun College, Yale University. The walls were stippled with some kind of wartime stucco that had the texture of dried oatmeal. When he ran his hand over it, a sprinkle of grit fell to the floor. "Paint will help," he'd promised Louise, hoping there was a chance she would see the possibilities. But she hadn't. She had stood in the middle of the room holding her pocketbook in both hands, and then sort of backed out the door. He guessed the house was a shock to her system, which was now a system of comfort and security and major real estate, a system she hadn't always been in.

"I'm not starving on purpose," he said, taking another shrimp. "I'm out of food. I've given it all away." He was not above fishing for a word of praise from Louise. The combination would be even better—pity for his hunger, admiration for his generosity. . . .

"The bridge is fixed," she said. "You can go to the Bi-Lo now. You can even get a hot meal free from the Red Cross, down at the inlet. Sit on the dock, eat a barbecue sandwich. I did it yesterday. Or hell, I'll give you some food to take home with you tonight. You're using this situation as an excuse to spiral downward. I know you."

"Hell" was one of her favorite words. He was charmed when she said it—by the ladylike choice of expletive, and by the force, unladylike, with which she shot the syllable into ordinary conversation. It sounded both prudish and profane.

"My refrigerator's not running," he said. "Albert got me a little generator he looted from the church, sent down by some Episcopalians from Pittsburgh, but it'll only run the lights and one appliance. I picked the TV, I can't live without TV." The networks were carrying nightly reports of the ruin. Every night he reclined in his recliner, warm beer in hand, and watched hours of footage displaying scenes that he couldn't see firsthand: copter surveys of the coastline, the President landing at the airport, food lines at the distribution centers.

"Was your house hurt?" Louise said.

"Lost some shingles, some windowpanes. Couple of feet of water in the living room, but it's drying out. Doesn't look that different from before. My house has a low profile. We didn't offer much of a target."

"I hate you living there. You promised me you'd get a decent place to live."

"My house is decent. That's the one thing it is."

"I was worried about you," she said. "I was huddled in the shower stall thinking the end was near, and all it meant to me was that I might not see you again. We might never play golf again."

"There's still the danger of that," he said. "I hear the course is trashed."

"Who cares? You might do better on it that way. You said it was so perfectly groomed it made you nervous and you couldn't concentrate. Let's go soon. I have to work at the shelter all week, but how about Saturday?"

He said okay. He never turned down an offer from Louise.

2.

At one time some years back, Louise had been the love of his life, but then she had gone and married someone else. He weathered it. Love fails on this earth a million times a day, so often that guidelines for recovery are published in newspaper columns. He did what a man is supposed to do under the circumstances: gave up hope, developed other interests. But the hitch is, hope isn't something you can give up. The ball is in hope's court. And it had not entirely abandoned him. There was a shred of it that hung on. A man can be fairly incapacitated by a shred of hope.

It wasn't hope for her, for winning her; it was a more general thing, a longing for—for what, he could not exactly say. It was sexual, it was spiritual (he could not tell the difference), but it was a longing that ranged without object, settling from time to time on other women but reaching always, it seemed to him, for something beyond women. Not something better than women but something *via* women. He didn't know what it was.

Louise was out of the picture, realistically speaking, and he didn't pine for her. In a normal town, that might have been the end of it. But he still saw her, Charleston being a place where people continually run into each other in spite of rifts and irreconcilable differences. Divorced partners find themselves in the same grocery aisle twice a week; men who have cheated each other in business drink together at cocktail parties. No one seems to mind. Rob certainly didn't. She had married his law partner;

she didn't possess full knowledge of his devotion. He could see a lot of her. Her presence still activated in him an awareness of good and beauty, which otherwise he had a hard time keeping in sight. He made the most of his opportunities, pretending to be her pal. Eventually, he was her pal.

She invited him to her parties; they fished and golfed. This had been going on for five years. Days with Louise were the energized parts of his life. The other parts had gone into serious stall.

"I'm still worried about you," she said.

"I'm fine. I fixed the roof." Actually, all he had done was to nail a sheet of plywood over the bad part.

"I don't mean that. You know what I mean. What's it all about?"

"Hank told you?"

"Why shouldn't he? You hand in your resignation, and he's not supposed to tell me? You thought you'd keep it a secret from me?"

The answer was yes. It was Louise's custom, while golfing, to discuss his life. She didn't like the turn it had taken, in the direction of melancholy and low-rent housing. She kept hoping he would show signs of improvement. He hadn't wanted to appear even worse.

"I found it difficult to go back to the office," he said. "Extremely difficult. Ultimately, impossible. So I quit."

"Oh, Rob."

"I'm in a new phase. Frugality and decency. You'll see, it will all turn out for the better."

"It's a posttraumatic withdrawal. You can't let the storm get to you like that."

"It was a pretraumatic withdrawal. I was withdrawing long before the storm. Before the winds began to swirl off the African coast. Listen, it's okay. I swear. It's a step in the right direction."

She looked dubious. But the good thing about Louise was that she trusted him, deep down. He could tell that she was not completely disappointed in him. She had his best interests at heart. One day she had confiscated his ties and replaced them with a whole new set. In the middle of their last golf game she had given him a bottle of 500 capsules of vitamin C. The golf had been her idea in the first place; she thought he needed a sport, and golf was good for a lawyer.

He put his arm around her shoulder and was surprised to see goose bumps rise across the back of her neck. "Look on the bright side," he said. "I'll have unlimited leisure time. We can play golf every day. We can go fishing. We can hop a flight to Brazil. Anything."

"Yeah," she said.

"Give me another pickled shrimp."

"I made them for you."

"They're fantastic. They're great." She was not a cooking woman, but she liked to be complimented on her shrimp. Or on anything else. "And the house looks great, and you're a knock-out," he said.

"We're lucky to be alive," she said. Her arm came up around his waist from the back. They stood there surveying the luckiness—the room, the porch, the sunset, the gathered fellow human beings.

"We are," he said. "Very lucky. Who's the girl?"

"Which one?" she said, and he could tell from her immediate glance in the right direction that she knew which one. There was even a chance that she had invited the girl for him.

"The one that looks like she just got out of bed. In the sort of wrinkled dress, with her hair—"

"That's Billie."

"Yes?"

"What about her?" Louise could be uncooperative.

"That's what I'm asking you," he said.

"You're interested?"

"Just a simple request for information."

"You can get it yourself. Here's how it works. You go up to

her and you introduce yourself and you ask some questions. Watch that guy with her. He's doing it." Billie was talking to a young lawyer he knew vaguely and disliked distinctly, a litigator.

"He's not asking questions. He's expounding," Rob said.

"Okay. What the hell." Louise drew a breath, held it, exhaled. "I'll introduce you. If you want."

"You sigh," he said.

"Sometimes you make me real mad, Wyatt." She moved her hand to the small of his back and propelled him across the porch. He liked her hand there, maneuvering him among the clumps of cocktailers. He tried not to think of the old days when he'd counted on marrying Louise—but made the mistake of not letting her in on the plan, and had to abandon it altogether when one starry night, in a green silky dress, she announced—without prior notice—her impending marriage to his partner.

Ex-partner now. He liked the sound of it. He had heard women use the term "ex-husband" with audible pleasure, as if the prefix canceled the man again, every time they said it.

And as Louise steered him past his former colleagues, he warmed inwardly, like an escapee glowing with false sympathy for his fellows still behind bars. Not that a one of them envied his freedom, consciously. When the word spread, to a man (and woman—there were a few lady lawyers here, identifiable by the blouses buttoned to the chin, minimal show of arm) they would view him as a lunatic. Hank had implied as much. But Rob had never been one of them. He had loved the law and hated the lawyers.

They were nearing the girl, Billie. She was even better up close. A heart-shaped face, top front teeth slightly prominent but small. Her high forehead was knit in concentration as she listened to the blather of the litigator. She was polite. She nodded as the litigator explained a personal-injury suit he had won. Rob liked that kind of female courtesy which will allow dolts to reveal their doltishness. Billie wasn't saying a word. She wasn't fooled. The litigator nodded to Rob and Louise but didn't falter, proceeding with the details of his cleverness. Billie was good, Billie was magnificent. Rob winked at Louise in gratitude, sure now that she had invited Billie for him. She knew the kind of girl he liked.

This wasn't a sex problem, his need for women like Billie. He didn't require conquests. The problem was not simple desire but desire complicated by imagination. Meeting a new woman, he saw more than the woman. He saw a whole possible life—into which he entered, imaginatively, on the spot. Up close he took a glance at Billie, her clean and healthy eyes over the glass she sipped from, her small nervous hands, the strand of hair across her cheek; and he was hers. They would eat good food together and drink beers in a boat, hike the Swamp Fox Trail and have some children and send them to well-integrated parochial schools (Billie would have a benign religious streak) and he would teach her the birds and they would make love in the National Forest—

He stopped his thoughts. Could anyone tell he'd been fading into life with Billie? No one was watching. Louise was alert for an opening in the conversation. Hank was a few feet away, but he was busy talking to a judge, the gravely respectful look on his face that you will see on the face of a lawyer when he is talking to a judge. You see it even on the faces of the best, even on the face of Hank Camden, who was known as a man of honor. Rob said to himself, Ha! I will never have to talk to a judge again, or if I do I can say to the judge that his recent decisions have appeared to me to be a little bit off base, a little bit fucked up.

The litigator noticed the judge just then, lost hold of his monologue, let his eyes wander beyond Billie's shoulder to the judge; he panicked, fearing he might miss the judge altogether and be stuck with a beautiful girl. Louise saw him miss the beat, and she seized the moment, stepping forward. The litigator edged out. Rob edged in.

Louise said, "Billie, this is Rob. Rob Wyatt, Billie Poe." Not your most gracious introduction. Louise could be perverse, often for reasons unclear to him. But Billie smiled. Her eyes were impossibly wide-set. He wondered how she could see a single image; it appeared there could be no overlap in the range of those two eyes. Outside, the eight o'clock summer sky was red and may have accounted for her color. He couldn't believe her color.

He'd been keeping an eye out for accidentals, maybe a wind-tossed frigatebird or spoonbill, driven from its natural range into his. A bird man believes in surprise; it is his faith, that at any instant some rare new creature may flit into view, something unfamiliar start into the midst of all the old familiar, and charge the old itself with that new beauty. It's a faith in the possibility of discovery. Billie was definitely a discovery.

But not entirely new to him. Not a complete surprise. A man prefers a certain type of woman. He can't describe the type; it's set in his brain from birth, and he carries it through life like a wallet snapshot; when he sees one, a moment of recognition occurs. *La femme déjà vue.* That forehead, that chin, and something about the eyes . . . Sometimes the paradigm resembles his mother, sometimes not; in his case not. Billie didn't look like Maude at all. But he recognized Billie as one of his. He couldn't believe his luck.

"Billie's husband, Carlo, is on a submarine," Louise said. "He's been underwater for—how long now, Billie?"

"Two months," Billie said. She looked embarrassed by this information.

Rob shot a look at Louise, who smiled. Billie Poe raised to him eyes in which he saw, or imagined he saw, a *plea*. It was there only for an instant, like an involuntary reflex; and then it disappeared, replaced by the ordinary polite gaze of attention that she'd given the litigator, as if she had seen something in Rob, or imagined or hoped she saw something, which on closer inspection was not there.

3.

In the company of more than one woman, he wasn't at his best (even his best was not that good). His attentions divided. Billie's peach-hued dress was made of something shiny. Her earrings—and he had to look twice to confirm this—were tiny nuclear submarines, dangling nose up. He thought of the man under a mile of ocean. What if Billie's shingles were off, what if she had a pine tree through her attic? Rob was a good handyman. He started to imagine climbing out on Billie's roof.

But Louise was at his side. Her arm touched his. He noticed her clavicle.

"Rob is one of my best friends," she said to Billie.

One of them? That was probably true, from her point of view. Louise had many alliances, a pantheon of friends. She had a way of taking people in out of their various storms, ferreting out their secrets, ordering their disordered lives. She wanted to know everybody's story. That's what had made her, at one time, a good newspaper reporter. But Louise was not a great confessor. Albert let Rob run on till he spilled his guts, but Louise *probed*. She gathered information, as a hobby, and Rob didn't always have it to impart. Sometimes she'd ask him something—about his parents, his childhood—and he would make up the answer. He didn't like to dwell long enough on those subjects to figure out the truth.

On the golf course she had been asking more questions, all the while trying to teach him the game. He hated golf, but would endure the entire eighteen holes just to watch Louise plant her feet and swing her thin but muscled arms—she worked with weights every Tuesday and Thursday—and whack the shit out of the ball, holding her elbows high and her right knee bent and the club motionless behind her shoulder until she saw the ball drop in the green distance.

The greenery distracted him. Here was civilization's thin veneer: all that sod pieced and fixed upon the sand dunes, and carefully maintained by fellows with degrees in golf grass. It gave him the creeps. But the presence of Louise counteracted the creeps. Louise golfing was a sight that made his heart ache. She looked brave and tough, when in fact she was neither. She talked brave and tough, and golfed brave and tough, but this was bravura, not bravery. He could see through it, to the Louise he used to be crazy about. He was still crazy about her. Tonight she wore her hair loose on her shoulders, a shark's tooth on a chain around her neck. He had given her the tooth, the prize of his collection.

"What do you do?" Billie Poe said, and he snapped back to the peachy sheen, the eyes.

"Rob is unemployed," Louise said. "He used to be an attorney."

"I think everyone here's an attorney," Billie said, brightening to the word, thinking no doubt of leather-bound books and mahogany furniture. He didn't feel the need to correct her impression. She would be less impressed to know that his practice had consisted mostly of title searches and little-league divorce, the kind where a secretary is divorcing a cop. No complicated legal theory. No big bucks.

"Billie's nineteen," Louise said.

She meant, *too young for you.* But Billie didn't look nineteen. Besides, she was married, and married to a submariner. That would put some years on a girl. What did it matter anyway? All he wanted was the close-up look, enough for his purposes—not the real girl.

"I guess I've come to the right place," Billie said. "Coincidentally. I need an attorney."

"I'm out of the game," he said. "But you've got a field of dozens before your very eyes."

"But you *are* one, right?" Billie said. "It's not something you stop being."

"I've quit." It still sounded good. As a boy he had quit many things—the basketball team, the Episcopal youth group—and always enjoyed the experience. People should do it more often; *walk,* scot free. But his quits had been penny-ante. This was the big quit.

"How come?" Billie said.

"How much time do you have?" he joked.

"Oh, I have all night," Billie said. With an odd little snort she added, "I don't have to go home at all. My apartment disappeared. The walls snapped out and the roof blew off. It looks like a dollhouse now, the kind that's all open on one side so you can reach in and move the furniture around in the little cubicles. But I'm glad. If it hadn't blown apart, I might have blown it apart myself."

He began to wish he had gotten more information out of Louise, preintroduction. Maybe Billie was one of Louise's loony projects. Louise was a do-gooder, and you could never predict who would show up at her house. She took in lost foreign-exchange students, her maid's daughter AWOL from Parris Island, women friends AWOL from marriages to some of these very lawyers present. She had, in fact, given sanctuary to some of Rob's own loonies: his brother Ernie at various down points in Ernie's up-and-down adolescence (still in rocky progress), and his mother, last year when Maude took it into her head to leave home and return to the stage, despite the fact that she was past sixty and had never been on the stage, professionally. The Camden house was a damn refugee shelter, Hank complained. But Louise was appreciated. In Charleston, where people would rather perish than seek professional counseling, she was a godsend.

But at the moment he didn't need a waif on his hands, and Billie looked to have definite waif possibilities. He liked a girl who needed a little help, but not one who needed lifesaving. Not now anyway, as he was engaged in a different sort of lifesaving operation: his own. He thought about politely excusing himself while the image of life with Billie was still sweet. There were several bad signs here.

But Louise departed first. "You two should get to know each other," she said, and left them standing together. He looked at Billie. Her skin was smooth; but when she talked a small furrow appeared between her nearly invisible eyebrows.

"I'm not kidding," she said. "I really do need a lawyer."

Drug charges? But she looked so clean and bright in the corneas. Maybe she had a stingy insurance adjuster. Lawyers would be making money off the storm, suing insurance companies on behalf of policyholders.

"Hank's a lawyer. You know Hank, don't you?" he said.

"Yeah, but he's—well, he's old."

"Forty-five. Hardly the age of incompetence. More like the age of wisdom."

"Louise said he does bank stuff."

"That's true, but he can handle just about any problem you've got."

"Tell me why you quit," Billie said.

"Tell me about your earrings."

"Oh, they're awful, I know." She reached up and pulled the wires out of her ears before he could stop her. Without the submarines she looked bare; she wore no other jewelry. No rings. Her arms were thin, her nails (on fingers and toes) were pink. But he could see, under the fingernail polish, thin crescents of dirt, the permanent variety that you see on kids and mechanics. "I'm not used to parties," she said, looking around the porch.

"Neither am I," he said truthfully, though he had endured a decade of them. There were certain rules to a Charleston cocktail party, and he had failed to master them. You couldn't sit down. You couldn't disappear into the kitchen or stand alone in the corner and drink too much. You couldn't sneak out early and go home. All of which he usually did.

"It seems weird, having a party. Now."

"Nothing slows the cocktail circuit," he said.

"You're on it?"

"Not anymore. I'm not a successful partygoer. In fact this may be my last appearance in the social world."

"What do you do, then? You don't do law, you don't do parties." She took a sip from her glass, but watched him.

"Ah. Household repairs," he said. "A little firefighting. And let's see, I also collect things . . . and I sit in the sun a lot. Watch the birds, listen to the Ink Spots." He tried to think of what else he did. He didn't want to say "play golf."

"You have a family?" she said.

"No."

"Divorced?"

"Congenitally unmarried."

She looked surprised. But her reaction was not the usual one. Usually, when women found out that he was unmarried, they wanted to know why. He had a stock of semifalse answers ranging from self-effacing (a list of his shortcomings) to cocky (a list of the shortcomings of women). But she didn't want to know why.

"Smart," she said, nodding.

"Why do you say that?" He couldn't settle on a tone of voice. The question ought to have been mock-sly but came out sounding sincere.

"Scripture says, 'He that is unmarried careth for the things of the Lord.' "

"I didn't know that."

"It's true," Billie said.

He'd been right. The religious streak. In his experience most Charleston women had a religious streak, and their men went along for the ride. Maude and Jack were the exception. But he hoped Billie's was only a streak. More than that, and they can turn unpredictable. The topic was one he wasn't anxious to pursue; luckily, Billie didn't pursue it.

"How old are you, anyway?" she said.

"Thirty. Thirty-one."

"Well, which?"

"Thirty-two."

She laughed. "That's thirteen years older than me."

"I know. I apologize."

"The same amount that Charles is older than Diana by."

"I'm drawing a blank."

"In England," she said.

"Ah, yes."

He had found it not always to be a bad sign if a woman followed with interest the life of Princess Diana. It signaled both innocence and longing, not necessarily dumbness. Billie was the kind of girl men might call dumb—from her looks and her language—but he often saw in such women a form of intelligence that most men overlooked, the form that can tell truth from bullshit and good from bad. He knew of many a so-called brilliant lawyer who could screw a genius paralegal for months and never have an inkling of the wisdom he had fucked. Should a day of reckoning ever occur (a possibility he doubted but did not entirely dismiss because he hoped for it—history's denouement, the moment when truth will out)—come that day, when the vast collective intelligence of paralegals and receptionists and waitresses shall be finally translated into terms that lawyers can understand, many will be taken by surprise.

He didn't pretend to understand women fully, but he did think of himself as a sympathizer. An ally. He had liked that part of lawyering, when he could stand as a woman's protector and squeeze money for her out of a tightfisted bastard. At the same time, a sympathizer might also be an admirer, physically speaking. For instance, as Billie spoke, he both sympathized and admired. Well, maybe admiration had the upper hand. He wanted to blurt his admiration, say, "You make my mouth water, Ms. Poe. You make my tongue hard." He didn't.

He tried to ascertain exactly what it was about her that he found alluring. One thing was that she didn't measure her allure. Wasn't monitoring her effect, wasn't using him as a mirror. She had a preoccupied manner, as if her thoughts were, if not a thousand miles away, maybe a mile and a half away.

"Well," she was saying, "it's difficult to not get married. You have to put some effort into it. Keep your guard up."

"Haven't thought of it in quite that light."

"It's true. Like not eating fat."

"It may very well be true," he said, honestly but without full consideration of the theory, distracted as he was. She rubbed her nose. It was a small and very wonderful nose, delicately made.

No matter how low he sank, there would always be certain pleasures that would buoy him. And most of them were free. There were a hundred thousand women in the tri-county area, and they could be seen any day of the week, in easily accessible public places. There was also a good county library and a good national forest. Those three things (women, books, woods) would always, respectively, lift the heart and stoke the brain and feed the spirit. How bad could life without money get?

He hadn't actually read a whole book in some time; his encounters with women were becoming progressively briefer; and word was, the National Forest looked more like a national stick-pile. But still. He thought of himself as having resources. It was the image of the resources that buoyed him, not necessarily the direct experience of them.

The moon belongs to everyone, sang the old singers, who ought to know.

"So," the girl said. "Tell me what you're doing with your life. Seriously." She wasn't settling for his evasive tactics.

It was a hard question, harder coming from Billie. He didn't know at what level to approach the answer, shallow or deep. Her two eyes were on him. He wanted to go for deep, lay out his true desires then and there; but he backed off from deep and went half shallow. Sometimes he was too eager with women, and showed himself too soon, and frightened them off.

"These days, I'm living in a bungalow on the scroungy end of the Isle of Palms. The rent is two hundred dollars a month, utilities included. I have twelve thousand dollars in a money market account, clear title to a 1980 Toyota, and the loan of Louise's extra knives and forks. I'm running an experiment. How long will twelve thousand dollars last an unemployed bachelor with no dependents and no costly tastes? My guess is three years. What do you think?"

"Six months if you eat beans and rice."

"Precisely my diet! Pinto beans, Mahatma rice, no fat."

"But then what, after the money is gone?"

"That's the most interesting part. *Then what?*"

"Something will happen."

"Exactly what I'm thinking."

"Louise told me you were self-destructive," Billie said. But when had they talked about him? He thought he had a fresh start here; he didn't like working against some image that Louise had planted. Christ, "self-destructive." What was Louise trying to do to him?

"And you agree?" he said.

"Well—I can't tell yet." He liked the implication of a future in that "yet," a future in which he would submit himself for examination and judgment by Billie. He had nothing to hide.

I place before you a heart that's an open book, the sweet-voiced tenor crooned. Over the sigh of the boneyard, his songs rose and fell. Louise knew of Rob's love for the Ink Spots, a devotion dating from the cradle. She had gone to some trouble to order these tapes. The lead Spot had the saddest voice Rob had ever heard. *You were only fooling, but I was falling in love.* If his mother had spun Mozart for him, maybe his musical taste would have been more refined. But she had loved the Ink Spots, sang along with them, even danced. To this day, nothing moved him like those honey-toned black men, or their descendants—the Platters, the Temptations, the great Aaron Neville and all his kin. But the Spots were the first and the best.

Albert could take the Ink Spots or leave them. He was a jazz man. Rob wondered if Billie had ever heard these songs before. They'd been old even when he first heard them. She had probably been raised on heavy metal and rap. The conversation lagged; her gaze wandered to the stars, two of them newly popped out over the black sea. Generation gaps are most noticeable to the younger of the gapped generations. He had little of interest to offer her.

"I'll show you something you've never seen before," Billie said.

"What's that?"

"Look at Venus. The one on the right. What do you see? What does it look like?"

"Like a star," he said.

"Okay, but focus a little bit off to the side."

"Yes?"

"Don't you see it? The crescent? Most people don't notice it, but on a clear night you can see the phases of the planet Venus without a telescope."

"I see it. I never knew that."

"I knew you didn't," she said. "Nobody does. I like to know things that no one else knows."

What could he say after that? He didn't know anything that no one else knows. Except maybe the habits of the Bachman's warbler. He'd found that women were seldom interested in bird lore.

"You need another drink," he said. "And another napkin."

"Sorry. I always do that."

"I'll be right back," he said, giving her a chance to escape him.

He headed for the porch bar; but Albert was still nodding and smiling, pouring, squeezing the limes. So Rob detoured to the kitchen, and the cabinet where he knew Hank's Tanqueray was safely out of reach of the guests. This kitchen was not one of his favorite spots. In it was revealed the scale of the Camdens' life. Even though they had no children, and even though Louise, when she cooked, relied on top-of-the-line frozen dinners, still the kitchen was outfitted to feed a battalion. A stove of restaurant capacity, six burners and a grill. Two ovens, or maybe three: there was something on the counter that was either a microwave or a television set, he couldn't make a positive identification. This did not seem like the right place for Louise.

His favorite people were all marooned in places unsuitable to their souls.

He mixed a weak gin and tonic and dispensed himself some ice from the automatic cube producer in Louise's monster refrigerator, then sat down at Louise's desk. He wasn't happy with the prospect of serving as Billie Poe's legal adviser. If he went back out there and gave her this drink and saw her pale eyelashes, he would be caught again in what he had just got out of. He would be *retained*. So he sat. Looked through Louise's mail, her appointment book, her phone bill, hoping to find some mention of himself in this record of her daily life, some documentation of his existence. Failing. Nothing but Junior League memos, errand lists, minutes of the art museum board meeting, a schedule of volunteers at the homeless shelter. Billie's name was penciled at the bottom of the schedule. Maybe they were volunteers together. The shelter was doing four times its normal volume of business these days.

He spun the Rolodex. At least he was in there. His name, along with the new phone number that he didn't even know himself. He liked seeing his name written in Louise's lovely cursive, "Robert M. Wyatt." But he wished she had written "Rob" or "Wyatt," the names she used in everyday conversation. Whenever she called him Robert, it meant she was establishing a temporary distance that might take a week to overcome. And here was his whole formal appellation, as if he were her lawyer or insurance agent. He wanted more intimacy on the Rolodex.

It affects a man to have two names, especially when they imply different worldviews. He was Robert the Serious, a believer; also Rob the Ironic, jokester and cynic. His two names had given him two philosophies. He espoused them both, simultaneously, in a kind of philosophical bigamy.

And he was true to both. How, he didn't know. One good philosophy like one good love ought to displace all others. Certainly it should not accommodate its polar opposite. For instance, he believed that everything mattered. Equally, he believed that nothing mattered.

Back when he was enamored of the law, he learned the importance of documentation. Without it you have no case. The human condition entails a longing for documentation, proof of

existence. Hence photo albums, souvenirs, diaries. But other creatures don't feel the need. Speedo could lie in the island sun fully
confident of his own existence; he knew he was there. It may
have been the only thing he knew, but he knew it at the deepest
level. Rob once showed Speedo a Polaroid picture of himself, and
he didn't recognize its importance. He didn't need it.

Speedo didn't need much at all. Of course, someone was filling
his dog bowl on a daily basis, with a high-protein, low-fat, special-
for-senior-dogs chow. Nobody was going to provide Rob with a
comparable service. He didn't have a family fortune like Hank
did; his father's surplus funds were earmarked for the Episcopalian old folks' home, where to get in you had to sign over fifty
thousand up front, per resident, and then pay an additional twelve
hundred a month. It was a cleverly constructed scheme. You got
your fifty thousand back when you died. His parents were on
the waiting list to get in. They would have their own cottage in
the pines (the image tempted Rob himself, he wouldn't mind a
cottage in the pines, had picked his own house with that image
in mind), and they'd walk an azalea path down to meals in the
lodge, and see all Jack's old Episcopalian friends, and have everything they needed right there on the premises, including hair-
dressers and laundry. They would be well cared for. They seemed
to sense that their sons would not be stepping forward to care
for them, neither being in a position to do so. Rob in his Isle of
Palms bungalow had no room for them; Ernie had been loose
on the road since February after dropping out of school.

"One of my sons is a lawyer and the other one is an adventurer,"
Maude liked to say.

He never expected any money from his parents; was in fact
surprised when they came into some. The Wyatt pharmacies,
three of them, had always appeared to be flops—corny drugstores
in declining neighborhoods, doing a major business in prophy-
lactics and suppositories, with a permanent inventory of cheap
candy and expensive cosmetics that no one ever bought. Only in
the back room, where Jack mixed possibly illegal concoctions,

was there any air of the apothecary's mystique. Rob grew up thinking of his father as a scientist-magician, the last of the breed, the Amazing Jack Wyatt. But he'd sold the stores last year to a southeastern chain; not to be incorporated into the chain, but simply to be eliminated, so that anyone needing a bulb syringe would have to get in the car and drive five miles to the warehouse-size discount drug palace.

Louise was right that he might face a survival problem, once First National's computer flagged his account. But he had some time to figure things out.

It wasn't that he didn't want to work. He'd have liked any number of tasks: cleaning out the Augean stables, for instance, or searching for the city of gold. But you can't tell a woman like Louise that you want to be a hero. She didn't believe in grand dreams; her pleasure came from the maintenance of daily order in the real world. She kept her shoes (as he learned when he helped her install a closet system) in the original boxes, labeled in a vocabulary obscure and tantalizing: "white slingbacks," "black espadrilles." She saw him as her chum, a cynical/innocent sort to whom she could place midnight phone calls—someone to joke around with and golf with. They didn't mention their past romance; and as it had never been technically consummated, had even in its heyday been ill-defined, a sort of mock romance by all appearances, maybe it didn't merit mention now; she seemed to have forgotten it, and taken him on as a sidekick. And he didn't make light of this role; on the contrary, it was a responsibility. But the nature of it did not allow him to tell Louise all the truth.

At the same time, he wanted to be the opposite of a hero—a Charlestonian. He wanted to fit right in, and present himself as proud citizen of the fair place. It should have been easy enough to do. Charleston didn't always welcome newcomers, but he was no newcomer, he was a native, old family on his mother's side, with her Bonnette ancestors under slate angels in the Huguenot cemetery. But something was wrong between him and his native

city. He felt less closely related to those successful merchant Bonnettes under the angels than to the dark and diabolic Stede Bonnet, no relation, hanged for a pirate in 1718 in the lowtide mud
off the Battery. Stede never settled into citizenry; but maybe he
wanted to, at one time—maybe saw through his glass those houses
along the bay and imagined himself ensconced, law-abiding,
wived, a townsman. But some men cannot pull it off, towns-
manship; as much as Rob longed for it, he could not even walk
the city's streets, between the white piazzas and the polished brass
knockers on dark green doors, the side-slung gated gardens,
without feeling like an interloper.

He fared somewhat better on the outskirts of the city, the
islands or the suburbs or the country, where newcomers accreted
and a certain degree of anonymity could be achieved. That was
why he could not be a real Charlestonian. There was nothing
wrong with the town, but something wrong with him, and it
was that he could not properly present himself, as a Charlestonian
can. He had to be able to hide.

"Mr. Wyatt?" a voice said from the doorway. Billie stood there,
and behind her Louise. He noted how much smaller Billie was
than Louise, in all dimensions. Even her head was smaller. And
yet they sort of looked alike, could have been sisters or, possibly,
mother and daughter.

"Are you on the phone?" Billie said, polite, backing away.
Louise put her hand at Billie's back as if to keep her in the room.
He recalled that hand at his own back.

"No, I'm just sitting. Just taking a breather. Call me Rob."

"I was afraid you'd left. And I really—I didn't want you to
think I was joking about needing a lawyer. Do you think you
can represent me? I can pay you, not a whole lot right now but
I'm going to get a job and then I can pay you."

"To tell you the truth, I'm not much of a lawyer. I've had
what you might call a limited practice. You'd really be better off
with Hank. He'll work out some terms with you."

Louise said, "Listen, Rob. Maybe you could just advise Billie, unofficially. You could do that, couldn't you? Just sit down with her for a few minutes and point her in the right direction?"

Louise knew as well as he did that there was no such thing as unofficial legal advice. If he was going to point Billie in the right direction, he would have to do it as a lawyer. He saw Billie's little upper teeth catch her lower lip.

"Let's talk about it," he said. He swung the chair around and pulled another one out from the kitchen table. Billie came forward; Louise stayed in the doorway, one hand high on the jamb. He ignored her and spoke to Billie as if they were alone.

"The only thing I'm really good at, legally speaking, is divorce," he said.

"See, that's what I need, sort of."

"You do?"

"I think so. But it's complicated."

He tried to hide his surprise. He said, "You'll have to give me a little more information."

"Now?" she said with disappointment, and he realized that she had in mind something more extended than a kitchen chat, and something more private.

"Well, we could get together next week sometime," he said. "But I'm afraid I don't even have an office anymore."

"I'm helping at the shelter until next Saturday, but I could meet you then at your house. She said that would be all right."

"She did," he said. He took a breath. He was no match for Louise's wits, her snookering capabilities. She'd have been a good litigator.

"Sure, that would be all right," he said to Billie. "I live on Tanglewood Street, in a blue house. You take a left off Palm Avenue—"

"I know where it is. Louise told me."

"Of course—what am I thinking of?" He touched his forehead. "Well, how about Saturday morning?"

Behind Billie, Louise shook her head. He had forgotten about the golf date.

"Or midday," he said. "Noon?"

"Good," Billie said. "Thank you." In the kitchen, without the benefit of sunset, she was still peachy: the color was her own. And she still didn't look nineteen. Louise, in the background, smiled at him.

Billie stopped on her way out, turned and said, "This sounds dumb, but were you in the navy?"

"Not me," he said. "Why?"

"I have a feeling I've seen you before. I don't know where. I thought maybe it was at the base."

"I probably remind you of one of the regulars at the shelter," he said, his heart racing. "Scruffy and shifty-eyed." He didn't say, *in your dreams, Billie, in your heart of hearts.*

He thought a lawyer could not be a hero, because a lawyer is removed. Even when the stakes are high, his battle is not his own and he has, therefore, nothing to lose. In this respect, a lawyer is less like Odysseus and more like Ares, who may participate in battle but—after all—what are the risks to Ares? He fights for fun. Lawyers are for all practical purposes immortal, and the immortals are a dull crowd.

The creatures Rob liked best were those whose existence was marginal, who might slip at any moment into extinction. Into the void. For that reason, he liked pelicans, he liked waitresses. Their battles were real. Their stakes (their lives) were high. He would have been happy to live among either group. Whether he could do it by act of will, he did not know. It was possible that marginality wasn't something you could earn. It might be like a state of grace, which falls upon you like a net whether you want it or not, whether you deserve it or not.

He slipped away from the party without formal farewell and trudged through sand toward his car, parked illegally on the shoulder for ease of getaway. Halfway there he stopped at the sound of his name; he turned to see Louise and Hank standing on the porch.

"Saw you sneak out," she called. "You're yellow-bellied,

Wyatt." Hank had his arm around her. She waved. He had reasons for disliking her little wave. He did not like to be waved to, by her, like that. He waved back and hoped she noticed how paltry a gesture it was.

He looked up. Saw the white crescent, tipped earthward. That planets wax and wane had not occurred to him, but there it was, the planet of desire, a thin curl in the uninhabited heavens, spinning through its phases unnoticed.

C H A P T E R   3

⮝⮟⮝⮟⮝⮟⮝⮟⮝⮟⮝

He drove home, or to what he called home. It was the kind of neighborhood where everyone who lives there is planning to move out. But Rob had a new rule of thumb: move in when others are moving out. He had wangled a low rent with no lease, and a little house of the type known to realtors as a "starter." He didn't mind the irony. A starter home is for young couples on the way up. And here comes the balding bachelor on his way down.

Of course, if he had followed through on the promise of his youth, he'd have made his move by now into a tall house below Broad Street, with a carriage house in the back for the aging parents. He suspected that was what his father originally had in mind for his golden years. But Maude came up with the plan to check into what she called "geriatric Elysium." Rob was surprised; but she seemed enthusiastic, and he didn't object. He was relieved of a worry that he didn't need, in his present circumstances.

Last year he'd made fifty thousand dollars and spent most of it. Fifteen hundred a month went to sublet a furnished luxury apartment at the top of Fort Sumter House, an ex-hotel now in condominiums. There was not fifteen hundred dollars' worth of luxury in it—a decorator's idea of southern comfort: artificial antiques and a Jacuzzi in which, alone, he felt not luxurious but deprived. However, there was a fifteen-hundred-dollar view. From his window he had looked out onto the tops of the oak trees in the park below; and past them the boulevard and the harbor. On Sundays, black people gathered along the seawall for what looked like a Latin American paseo, youth parading its charms; the sidewalks of the boulevard became two long lines of saunter and joy, each herd of girls melded to a herd of boys, their portable music wafting over the harbor.

On occasion up there he thought that an official day of reckoning might not be necessary; it seemed possible that if you could just get the right vantage point you might be able to reckon everything yourself, see the big picture or at least get glimpses of it. What was life but trees and water and a parade of folk jockeying for love? A little carnival? From up in the Fort Sumter House, all those black people looked happy.

But white residents in houses along the boulevard had complained to the cops about the music and the litter, their real worry the sight of so many black people gathered in one place. Ordinarily, the city was a model of racial harmony. Blacks stayed uptown, quite harmoniously. But if they came downtown, if they *congregated,* the white people got nervous. Currently, certain indicators were ominous. Uptown, there were young men gathering on corners during the daytime. Downtown, new street signs had sprung up depicting the neighborhood crime-watch logo, a large and somewhat demented eyeball.

Rob had noticed those messages that had frightened Jack. "Behold God Army." Of course, they were only the work of some Christ-crazed graffitist ignorant of the possessive case. But they were all over Uptown. Shopowners painted them out, and they reappeared the next day. Then the hurricane hit. Since then there had been no new messages. Maybe there was a shortage of spray-paint. Maybe the graffitist was busy fixing his roof.

Fifteen hundred was what people paid to be above it all. But a view from on high is not the most accurate. It's pretty, but it's not entirely true, omitting the single heartbreak. He'd had the view a couple of times before in his lifetime, once as a child from the steeple of St. Mark's, and once from the Isle of Palms water tower, which he had climbed drunk the night of Louise and Hank's wedding.

At that wedding (gotten together on surprisingly short notice, he thought, yet formal and enormous) he was sick with a flulike malady that had not responded to NyQuil. Upping the dosage to three cuplets hadn't helped. His mother gave him some sherry before they set out for the church, and then he'd found a half-pint of bad rum in his glove compartment. His head swam and his eyes ran; he had to breathe through his mouth. In his wrinkled tan suit (he'd forgotten to pick up his rented tuxedo) he must have looked, standing in the pew with Maude and Jack, like a slack-jawed adult child in the custody of its parents for reasons best not inquired into. (Has it murdered dogs? Sent obscenities in the mail to prominent citizens?) At his side, Maude frowned. She snapped her pocketbook open and shut.

"What happened to good old-fashioned hippie weddings?" she grumbled. "Why couldn't they have gone down to the Battery and read Kahlil Gibran to each other in the setting sun? I'm disappointed in Louise. This man isn't right for her." Rob thought her diatribe was for his sake; she must have sensed his heart was broken. "It's a travesty," she said. "It's all wrong. It's a damn shame."

"Maude, we're in church," Jack said.

"That's what I mean," she said.

The stained-glass lamb of God above the altar looked dim and gloomy. Then he realized it was night, and the light that usually lit the lamb from outside wasn't there. He was dim himself and swelling with fever, his skin suddenly a size too small. He must have groaned.

"Are you all right, Rob?" his mother whispered.

Her sympathy touched him. He wasn't all right, grief and influenza were wrecking him. But he appreciated her concern; he nodded nobly. The cherubim at the shadowy corners of the ceiling mourned with him, their mouths downturned. Everyone craned to watch the approach of the bride, and Maude's hand touched his arm, in what he took as an attempt to comfort.

But her fingers dug hard. He had misread her. She said, "How could you have let this happen? What were you thinking of?" She was furious.

Louise's face was shrouded in veil. He couldn't tell whether she saw him or not, as she passed on the arm of her father. The Wyatts were standing on the bride's side, with a motley assortment of the bride's relations and friends, including the entire disreputable-looking staff of the newspaper, where she worked, and a gay contingent made up of Louise's pals from the art museum, where she was a docent, and a number of other unusual characters she had befriended along the way. Across the aisle the groom's people occasionally glanced in horror at the other side. But they knew they had won. Louise would soon be theirs. She was considered a wild girl who only needed reining in, and Hank was the man to do it. He was "established," "steady." Hank's mother, who was the twin of Nancy Reagan, perfectly coiffed, and confident of victory, smiled at the losers.

He discovered that he was unable to swallow. Would he stand and dribble?

Surely Louise, if she had been blind in the preceding month, would now see her error. Even through the veil, the scene could not be lost on her; she'd notice the dichotomy here, the unbridgeable gap between His and Hers. Her side had real black people, Hank's had maids and retainers. Hers had waitresses, his had debutantes. Hers had Rob! He wanted the bride's side to rise up as one and spirit her away. But she was already at the altar. Her father was handing her over.

He could see only her back and the costume of white satin puffing and spilling onto the floor around her, and the headdress of mammoth proportions shooting outward from her head. The minister asked if anyone wanted to stop the marriage. Rob didn't think it would go over well if he raised his hand to explain that he'd been meaning to marry this woman himself but just hadn't gotten around to it in time: the explanation would have required eloquence, and he couldn't even dislodge his tongue from the back of his throat. He half hoped Maude would speak up. But she was sucking her lips in, mum.

Was the groom willing to swear fealty? Hank answered loud and strong, a little too loud and strong. Bride? Rob strained but heard nothing from Louise. He thought, *She's backing out!* Hope jumped in his chest. *Attagirl.* He made ready to step forward and hustle her out of the church. They'd keep right on going, out the door, up the street, into a cozy cottage by the sea for the rest of their lives.

But the minister went on from there to the final pronouncing. Had she spoken? Or had she maybe only mouthed the vows, in which case the pronouncement might be technically invalid, or at least vulnerable to later appeal? He grasped at straws, like a good lawyer.

She turned around. He hoped to see second thoughts written on her face. They weren't there. Her face was the one in photos of radiant brides. She walked toward him, beaming, and her eyes landed on his, maybe accidentally or maybe she had sought him out—and she smiled bigger. She gave him a little wave of the hand, the cute high coed variety of wave in which only the fingers move. Not the gesture of someone having second thoughts.

He preserved that wave in his memory, as reassurance: nothing great had been lost, if she could wave to him like that. It was a gesture of double function. Hello, goodbye.

Albert was standing in the vestibule overseeing the logistics. He followed Rob to the car. Rob got in; Albert got in. "Well, fuck," Rob said by way of conversation, and drove to the island.

Albert remained politely in the car while Rob climbed the water tower. It was something he had always wanted to do. There was a light wind and a wide sky. Hand over hand he pulled himself up the metal ladder, past the ten-foot letters spelling out the name of the island, onto the sloping silver cap of the tank. He crawled to the center and sat. It was immediately restorative. He was sitting on top of the world. Below him the island bent like an elongated banana, lit with the lives of normal happy people at home in their dens and rec rooms, and beyond them opened the black Atlantic. The wind carried in the sounds of teenagers on the beach. Shrieks, laughter. The firemen's fair was in progress, and its small Ferris wheel turned in the sky to a tinkling tune.

He leaned back against the cone of the ancient alarm, mounted there in the fervor of civil defense to signal meetings of the Volunteers (one blast), wrecks (two), water rescue (three), fire (four), and on up through rarer and rarer catastrophes (tornado, hurricane) to those for which alarm seemed superfluous. Nine was earthquake. Ten was war.

He had not, at that point, ever heard it go past four. The thought occurred to him that there were ten categories of possible disaster in the world, and that his life was the sort of life, this was the sort of place, that would never reach past category four, a modicum of disaster. Louise's wedding had not even merited a peep out of the cone. He watched the Ferris wheel rotate. The little carnival, a civic event produced annually by the Volunteers to raise money for new equipment, never raising enough to buy more than hoses, was nothing in the great scheme of things, under the enormous void. Just a brief and pleasant gathering, well-intentioned, continuing year after year in spite of everything. No grand carnival—no shouts of *"Carne vale,* O flesh, fare-well!"—but only a local fair, a little tomfoolery in the darkness.

He heard Albert coming up, the scrape of shoe leather on the metal ladder, a muttered curse at the top.

"Rob?" said his voice through the darkness.

"Over here." He was glad to have Albert's company here on the top of the world. Albert's very existence seemed a balancing factor; without Albert one could think the human race a race of merchant mentality, all lawyerly in one way or another, transacting daily business without a nod to the possibility of sorrow. Albert seemed to know sorrow. Exactly how he'd become acquainted with it, beyond the obvious general conditions of his life (taken from his people and trained like a pet), Rob didn't know for sure. But there was something, some kind of specific woe.

Rob felt a hand on his shoulder. "You all right?" Albert said.

"Course I'm all right." Rob's speech was more slurred than he would have expected.

Albert sat down next to him. "Hard times," he said. "You have to shake them off and move on."

"Right."

"Best way to do that is go home and sleep. Mornings, everything looks better."

"How did you get out?" Rob said.

"Of what?"

He meant *out of the spin, the whole spin and rush of trouble,* but even to him it was not a clear concept. He said, "Hard times."

"I don't think I did."

"You did, you removed yourself. No family, no taxes, no women. A simple life, no one to worry about except yourself."

"Till you go and climb a water tower. You ready to go home now? I'm dizzy sitting on this round thing, that Ferris wheel turning."

"She made a mistake, Albert," Rob said.

"Yeah, come on now." Albert tried to stand, but the slope was too steep and he sat again. "I got to get down from here. Let's go."

"You go. Take my car."

"Can't do it," Albert said. "I'm not leaving you up here."

"You don't understand."

"I understand all right. Women. Can't live with 'em, can't shoot 'em."

"That's how you see it?"

Albert wouldn't elaborate. "You're a stubborn fool," he said. "Acting like a baby just because you got your feelings hurt. There's a lot worse things than some woman busting your heart, a lot worse. A bust heart is a luxury item. And I'm not leaving you up here so you can go and jump. If you had a good reason, I might let you. This is nothing."

"You thought I was going to jump?"

"What else does a man climb a water tower for?"

"For the view. To get my bearings."

Albert shook his head.

"I'll go down," Rob said, "if you'll tell me one thing."

"What's that?"

"Where you go every Wednesday."

"That's my day off," Albert said.

"I know that, but where do you go? You disappear. Where to?"

"That's my business."

"You've got a woman somewhere. If you didn't have one, you wouldn't be saying it's nothing. It's easy to tell me it's nothing if you're set up yourself. You've got a woman."

"If you say so."

"And you see her every Wednesday, and keep it secret, because maybe she's married? Or she won't have you, or you can't afford her, or you yourself don't want her more than Wednesdays?"

Albert narrowed his eyes to study Rob's face. "What good's this information going to do you?"

"Keep me from leaping. To know you're fallible, you're in a mess, I'm not the only one."

Albert sighed. "You're not the only one," he said.

"I knew it. So who is she?"

"I'm getting you down from here now, whether you cooperate or not. If I have to knock you out and carry you. If I was you I wouldn't want to be hauled down from here by a man whose knees shake in a high place."

Before climbing down, Rob took one more look out across the island. Of course he'd had no intention of jumping. All he'd wanted was a view of festival and revelry. From the water tower, things looked okay. Things looked small and happy.

Sad to say, during Rob's income-producing years he hadn't salted away much money. Now he was obliged to break the big rule: he was spending capital. Since there wasn't very much of it, the infraction seemed hardly significant. In fact, it seemed like a good idea. Maybe the rule was wrong. Maybe the real rules are the opposites of the ones you hear. Spend your capital, keep your guard down, build your house on sand. A wise man and his money are soon parted.

His most recent communiqué from First National showed a beginning balance of $17,376, dwindling rapidly to $13,201. He'd bought his way out of the condo, traded his half-paid-for Alfa for a car probably worth a negative sum, put down a deposit and a month's rent on the bungalow, sent a check to the Red Cross lady on TV. Today there was another thousand-buck outflow for insurance. By his calculations he was down to $12,006.

Insurance! Why had he bought it? A moment of weakness. Hank was levelheaded, and he wanted Hank to believe he was still somewhat levelheaded himself. Levelheaded men cover their lives and their health.

Actually, the deal was sufficiently cockeyed to appeal to Rob. He was entitled to name a beneficiary, someone who'd need help if Rob were no longer around. Speedo was the only logical choice, but he put down Albert. Then the new policy promised him a windfall should he ever lose one eye and one limb, even more if he lost both eyes and two limbs, double this if the misfortune should occur while he was in the process of being transported by a public carrier. "I guess if I'm low on funds I can always board a Greyhound and hope for a moderately tragic bus wreck," he'd said to Hank, who didn't laugh.

Hank was Mr. Charleston. Of ancient and distinguished lineage, educated at Woodberry Forest School and the University of the South, the last of the southern gentlemen-scholars. Rob's own lineage was somewhat suspect, the upcountry Wyatts and the French Bonnettes. Hank was a member of the St. Cecelia Society; Rob was a member of the Volunteer Fire Department. Even his Yale University degree, which might have been a badge of distinction somewhere else, was in Charleston only a sign of aberration. He had done well at the state university law school, and Hank had taken him in on the basis of his grades there. Rob had been under his wing for seven years, a protege of sorts, a promising young man. That promise had not been fulfilled, and he was aware of Hank's disappointment. But the failure of the protege was in part the fault (unintentional) of the mentor.

Hank was unassailable on all fronts—smart and honest and "ruggedly handsome" (as Louise had once put it, to Rob's considerable disgust). Worse, he was taller than Rob. All of which triggered in Rob, while in Hank's company, a sensation of shrunkenness. He felt thrown into the role of a younger brother, perversely compelled to become the opposite of the one he should emulate. In the office he had found himself turning clownish and cynical, the underdog showing a belly. With men other than Hank he was his normal self, or better. With Ernie, for example. With Ernie he was like Hank.

Hank was the only shadow on his horizon—or not Hank himself but Hank's disappointment. But fuck Hank. He had quit Hank. He had other things to think about.

Debt, none. Assets, minimal: the money market account, plus one hundred shares of pharmaceutical stock that was now worth a little more than half of the five thousand he had paid for it in 1987 (his timing off, the purchase occurring four days before market meltdown).

He had lost money, but he had gained strategy. It was that crash that had suggested the countercourse, the rule of moving in when others are moving out. His loss was minor compared to the losses of big investors, and yet when it happened he was grief-stricken, embarrassed, and finally relieved. The market had crashed in order to reveal to him his own stupidity. He was not a money man. Let others make the millions. He would stand back and admire. Money-making was a talent as odd and mysterious as the other talents he did not possess: musical, artistic, athletic. Some people are blessed, some are not. The day after the crash, with the Dow Jones at 1680, Hank had leapt into the market and watched the average climb to 2660, then got out with what had to be close to three hundred thousand new dollars. That was artistry. Rob, on the other hand, had chosen his drug company stock out of loyalty to his father's profession. Housewives had done better. One of his clients sank her entire settlement check into steakhouse securities and parlayed it into a fortune. She had gotten her tip from a radio show.

He hadn't even bothered to sell the damn drug stuff, planned to keep it till it went to zero. He was curious: What exactly would happen when everything went to zero, and First National would no longer honor his checks?

2.

In the moonlight his blue house looked white as a shell. Originally, these tiny houses had all been identical: peaked roof, three rooms and a bath, front and back door. But over the years some had gained screened porches and various add-ons. His had an extra room in the back and a carport on the side, a lean-to of aluminum poles and corrugated green fiberglass. He pulled into it, and heard his phone ringing. He hadn't realized it was back in operation.

The windows were open; the telephone rang into the night air. He took his time getting to it, half hoping it would stop ringing before he answered. It could be Albert, who sometimes stopped by after bar duty to sit on the porch and demonstrate gloom personified. Rob understood that he was somehow privileged to witness Albert's moods, since nobody else saw them. Albert trusted him enough to indulge, in Rob's presence, in both moodiness and alcohol. But the moods could be contagious. He didn't need one right now.

Or maybe it was Louise, ringing him up for jokes. He didn't need those either. There was no one he wanted to talk to.

Including Ernie.

"How's it going, Rob?" Ernie said.

"Where are you?"

"Hey, that's my question to you, man. You weren't easy to track down. I had to make the supreme sacrifice to get your number."

"You called home?" Ernie didn't check in often with Maude and Jack. He was more likely to call Rob and relay a message.

"I disguised my voice. I don't think Mom recognized me. I said I was an old friend of yours and had tried to call you but your line was disconnected and did they know where you were."

"Ernie, she had to recognize your voice—"

"She wasn't all the way awake, and I talked funny—she thinks you've got a redneck friend. I don't know, maybe she knew it was me. She went along. Gave me your number. So where are you?"

"Isle of Palms." He suddenly realized he didn't want Ernie to know his situation. Ernie looked up to him; he didn't want to disturb that perspective.

"I got the idea from the news that the Isle of Palms was no more," Ernie said.

"It's here. Not in the best of health, but here. Where are you? How's the rampage?"

"I'm not exactly on it anymore. It's tough to keep one up. I mean, after six months you just don't have the brain cells left. And then I saw the news photos. Thought I might, um, come home. I'm on the way, in fact, sort of. I'm still in Gainesville, but I'm making my move soon."

"What happened? You're in trouble?"

"No, you are, right? I got worried. You, them, the old hometown."

"Last time we talked, it seems to me you said you never wanted to see the place again."

"Yeah, well, that was true then. I've mellowed and matured. Seen the error of my ways. I didn't mean I hoped the place would be creamed."

"Run out of money?"

"That, too."

"Okay, good. Come on home. You need money to get here?"

"No, I've got enough. Had a sort of benefactress in Gainesville. She's paying for a new carburetor. Soon as the bike's out of the shop, I'll ride on back. What I'm calling about is, if I could come stay with you for awhile. I can't rent a place. And also, Rob, look: I don't want Mom and Dad to know I'm back."

"That will be hard to manage. You're going to wear a disguise?"

"I don't see why it should be so hard. My path won't cross theirs. I mean, I'll see them sooner or later, but not right away. So what do you say?"

"I'm in transition, Ernie. I don't have room for you."

"Ah."

"I'm not putting you off, it's the truth. I've moved into . . . a new situation, let's say."

"That's okay, don't worry about it. I can stay with the Camdens. Could you fix it up with Louise? Louise is hot for me. And I'm doing good, Rob. I'm in extremely good shape. Seeing the light. I'll call you, okay? But don't tell them. Don't even do it if you think it's for my own good."

"All right."

"Well—I'll need your word on that."

"I am not going to tell them. You have my word."

"I'll call you."

Ernie sounded good, he thought. But then, he had never really been worried about Ernie, who liked to fool people into thinking he was a wild man, when he was really not. Ernie's problem was cerebral: too much brain, the kind of brain that doesn't fit into a school system. Ernie had been in trouble for his brain since the first grade. Teachers don't receive adequate training in how to deal with someone like Ernie. They called him hyperactive, pressured Maude to put him on drugs, which she steadily refused to do. When she told them that Ernie was gifted, they sighed; many parents think their sons are gifted, she was told. They proved Ernie's lack of giftedness by trotting out his permanent record, a history of failing grades and insolence. Even the coaches hated him. Ernie was six two, a hundred and eighty. He told the coaches football was a sissy sport. He got kicked out of two private schools before finding relative equilibrium at Charleston High, where he was the only white kid in an enrollment of nine hundred. When he took the SATs in his junior year, he scored an even 1600. The scores came in the mail; Maude opened the envelope and danced for joy and sent copies to the former teachers. Ernie didn't give a damn. In February of his senior year he bought a Harley and rode it to Florida.

He called home often at first for hour-long talks with Maude, whose faith in him was unflappable. She didn't urge him to come home, only to wear his helmet and to tell her all about Florida. She loved Florida. She'd never been there, but that didn't matter; she loved the concept of Florida. She wanted to know about everything he saw and did. She wanted to hear descriptions of the places he went and the girls he encountered. After the first calls, Ernie slacked off, reluctant to engage Maude's interest, which could at times be burdensome. A fellow doesn't like to file rampage reports with his mother.

Maude's enthusiasm for Ernie overrode any doubts Jack might have had about his younger son's activities; Jack wasn't allowed to raise an eyebrow. Long ago Maude and Jack had staked out their territories. Ernie belonged to Maude—and Rob, after age thirteen, to his father. Maybe any two-child family falls into patterns of alignment like that, but in most families the alliances shift from time to time. These were rigid. It was as if Maude and Jack had come to some formal agreement, like a property division, an agreement roughly coinciding with their adoption of Ernie when Rob was thirteen. They had gotten him for Maude at a time when her spirits had been low—had been, in fact, rock-bottom.

Maude was eccentric. She was an actress. Which came first, the eccentricity or the drama, Rob didn't know. Either one can be the cause of the other. Rob and Jack had learned to live with both, not always knowing which was which. Sometimes when she said something particularly nutty, he'd decide she was off the deep end—but then he'd realize it was only a line from a play:

usually Shakespeare, left over from her days in a girls' school, when by virtue of height and angularity and a photographic memory she won the roles of Mercutio, Prince Hal, and Hamlet.

When a boy is young, a mildly eccentric mother is no problem. Rob was her rapt audience, especially fond of her Hamlet. The lines didn't always make sense to him, as she remembered only her own (not necessarily in order) and couldn't always fill him in on the other characters. He got Hamlet in pieces, over breakfast. Hamlet was, it seemed to Rob, mildly eccentric himself—but not mad, not lost to reason and human sympathy. She said Hamlet was a damn fool. She'd do the soliloquies and then correct them, telling Rob what Hamlet should have said, and what he should have done, if he'd had an ounce of sense. Go for the girl, get the hell out of Elsinore.

"Hamlet is a wimp," she said, buttering his toast. "So what if his mother married his father's murderer? That's history. The man should get on with his life, make something of himself. It's the thirteenth century, for goodness' sake. You know what that means, Rob?"

"No," he admitted, and did not, beyond the fact that it sounded familiar, the thirteenth century. He had just turned thirteen.

"Think about it," she said, setting two slices of toast on his plate. "Twelve hundred A.D."

"What?" he said. "I don't know."

"America, Rob. *America has not yet been discovered.* The man could have set sail; he lived in a seagoing country. He could have discovered the damn thing. But no. No, he'd rather mince around—'To be or not to be.' Ha! That's not the question at all. To be or not to be is never the question, Rob. And revenge! The stupidest motive on earth, just an attempt to change history."

He was her great admirer, those mornings, and she knew it. She was on stage. He was a good audience for her, for a while.

But there came a time later that year when he had to conclude that she was lost to reason. She had by then quit the Footlight Players, too old for the ingenues and unwilling to take the ma-

ternal roles requiring wrinkle makeup and silver hairspray. Without stage drama, her eccentricity blossomed, and drew Jack and
Rob into it. The scenes consisted of Maude raving; Jack at wit's
end, his magic unavailing; and Rob longing for escape, hoping
for a miracle. She imagined herself old and ugly; she imagined
them against her. They were plotting to abandon her, she said,
to pour poison in her ear; Jack was seeing other women, Rob
was aiding and abetting.

One night his father came home late, when supper was already
over and Rob and his mother were at the dining table leafing
through his Peterson field guide. Rob sometimes showed her
pictures of the birds that came to his feeder. She knew nothing
about birds, and she seemed interested; he felt good, teaching his
mother. But tonight her interest had been only halfhearted; she
seemed sad, and he hated sadness. He had tried to be as lively
and talkative as possible, so that she wouldn't go to bed. Sometimes when she was like this she would go to bed at six o'clock.
Sometimes she would stay there for days.

When Jack came in he was jovial, he was charming, "the little
magician," as Maude had once called him. He came up behind
her and leaned down to nuzzle her neck, and she went stiff.

"You smell, Jack," she said.

Jack looked at Rob. "What kind of thing is that to say to a
hardworking man?" he said, more to Rob than to Maude.

"You know what I mean," she said.

Jack sat down at the plate set for him hours earlier, looking
not quite so jovial. But he smiled at Rob. "And what was the
bird of the day?" he said. "Anything spectacular at the feeder?"

"This one," Rob said, passing his father the field guide.

"Evening grosbeak? I've never seen that one before."

"You're poisoning me," Maude said.

Rob and Jack pretended not to hear. What else could they do
when she said things that made no sense?

"Can't you see that?" she said.

It was like a nightmare, Rob thought, to have your mother go crazy. Craziness was a thing he understood as being like a deep hole, and she was slipping into it, out of his reach. He saw a look of helplessness on his father's face.

"Maudie, Maudie," Jack said.

Her eyes filled with tears, and her hands shook. "I just can't— I don't know what to do. You think it's nothing, but honestly, it's very bad"—she stood up, her napkin fell to the floor, and she reached toward Jack with both arms across the table—"and I think you have to help me, I think I'm in danger."

Jack took her hands. "Maude, let's wait, all right?" He nodded toward Rob. "We can talk about this upstairs."

Rob looked at the floor, he could not let his eyes fall on her frightened face.

"There's not enough time," she said. "I have to figure out— I'm growing old, is that it? Have I gotten too old? I used to be pretty, I really was, but now I'm thick, my neck is thick. Do you think my neck is too thick, Rob?"

He was horrified that she would ask him such a crazy question. He couldn't answer.

Jack came around the table to take her in his arms, and for an instant she seemed ready to fall into them, but then she leapt away.

"Leave me alone!" She backed into the corner, her hands up to stop his approach. "It's you," she said, a wild look in her eyes.

Jack moved toward her. "It's just me, Maude."

She dodged to the sideboard and picked up a decanter by the neck, spilling sherry onto the floor. The sweet brown smell of it made Rob's stomach turn. She held the decanter not as you would to pour but as you would to strike, like a club.

"Please," she said. "Don't touch me."

"For God's sake, Maude. Rob's here. Think of Rob."

For a second her face was blank, and Rob thought she didn't recognize him. But then she did, she said his name and put the bottle down. She sat in her chair, frowning. When she looked at Rob again, she said, "I apologize to you. I'm very tired. Sometimes I— I am sometimes a little bit confused. Please forgive me."

He was ashamed to be asked for forgiveness, when it was not a matter of that. Craziness could not be something a person does on purpose. It was an accident, like something breaking or wrecking.

"The truth is, Robby, I love your father very much and we both love you," she said.

Jack, behind her, put a hand over half his face.

"I'll need something to sleep," she said, without turning to look at him.

"It's in the medicine cabinet—"

"Please, get it."

When his father left the room, she picked up the field guide. "Oh, what a mystery," she said. "Why do you love them so?"

He was at a loss.

She said, "Because they're a mystery. Because they are so beautiful. Because you cannot make them love you."

She took the pills Jack brought her. For a while she continued looking at the field guide. His father washed the dishes; Rob sat still in his chair at the table across from her, afraid to move, afraid that if he did, she might speak again and say more things that made no sense.

After she was asleep in bed, and Rob had taken the book up to his attic room, he heard his father knock on the open door. "Mind if I come in?" His father was so *polite*. The politeness made it sometimes hard to tell what was really going on. He sat down at Rob's desk and twirled the globe with his finger.

"I think we should get some kind of help for your mother," Jack said. "Get treatment for her."

"What kind of treatment?" He had not known there was a treatment.

"A doctor, hospital care."

So it was a *sickness*. Rob felt his whole body ease, and a great swell of hope rise in his heart. "Is there a cure for it?" he said.

"Rob," Jack said, laying a finger upon the Sahara to stop the globe dead, "I have to tell you there's more to this maybe than you might understand right now."

"I understand," Rob said, thinking no longer of something cracked and broken beyond repair but of something as temporary as a fever, an ache, caused by germs, curable.

"Maude is—sensitive," Jack said. "And smart, unusually so. But she can get an idea in her head and blow it all out of proportion, until it's a life-and-death thing. She doesn't really think I've poisoned her, of course. She only thinks—well—she thinks I've been seeing other women, and, Rob, it's not that she made it up, I do have a weak spot, I've always had a weak spot . . ." Jack got the earth going again, faster this time. "But I never wanted to hurt her, I want you to know that. I only hope I haven't caused anything serious, for her, God I hope that." His shoulders shook, and he was about to cry.

"You didn't cause it, Dad," Rob said. "You couldn't have caused it. It's a disease, right? You said, doctors—"

"Yes, but I've tried before to get her to go, and she won't. Her own doctor tried, just for a week maybe, for a rest and some tests."

"Let's do it right away."

"Right away?"

"Tomorrow," Rob said.

"It would be complicated. It would have to be an involuntary commitment. That means a judge has to rule that she needs help, he talks to her, and us, and her doctor."

"And he could make her go."

"Yes."

"How soon could we do it?"

His father looked at him with gratitude, with admiration.

He knew his father was a good man, a kind man, honest, meaning no harm to anyone. He wasn't like other fathers, he had always been soft-voiced and gentle—so gentle that sometimes Rob felt the need to protect him from those other men, his buddies Judge Barkney and Dr. Price. He didn't want his father to turn into someone like them, loud and mocking. On fishing trips he heard those men make fun of their wives and their children. They complained about their work, Barkney griping about his low pay in family court, Price about patients who called him at home in the middle of the night.

Jack loved his work. When he talked about it, a light came into his eyes. It was more to him than a way to make money. In the back of the King Street pharmacy he worked on new concoctions, cures for minor dermatological problems. One of his powders was good for heat rash. The FDA knew nothing of his potions, but Jack wasn't selling them anyway; he dispensed them free of charge. People adored him. At Christmas they sent hams and bourbon to the house. Who could help loving him? He believed in cures and he believed in God and he was always courteous. He would never have harmed his wife; he wanted the best for her, he wanted to help her get well.

It was done privately—in the dining room, with the judge and the doctor, and a young man writing things down. Maude took a seat at the end of the table and laid her hands flat on the dark mahogany. She looked straight at the men. "If you all knew how funny you look," she said.

On her face Rob saw an odd expression that he had seen before whenever he was about to embark on something she considered dangerous—when he took his sailboat out alone in the harbor, or when he talked her into dropping him off for the day in the National Forest. She would let him go, but she got that look on her face that meant she had willed her fear away. It was a distant look. She told the judge that she did not want to go to a hospital, she didn't think she needed to go to a hospital. That was what she was afraid of, Rob thought.

Dr. Price said he thought she could benefit from a week or two of treatment. Judge Barkney, reading a document, asked the doctor whether she was a danger to herself or to others. "Possibly," Dr. Price said. Maude made no objection; she was looking out the window, not even listening.

"And Robert," the judge said, "have you ever had the feeling that your mother might harm herself or anyone else?"

Rob had not been told that the judge would ask him anything.

Maude turned, bristling. "This is going too far," she said. "Asking a child something like that."

"We're in an informal situation here, Maude," the judge said. "I'm just trying to do it right."

"Well, you're doing it wrong, damnit," she said. "I'll go, how about that? I give up. I'll do what you want."

"Robert, I think we need to hear from you. Do you believe your mother is a danger to herself or to others? Would you say that she needs help?"

"Yes, sir."

She said nothing after that. When it was over, she picked up her suitcase in the hall (already packed! she had known what would happen) and hugged him at the front door. He began to feel his hope fast turning into its opposite. He wanted to change his answer to the judge's question.

"You can come visit me, okay?" she said, hugging him. "I'll be back soon anyway." By then he was sure he had made a mistake. He was sure that she would not be back.

The first month she was gone, Jack went to see her often, but Rob did not. Albert, who had just come to work for the church, said that in those hospitals the patients were strapped to their beds. Rob said that wasn't so; but for weeks he couldn't get the picture out of his mind, his mother tied up. He asked his father if it was true. "Of course not," Jack said. But Albert insisted on it, and worse things as well. What did Albert know, an orphan dropout? But Albert could be convincing. Rob hadn't had a black friend before; his school was a private school, all-white, but that summer he was as alone and strange and gloomy as Albert was, and they spent long hours together in the graveyard that ran to the harbor's edge. Albert didn't have much to say, but what he did he said with authority, and he stuck to his story of locked and padded rooms, bed straps, electric shocks.

Finally, Rob had to see for himself. He went with Jack to the hospital.

The place looked more like an old plantation house. He was relieved to see his mother appear on the porch, looking well, wearing her flowery skirt and a white shirt knotted at the waist. The three of them sat in rocking chairs on the wide veranda; she rocked, while he and his father kept still. Now that he saw she was free and not mistreated, he wanted to go home. She was saying what a wonderful place it was, what a wonderful doctor she had, how wonderful she felt. The wonderful doctor joined them, pulling up another chair. Rob concentrated on a small noise he heard in the oak tree next to the porch, the tiny *chink* of a downy woodpecker. The doctor was talking about Maude's depression, and Rob didn't like the word. Depression wasn't an illness. It was only sadness. He was glad when they left, and he didn't go again.

She came home in August. He was waiting behind a camellia bush, to see her get out of the car, to see her before she saw him. When the car door opened, she swung her legs out but hesitated; for a while she looked up at the house, and he imagined she might even then pull back into the car and refuse to come home. But then she saw him. She came running to him.

It was more than he had hoped for: she was back, and she was cured. She played her old Ink Spots, she was Mercutio at breakfast. He watched her closely, to see if she was her old good self, and she was—except for one new thing. She said, on the second night home, that she wanted another baby.

Jack looked up in surprise. And in joy, Rob thought. "I had no idea—" Jack said. "Yes, a baby . . ." His voice was low, and tears jumped into his eyes.

"Yes, but I mean adopt one," she said.

"Oh."

"I like the idea of new blood, someone completely new, different from us."

Jack cleared his throat and picked up his napkin and put it down again.

"What do you two think?" she said.

"Fine, it would be fine," Jack said.

"Fine," Rob said.

So it was decided. The adoption was arranged by the same doctor and judge who had four months earlier declared Maude incompetent—a private adoption, the details unknown to Rob. He didn't ask how it had been done. He only recognized that it was, in an elegantly simple way, his punishment: not something *she* thought up, as revenge, but the result of a separate justice at work on its own, set in motion by none other than himself. He didn't blame her—it made sense that if your son proved faulty you might want another one.

They saw her take the baby in her arms for the first time and then sit with it on the sofa. Rob wasn't jealous. He was even maybe a little bit relieved, because immediately it was clear that Ernie was what she needed. She kissed the baby's knees. "Hey, honey," she said, "you and I are going to have a grand time."

Across the living room he saw his father also watching, also relieved. Their eyes met. That was when the lines were drawn. Maude turned her attention and her heart to Ernie; Rob and his father were coupled.

Even now, eighteen years later, there was still that bond between Maude and Ernie, and he couldn't figure out why Ernie would be avoiding her, on his first trip home in half a year. After Ernie's phone call, he went to bed without showering, aware that at the back of his mind was a secret fear. Alliances can break down. The equilibrium of a family, even a hard-won and long-standing equilibrium, can disappear overnight. His secret fear (for all his professed concern, his posturing as the attentive son) was that he might be called upon to take care of them—Maude, Jack, Ernie, all of them. Twice now he had failed to provide shelter for them. He should have taken his parents in, taken Ernie in. But sometimes sheltering one's kin may not be in the kin's best interest. It was not a clear-cut case.

He spent the night dreaming of things just out of reach, things meant for him but not yet in his possession. The dream was interrupted once by Speedo, who sneaked into the room and laid his head on the bed; but Rob pretended to be asleep. Speedo, ignoring the law, jumped onto the bed, and Rob let him stay. Speedo was worried about him. You have to be kind to those who are worried about you, because that is about all you can do for them.

C H A P T E R   4

~·~·~·~·~·~·~·~·~·~

In the morning he made a list of the things he had to do this week—patch the shingles, order half a ton of flounder, put up signs on the road to say the fish fry was still on, then Saturday golf with Louise and meet the girl. Maybe pull the cockleburrs from his yard and plant some grass. He numbered the items one through six, and then walked down to the beach to get the list out of his mind.

To-do lists made him uneasy, reminders of the unaccomplished future. He preferred a retrospective list, and kept several to remind himself of what had been accomplished. His life list, in an old mottled black and white notebook, was one he could never quit, as the name implied. When he died there would be a number on the last page representing all the birds he had ever seen. But he kept sublists, too, which tracked certain categories—birds seen on television, birds seen mating, birds in dreams, birds found dead.

That last one had stood, before the storm, at fifteen, starting with a warbler he'd found in his yard when he was little—in fact, the very bird that had sparked his first interest. Even though it was dead, or maybe because it was dead, he was moved by the bright yellow throat specked with a necklace of black, the feathers soft in the palm of his hand, the curled leathery feet. Then there were road kills and other accidents, usually pigeons and sea gulls, and some shot ducks, and a kingfisher caught in a spring-jaw trap at a trout farm. Why he felt the need to record these deaths he could not explain. He had preserved some of the specimens and still took them out now and then to look at them. As a boy he had thought that he was doing the world some service by keeping his lists, collecting his specimens—not only birds but shells, too, and seeds and bones, anything of beauty not attributable to human design.

He could find good things on the beach, especially now that the storm had washed out the belly of the ocean. He pocketed a giant bull's-eye, the olive-green shell bulbous and unchipped. That shell meant something. He scanned the flat sugary beach, his treasure-hunting instinct alerted. What had come to light, what lay waiting for him, washed and perfect? He might find conchs or fossils . . . but what his eye lit on (a slight movement of feathers, the unmistakable form of twisted neck and angled wing) was three dead pelicans, already disintegrating, wedged among the rocks of a revetment.

He took a feather, but there was nothing else to be salvaged. He stared at the carcasses for several minutes. There were others down in the rocks, terns and plovers and willets, some so far gone he couldn't identify the species. He went home. The next day he walked the creek instead, but along the bank there were dead herons, egrets, oystercatchers, and a wood stork. The death list climbed to twenty-two. He decided to close it out and quit the morning walks for a while, watch television instead. Methodically he did his chores and ticked them off the list. Standing in his yard and flinging grass seed, he doubted anything would grow there. He needed a golf game, he needed Louise. By Saturday morning he was desperate, and got up at five-thirty to practice his swing in the living room, his father's old fishing rod as club.

At the entrance to the Sewee Club he had some trouble getting past the security gate. The guard was outfitted like a junta general. Rob wanted to discuss with the guard the concept of security. Who were the dangerous characters—golf course saboteurs, looters, or just the usual riffraff? Evidently, Rob gave the appearance of a dangerous character. The guard consulted his clipboard and requested identification.

"Sorry, no visitors. The club is closed," he said.

"Look," Rob said. "I've been in here seventeen times. You never asked me for identification before. I'm meeting Mrs. Camden. You know Mrs. Camden."

"Yes, sir. I remember you now. And the dog. You've got a new car."

"Yes. I've got a new car."

Clearly, it hurt the guard to let in a Toyota, the driver an unshaven nonmember, the passenger an upright front-seat dog who was neither golden retriever nor deerhound but was maybe related to both. But he relented. Rob hit the speed bumps fast, a nonverbal message to the guard. The Toyota took it well.

And then he was cruising down the smooth black asphalt road, which seemed unusually sunny. For an instant he wasn't sure where he was. The club prided itself on being woodsy, pruned and spotlighted its oaks, ran a little bike path in and out of the pines and palmettos. The effect had been a kind of loveliness adored by newcomers, but too tame and neat if you were a native old enough to recall the original woods—if you were one, like Rob, who had camped out here in the old days in the swish of pine and the clack of palmetto, the intricate jungle of briars and underbrush, the secret liveliness in which you in your tent did not belong but only the deer and the raccoons and possums belonged, moving silently without even the crack of a twig, through all that vegetative tangle. Someone like Rob could be surprised by the politely wooded villa sites.

But now the woods were wild and jumbled again, the bike path invisible under a six-foot layer of tree trash from which rose the spikes of snapped pines and amputee oaks. And the green was gone. All was rich deep red, and reddening still as the pines dried and the wild vines withered. The forest had collapsed. Sun glanced off the red litter and the raw yellow of opened wood.

In the past, he had scorned the club. Now he found himself longing to live in one of those villas, around which the strange beauty of disaster was heaped, haggard and gorgeous in all directions. The villas themselves looked better than before, deserted except for the few that were privately owned and still habitable. The others were rental units for vacationers who had canceled out. It looked like a ghost town; it was beautiful. Even the golf course, visible ahead, was a splendid sight.

Drained of all green, it was a shade of gold matching the adjacent marshes. Parts of the fairway had reverted to sand dune. He saw the maintenance crew posed disconsolately on a hill. They couldn't figure out where to begin. They thought their life's work was down the drain. But a small gator sunned himself on a bank, an egret leaned forward knee-deep in the standing pool. Here were the hazards a golf course ought to have: a sense of hazard itself, a sense of mortality. Let the golfer confront not sand traps and bunkers but the real thing, let him look into its face—and *then* take his shot. On this course Rob's game could not fail to improve.

All was not lost.

The Toyota sped on, a good car. It had a bashed fender and no brake lights, and sometimes couldn't get up in the morning, but it had spirit. It was decent. He and the car and Speedo were a team. A man needs a team. Those he had been on in his lifetime had not been satisfactory: fake teams, assembled for some ulterior motive like athletic victory or year-end profit. His new team had no motive. It would meet what came. He felt good about their prospects. He was extremely optimistic.

He parked the car at the far end of the lot, and let Speedo out into the woods, where there would be plenty to keep him occupied, and if not he could go down to the beach and catch minnows as boys did, herding a school into the shallows, then pouncing.

"Meet me back here in three hours, son," Rob said.

· · ·

Louise was waiting, taking practice shots from the ladies' tee. Pink golf skirt, white golf top, pink and white golf shoes with lapping tongues. But Rob would not be distracted. He would find out what her scheme was. She would be made to talk.

On the first hole, he accused her of intimating to Billie that he was not entirely a responsible fellow.

"What do you mean?" she said. "I told her you were the best lawyer I knew."

"Also that I was self-destructive. Jesus, Louise. Call me an asshole, but don't call me 'self-destructive.' "

"Those terms aren't interchangeable," she said. "You're not an asshole; you are self-destructive. What can I say? You fit the profile of those people who're carefully planning to end their lives. They get real calm. They start giving things away. They detach. Don't spread your feet so far apart, Rob. Keep your eye on the ball. They don't shave, either, because why should they, right?"

"I'm not detaching so much as divesting," he said. "There's a difference. Anyway, you're partly right, but it's over and done with. I already ended my life. And started up a new one. The new life doesn't require a daily shave."

"But what are you going to do?" she said. She was subdued this morning. He liked her subdued phases. As she damped down, he tended to rev up.

"I'm going to wait and see," he said.

"Wait and see what?"

"Wait and see what I'm going to do." He swung hard and clipped the ball. It popped off the tee like a Ping-Pong ball and bounced behind him.

"You're hopeless," she said.

"Not entirely. I have hopes for world peace—that's a big hope. I have hopes for the Bachman's warbler, which I believe not to be extinct despite the pessimism of the American Ornithological Union. I cannot say that I am a hopeless man."

"But, Rob. It doesn't make any sense. People like you don't just quit."

"Who are those people, people like me?"

"The good guys. Okay, so maybe you don't want to practice law. Fine. I can accept that. Pick something else to do."

"I've picked it."

"What?"

"Golf."

"I can't talk to you when you're like this." She meant it. She'd done it to him before. He saw her set her mouth, pushing her bottom lip up, and it meant she wouldn't talk again until he demonstrated *sincerity*.

"All right," he said. They climbed into the car and she took off at maximum golf cart speed. She was coming out of the subdued state, edging over into the stubborn state.

2.

The one thing he did like about golf was the ride. Whoever invented the golf cart deserves an honored place in the annals of sport. He used to hate golf carts. They looked ridiculous, and the men in them looked ridiculous, without dignity. But in the cart himself he changed his mind. The silence! The buoyant bumping! Now it was like flying in a dream, with Louise sitting tall at his side, the two of them riding into golden glow, dodging puddles and downed trees. During the ride, he was incapable of speech. Louise at the wheel still had her pout on, but he was grinning like a golfing fool.

She stopped, and ascertaining that he was not yet sincere, she drew a club from her bag, actually Hank's bag, a maroon and silver leather quiver with matching socks for the clubs. Lips sealed, she strode to the tee. He couldn't help smiling. He lit a Marlboro Light.

Part of the countercourse. At a moment in history when the whole world was coming off cigarettes, he had taken them up.

From the cart he watched Louise. Here was where the bravura would cut in. Once she connected with the ball, she'd talk. So he waited the process out: the bend-over (lovely, heartbreaking, straight from the waist); the assessing glance down the fairway, then head down, rear end out; the settling in, little dance of the feet, grip, glance-up, waggle, swing, and contact. Perfect follow-through (as far as he could tell), smooth and balletic; perfect flight straight toward the green-no-longer green. That would make her happy.

"Your turn," she said, smiling, nodding him out of the cart.

He took her club and tried to do the thing properly. But he felt like an idiot, a golf impostor. Anyone watching would have known immediately that he was out of his element. He didn't look right, for one thing, in his jeans and canvas shoes. But even if he'd been wearing Hank's golf togs, he couldn't have played the part convincingly. As a golfer (and as lawyer and lover) he could only improvise and hope that in the end what he'd done might make sense.

Once when he was twelve he had watched Maude and some other people do an exercise in improvisation, without a script or a plan. From his front-row seat he was admiring her cleverness, when he began to itch with the fear, gradually confirmed, that this was *going nowhere.* After fifteen minutes, the director ended the scene and summoned the actors from the stage, complimenting their performances. But Rob was bewildered. There had been moments of significance but no possibility for overall meaning. The scene was over when the time was up.

It frightened him that his life itself might work the same way, might never amount to anything but random extemporizing. He had his moments: of truth, of weakness, of existential sparkle—but that was about it. They came and went, like this moment (the dying fairway at 8:30 A.M.), this detail (Louise's mahogany-colored hair, sun-streaked, loosely swinging).

They golfed on down through the goldenness. He expected a club official to appear and run them off; but the place was deserted. The few groundskeepers in evidence had taken up chain saws now, intent on clearing the course and dragging the debris into burnpiles. They showed no interest in the two distant figures making their way along the littered fairway.

"I'll tell you what, honey-pie," he said to her. "You are the most beautiful golfer this club has ever seen. You're too good for the course, beauty-wise. Where are the spectators? You deserve a crowd of onlookers."

That was true. She deserved fame. The world should have known about Louise. It seemed a waste, that she was not on television or in a book. Maybe he would write her biography. But it would be difficult to get Louise down on paper.

"You're it," she said. "You're my public. All I've got. And that's why I'm worried. If you self-destruct, who will I have to tell me I'm a knockout? I need you alive and well."

Here was a lie so big, and so deftly delivered, right at the top of his swing, that he lost everything—stance, grip, the whole action. The iron did its best without him, came down wild, lobbed the ball into the lagoon. Who would she have? Well, she'd have her ruggedly handsome husband, for one. But it was not part of the repertoire for him to point that out. The operative pretense was that Louise's happy marriage was invisible. She protected him from it, and he was willing to be thus protected. Only occasionally did an awkward moment occur, when she went too far in her protective efforts, and the truth was revealed by extravagant falsehood.

"I am alive," he said, "and moving toward well. It may take some time."

"So you do have a plan. Tell me what it is."

"It's to ride out the years with you in a Happy-Go golf cart, and eat your pickled shrimp till the cows come home."

"You couldn't afford it, Wyatt. The ride is three thousand dollars a year and shrimp are nine dollars a pound."

"Okay, we'll hike the Swamp Fox Trail and eat mullet."

"Listen, I don't really care if you want to starve to death. That's your choice. But there's something immoral about what you're doing. You're smart, you're educated. People need help. That's what lawyers are for, when people are in trouble. You can't just abandon the world. What about your contribution to society?"

"My contribution to society over the past five years has been minimal. The people out there who need help never got it from me. You could do a follow-up and you wouldn't find a single client doing better, really better, now than before. They think all they have to do is get rid of the person they're married to and happiness will occur. I was perpetuating a big myth. I didn't save any lives. There wasn't anyone I really rescued."

"There's Billie."

"Billie. Yes. But I'm not rescuing Billie."

"You liked her."

"Of course I liked her. But that doesn't mean I want to get mixed up in some nutsy case that I don't know a thing about and don't care about and don't want to care about."

"So when you say you liked her you just mean you liked her looks. You liked the way she stands like this with her little abdomen poked out—"

"That is, in fact, a fairly good approximation of Billie's posture."

"Then it's sexual. You didn't really like her. You only thought about Billie in bed, not Billie as a person."

"No, wrong, I thought about Billie as a person."

"But you don't want to do anything to help her. You just want to stand back and ogle her and—"

"You forget. Your little scheme, whatever it is, worked. It's on track. I have an appointment with Billie Poe at high noon. I'm looking into her case. Now you tell me what's going on. How you got hooked up with her. What your plan is."

"She showed up at the shelter the day after the storm. It was full. I gave her money for a motel room."

"I want the whole story," he said. "I can tell from your eyes that there's more."

Louise putted. The ball did one of those magic tricks where it takes two spins around the rim of the cup and jumps out. She was startled by its willfulness, stared at it in displeasure.

"Well, you're right," she said. "There is more. But it was told to me in confidence."

"So were all those stories I told you about my clients."

"It's a bad story. But I'll tell you. She was abandoned by her parents. In fact, she was sold."

"Sold? For money?"

"Four hundred dollars. She was thirteen years old."

"Who to?"

"The man, whatever his name is. Carlo."

"Christ," Rob said.

"There's something real strange about the marriage—"

"Don't tell me any more."

"I don't know any more. That's all she said. I don't think she wanted to tell me that much, but she was grateful to me, and she's dangerously lonely."

"What do you mean, dangerously?"

"The kind of lonely that makes you latch onto anyone who shows the slightest kindness. All I did was lend her forty dollars. You'd think I'd saved her life."

"Why didn't you tell me this last night?" he said.

"I couldn't. She confided in me. And it's so—gruesome. I don't even like to think about it. How can a child survive something like that? I was just hoping that you would be able to help her. But to tell you the truth, I'm not real sure about it now. You might get carried away. I can tell by your face that you're going to rush into this. You're going to take over, and Billie doesn't need that. Maybe she should just go to a lawyer, I mean someone who's neutral."

"I'm neutral," he said.

"You're not, you're *interested* in her. I did invite her to the party so you could meet her, but I didn't think that you'd want to—"

"I don't," he said. "I promise. I won't touch her."

"Good, because she's—vulnerable. Just help her, that's all."

"You can trust me," he said.

She looked at him. "You're a good guy."

"I am that." He couldn't tell if either of them believed it.

Louise and he did a banter thing, a swap of joke-and-tease. It had built up to such a level that truth was hidden pretty deep. Half of everything they said could be taken to mean the opposite; they were caught in the habit of irony.

3.

They played out the front nine. She had told everything she was going to tell. He could concentrate now on her pink and white outfit and her good legs. He tried to let Billie and Carlo slip to the back of his mind. But it was hard. Moss moved on the broken trees at the periphery of the golf grass. Woodsmoke rose in the air, from the burnpiles. In the distance he occasionally saw his dog sniffing in and out of the woods, tracking some animal he would never find, with no thought of giving up. Rob was tracking something similar, something he couldn't name but could sense.

To have tried to name it, especially to Louise, would have sounded foolish. "The meaning of life"? "The hand of fate"? He trundled along behind her, knocking balls into traps and roughs and trees. He remembered Billie's small hands.

After the ninth hole, Louise totted up the scores—her 44 to his 63. She was a cutthroat competitor; she liked to win, no matter how lame the competition was. He handed over his dollar (she had reduced the stakes from five dollars, in view of his lack of funds). They stopped for a drink in the deserted bar. The door was locked, but one of the big blue-glass plate windows was smashed. Louise leaned in and halloed to the bartender, a twenty-five-year-old bodybuilder who let them in and called her Louise and gave her a Bloody Mary without asking her preference. While they drank the bodybuilder swept glass. The room was dark. Tables were overturned, chairs upended. They sat at the bar on elevated stools that made Rob feel infantile. He preferred to keep his feet on the ground.

"What's wrong, Wyatt?" she said, crossing her legs and letting the top shin touch his knee.

"Too dark," he said. He wasn't sure whether he meant the bar or the image of the child abandoned. In his previous life as a lawyer, he'd sometimes had trouble with clients' stories. The great majority of them were tales of folly with which he regaled Louise, but now and then there'd be one that couldn't be turned into a joke. He'd learned to keep his guard up against that kind. As Louise had said: sometimes you don't want to think about big things, sometimes you'd rather just play golf, or quit something, or move.

"Run away with me," he said.

"Where to?"

"I don't know. Into the woods, into the jungle. Out to sea."

She sighed. Her disappointment was visible. She was the person he wanted to please, and she was not pleased. Lately she had been sighing a lot in his presence, and then lapsing into sullenness, as if she wanted him to be somebody else. He should have left her alone. But he didn't think he could do without her.

"You used to tell me such good stories, Rob. God, all those marriage stories."

"I prefer not to recall them."

"The couple who didn't screw. She wanted an annulment after four years."

"Five."

"And the guy who was married to two women. And the wife whose identical twin seduced her husband—"

"Stop. Enough. I'm through with it."

She swiveled on her barstool. The beautiful shin grazed his thigh.

"I know why you quit," she said.

"Tell me."

"You're a dallier. You play around with something for a while and think you're in love with it, and then you want something new, you're tired of the old thing. It's the pattern of your life."

"It is not," he said.

"I've seen it. You forget: I know you well."

"I've never gotten tired of you, have I? I think I've shown remarkable fortitude and fidelity."

"Is that what it was?" she said. "I always thought it was full retreat." Something in her tone surprised him. What did she mean by "retreat"? She seemed very sad now, suddenly, as if she had stumbled and fallen into sadness unexpectedly; but she recovered. She recrossed her legs on the other side of the stool, away from him, and looked at herself in the mirror behind the bar. He wondered what thought or memory had tripped her. There was something she wasn't telling.

"Well," he said. He had the feeling that a moment of truth was within reach, and that he ought to have leapt for it, but he didn't know what to say.

"Ernie called," he said. "Wants me to ask you if he can camp out in your rec room again. Temporarily."

"He's coming home?" she said.

"More or less. But doesn't have a place to stay, what with the rest of his family scattering to the winds. Can you put him up?"

"You can put him up."

"No, I can't. I admit, I have failed my parents and my brother, but I just can't have any of them in with me now. It's time for all of us to find separate quarters. That's what a family is supposed to do, eventually, when the offspring reach adulthood."

"*Ernie* has reached adulthood?"

"Okay, maybe it's a premature breakup, from Ernie's point of view, but you forget, Ernie decamped voluntarily. Ernie's out on his own."

She sighed. "Hell. All right. You win, Rob."

"What do you mean, win? I'm not fighting you on anything."

"You win," she said. "Give me Ernie. I'm crazy about Ernie."

"That's what he said. And he's crazy about you."

"Convenient. Mutual craziness."

He looked at his watch. "I'd better go. I've got to meet Billie."

"Ah, yes, Billie," she said, coming down smooth off her stool on his side, so that now what touched him was her abdomen. She gave him a kiss on the neck, and picked up her purse off the bar. It was a little wooden box with houses painted on it. It looked like a lady's tackle box.

"You know," she said when they were both standing, "sometimes when I say goodbye to you I feel scared."

"Because you can't do without me," he said.

"I don't think that's what it is."

"You still don't trust me with Billie."

"Be careful with her," she said. She stood gazing out onto the rolling, salt-burned grass. She said, without looking at him, "I may be making a mistake."

"I gave you my word."

"That's not all there is to it. I'm not only worried about Billie. I'm worried about you. You're a sucker for helpless girls. I know that. What am I setting up here?"

"You're not setting anything up," he said. "Don't worry about it. It's out of your hands now."

"That's what I'm afraid of. But what the hell, right?"

"Right."

She seemed to want to add something else, but she hesitated.

"What is it?" Rob said.

"I just want to remind you—a thirty-two-year-old man and a nineteen-year-old girl—there's something disgusting about it."

He thought that over. He might admit there'd be some imbalance in such a match, but "disgusting"? That was overstating the case. He wasn't convinced. But he made a note to remember something important: *Louise* found it disgusting.

"And, you'd be making a fool of yourself," she added.

Ah, she knew him well. He didn't mind the possibility of being disgusting, but he greatly, secretly, feared making a fool of himself. He tried, by shrugging and grinning, not to let on how close to home she had struck.

She looked at him and sighed. "So long, Robert," she said.

He followed her out and watched her walk to her Peugeot. Something was different about her. She was as beautiful as ever. She passed a couple of groundskeepers, who turned as if on cue for a second look. But she had the slightly forlorn slump that beautiful women acquire over time. He'd never seen it before on Louise, but there it was. Beauty on the verge of surrender, and thus all the more beautiful. He was a fool for haggard beauty.

He wanted to run after her and grab her; but he hadn't done it before and he couldn't do it now. She'd have thought him insane. He watched her get in the car, smooth her skirt, look at herself in the rearview mirror and run her fingers through her hair, then start the car and pull out of the lot. She was a terrible driver. He feared for her safety when he thought of her morning rounds, the yellow lights she'd run, the way she drove slow on the interstate and fast in the suburbs. He knew she would not readjust the mirror; she kept it, always, trained on her face. He'd seen her apply lipstick while passing an eighteen-wheeler on I-26.

Louise's vanity, however, was one of her endearing qualities. It arose from deep doubt. Like most good-looking women, she was never sure of her beauty, and had to keep checking on it, to make sure it was still there. He stood alone for a minute, until she was out of sight. Failed love has a paralyzing effect. What can you do but stand and watch? He watched her car, and then he watched the empty road.

Something flew low over the humped myrtles at the edge of the water. White, flying oddly. He lost sight of it as it dove. Maybe only a gull . . . but then up it swooped again, and yes, the long split tail, the black mask of the swallow-tailed kite, a bird he'd never seen before though it nested secretly in the deep swamp of the National Forest fifteen miles north. Maybe its habitat had been destroyed. It worked the margin of the woods— for frogs, he guessed, or grasshoppers—and Rob went into the suspended state that a sighting can trigger, for a few seconds unaware of any other thing, only the white bird, until it was gone.

After a sighting there is a sense of victory. The kite would be number 316 on his life list, a tally that wouldn't have impressed a serious bird man; but he was only an amateur, a lover. He loved the instant of the discovery, that flash of astonishment. But after a sighting there is also a sense of loss, and you must stand bereft, searching the empty sky.

After a while, he went to retrieve his retriever, down in the dark woods.

CHAPTER 5

He was late for his appointment with Billie, but so was Billie. When he got home, she wasn't there yet. He wasn't feeling too good. Antemeridian darkness, his hour in the bar gloom, had thrown him off schedule; he had a late-in-the-day feeling. In the bathroom he took a look at his face and decided to shave it, in hopes that shaving might trigger the sensation of dawn.

The face was foreign. He could have been convinced by a good lawyer that it wasn't his: too boyish, small nose and chin, and yet not youthful. The hairline was receding, the eyes were tired. You could see both a lad and a geezer in this face. He wanted the face of a thirty-two-year-old man.

He rinsed his skin and abandoned the mirror. He would rather look at his house than at his face. He went into his living room and sat down on his sofa. The pleasure of the house was a surprise to him, he hadn't expected to like it so much. The proportions were right, the house fit him. He could touch his ceiling; his bed filled the bedroom, his table filled the kitchen.

He didn't feel lonely in the house, but there was something lacking. A witness. He admired the place so much, he wanted it to be admired by someone else. It was like Louise on the golf course; it needed appreciation. It had gotten none from her, and none from Albert, who stopped by but wouldn't come in, just sat on the porch and jiggled his feet—funerals on his mind, probably. When there were weddings, Albert was in good spirits. A spate of funerals could lay him low. He said he just wanted to sit in the breeze awhile, under the stars, while Rob expounded the Principle of Purposeful Marginality.

"Get to the edge, that's the secret," Rob said, rocking back in his philosophic lawn chair. "In biotic communities, the edge is where things happen. So also in human lives." He babbled bogus law and principle for hours, those nights, the porch his stoa, Albert his listener.

But Albert didn't cross the threshold of the blue bungalow; he stayed on the porch. Rob couldn't tell whether this reluctance was based on some notion of social-racial propriety or was just another quirk of Albert, who had his quirks.

Speedo had been the only other eyes in the house, and though Speedo clearly liked the place, he wasn't what Rob had in mind. The witness had to have language.

Sometimes Speedo did seem to have language. At least he seemed to understand almost everything Rob said, even new things that he had never heard Rob say before, so they could not be simply signals. Maybe Speedo understood by some different method, other than the words themselves; tone of voice, body language . . . but the problem was Speedo's silence. Even when he understood, he didn't answer. A good witness speaks. Speedo was nine years old and had been Rob's companion since puppyhood, when Rob found him in the National Forest, hairless and starving. A bald dog is not a pretty creature. There was no way to guess what kind of dog it was.

"Nigger dog," the vet had said years ago. "Best kind to have." And there was the riddle of the South. The vet, old Percy, was an islander, a Volunteer. Rob was then just home from New Haven, looking to fit in; he wouldn't have minded shooting the breeze with Percy, learning what he knew. The vet's big, gentle hands caressed the flanks of poor Speedo, the nigger dog, with love. The riddle of the South was, At heart is it good or bad? Rob couldn't tell. He couldn't see into that heart.

"This dog'll lay down his life for you," Percy said, "once we get him in shape. But it's going to cost you a fortune."

Speedo harbored every kind of parasite and fungus that can

set up housekeeping in the canine host. Percy prescribed raw eggs and cod-liver oil and an assortment of medications; finally Speedo was restored to health, after months of treatment and a vet bill in excess of two hundred dollars. His hair came in yellow-red, a luxurious coat that was thick and oily to the touch. The vet saw some golden retriever in the hide and some hound in the jaw. "But I wouldn't put it in writing," he said.

Speedo knew that he owed his life to Rob; he was grateful and loyal. But he never spoke. Sometimes Rob dreamed that Speedo could talk, waking in the morning with a sense that during the night Speedo had said something important.

2 .

While he was waiting for Billie, he tried to clean up—gathered stray socks, made his bed, straightened the towel in the bathroom. He hoped she would like the house. Maybe he should have swept; he noticed dust he hadn't seen before. As he was going for the broom he heard an odd tune, something vaguely religious, as of church bells, chiming from the kitchen. It took him a couple of seconds to recognize the sound as his doorbell. He had not heard his doorbell ring before. He took one last look around. Billie was probably fastidious.

But from the living room he saw that the figure standing on the other side of the screen wasn't Billie. It was his father, who in his seersucker suit gave the impression of a little costumed puppet.

"Rob?" he called, peering through the screen.

"Hey, Dad." Jack had on his new contact lenses, tinted blue. He was a dapper man; he liked to look good. But now he was unkempt. His shoes were polished only across the toes. He was missing a cuff link.

"I wasn't sure which house was yours," he said.

"This one. Come in."

Jack looked around the living room.

"It's a deal, Doc," Rob said. "Two hundred a month. I lucked into it."

Jack nodded.

"Quiet neighborhood," Rob said. "No one knows these houses are here. You can't see them from the main drag. No traffic. Got a fenced backyard, plenty of space, nice breeze from the south."

Jack's expression didn't change. Rob hadn't hoped for enthusiasm, but he hadn't expected a total lack of interest.

"Let's sit outside," he said. "It's cooler." He opened the lawn chair for his father, out on the little slab that passed for a porch, and he sat on the concrete.

"Well," Jack said. "It's about your mother." He spread his fingers on his knees. "She sold the house."

"What are you talking about?"

"She signed a contract this morning. Without my knowledge. She asked me to walk up to Burbage's and get some cream of wheat. I wasn't gone more than forty-five minutes. When I got back the realtor was just leaving, and she had signed the contract! She sold our house!"

"Calm down, Dad. That's just not possible. Maybe she's having a bad spell and doesn't quite realize what's going on. She could be going under again."

"No, not at all. It's not like before. She's fine, she's never been healthier. That's what's so strange. She's clear and rational and, um, *happy*. I saw the contract, Rob. She signed it."

"Well, it can't be valid. A contract for the sale of that house would have to have your signature on it too. It's jointly owned."

Jack didn't say anything.

"Isn't it?" Rob said.

"Yes."

"Then you have nothing to worry about."

Jack groaned. "She has power of attorney," he said. "She signed both names."

"She has power of attorney? What for?"

"She said it would make things easier for me, back when we

sold the stores. She handled all the details, I'm not much of a businessman. She says the offer on the house was something we shouldn't pass up. But I think there's more to it. I think there's something terrible."

"Like what?"

"I have thought—there have been moments when I thought—there was another man."

"Ridiculous."

"Not so ridiculous. If you knew how she was acting. She's so cheerful! She hums! Old songs, ones she hasn't hummed in fifteen years."

"This means there's another man? She's sixty-five years old, Dad."

"She's a very attractive woman. And she's—well, lively. She hasn't lost anything at all, nothing at all. She's *active*. And to tell you the truth, I haven't been able to keep up with her." Jack fixed his eyes on Rob to make certain that he was understood.

"What would that have to do with selling the house? It doesn't make any sense," Rob said.

"She found out we could get into that place now, if we want to. Says she doesn't want to face renovations, we'll just unload the house and let the new owner renovate. But we didn't have that much damage. There isn't that much to renovate."

"It still doesn't make sense."

"You don't get it?"

"Get what?" Rob said.

"I don't mean that she has no feeling for me. I believe she has a certain amount of concern for my well-being. So she's going to get me moved in over there, where someone checks on you every day and makes sure you show up for meals—she keeps saying how happy I'll be there, she doesn't say *we*—and I think she plans to get me settled in, and then she'll skip town."

Jack had never talked like this before. *Skip town?* Rob closed his eyes. "And why would she want to do that?" he said.

"I don't know. Revenge."

"For what?"

"I don't know. I know there were—multiple transgressions. But none of it ever meant anything to me, Rob, you know that. I've loved only one woman my whole life. The others, they were nothing compared to your mother. Nothing!" He slapped his knee. "I don't even recall the names. But *her* memory is a hundred percent. Some of this information is thirty years old! That gallivanting phase of my life—or at least the serious part of it— was over long ago. In the past five years I've been exemplary. To tell you the truth, I've had no choice. This last year—I couldn't have gotten into trouble if I'd wanted to. But the thing is, why didn't she leave me before now, if she held the past against me? I know why. She's waited until I *need* her. Until I'm old and decrepit and can't polish my own shoes. Can't do a thing."

"You know what this is?" Rob said. "This is a guilty conscience. You're imagining the worst penalty."

"You think so? You think it's unfounded?"

"Totally unfounded."

Jack rubbed the back of his neck. "Maybe so," he said. "But then this morning I found a little suitcase, all packed, hidden under her bed." He spoke in a low voice, looking down at Rob.

Rob laughed. "She's *moving,*" he said. "She has to pack a suitcase."

"All the clothes were new. Brand-new slacks and shirt. She doesn't wear slacks. When she wants slacks, she wears mine. And brand new underwear, of a certain style that is foreign to her taste."

"So what? She said herself that it was time for a new lease on life."

"Exactly," he said. "I remember that remark too. Listen, Rob. You know her as well as I do. You know it's within the realm of possibility. She's threatened to leave before, that time when she ended up at the Camdens' house and Ernie had to talk her into coming home. But this time, what scares me is, there's nothing being said. Just the humming, the little smile. I thought maybe there's some message in the songs, you know, if she's humming a particular song maybe it means something . . . but I can't remember the words, I recognize the tune and maybe remember a line or two but nothing past that—but I'll tell you, Rob, I don't know what I'll do if she leaves me over there with all those doddering old fools. And listen to this—she's thrown away all my old fishing pants, my old khakis. I'm down to this suit and one sport coat and two pairs of pants. She says that's all I'll need."

"Dad, why would you give her power of attorney if you have these suspicions?"

"Because I love her. Because she's right. I owe her. I was a son of a bitch, all those times, and then the worst, the time we put her in the hospital . . . I'll do anything to make up for it, only I think it's too late. I think there's nothing that will *work*. It all accumulated. It was too much."

"Then talk to her about it. Just ask her."

"I did. I said, 'Maudie, listen, you aren't planning on depositing me out there and then absconding are you, ha-ha?' "

"What did she say?"

"She laughed. She *didn't deny it*, Rob." His hand shook, his knee twitched. "What I'm wondering is, if you would ask her. Ernie's not here, I know she'd tell him, but I think she might tell you."

"Me? What would I say?"

"Just ask her, point-blank. Find out. What her intentions are."

"Okay, Doc, I'll ask her."

"Soon."

"Yes, soon. I will. Don't worry about it. You've got nothing to worry about."

Jack made his way down the walk to his car. In the rear window was a decal that said DECOLORES in multicolored letters. Rob had seen the decal on a lot of Mercedes-Benzes and Volvos downtown. Jack said it was a renewal group; Maude said it was a cult.

He shook his head as Jack drove away. The long and raucous marriage of his parents was nowhere near its end; it was like a transcontinental bus, with maybe a few mishaps along the way, but it was not about to break down; it had gone too long to break down now. They were bound to each other in ways they didn't even know about.

As Jack had said, for example: "the time we put her in the hospital." He and Rob had done it together. If Jack had done it alone, she might have left him, but their collusion bound her. Women leave men without a qualm; but leaving a child is in a different category. Instead of quitting the marriage, Maude had chosen to shore herself up. With Ernie. Ernie was the linchpin of the whole thing.

3.

After Jack left, Rob sat in the folding chair to wait for the girl. The experience of waiting in vain for women wasn't new to him. He ought to have learned by now not to draw it out past half an hour. But he always made excuses for them, thought up good reasons for their being late. Once he waited three hours for Louise, sitting in the golf bar. It isn't so bad, the waiting time; right to the final moment there's a chance she'll appear—she's had a flat tire, flagged down help, it's changed now and she's on the road, on her way to you. What is more worth waiting for? The time's not wasted. Time spent in anticipation and hope and rumination is never wasted. You just sit back and look around.

Isle of Palms: the name was good, strong as a spell, with an effect on him like music or the smell of women. And once the island had been just as good: a jungle of palmetto and scrub oak in a sandy soil, a curving beach, clean sea sparkling like the sea in dreams, a shabby beach town at one tip, summer people at the other. It had changed since his boyhood summers in all the different cottages—but what had not changed, since that boyhood? He was still drawn to the place as if it were his real home.

In those cottages, those summers, his family seemed different, loosed from the habits of town. He and his father fished a lot, in the boat just past the surf, never too far out because Maude wanted to keep them in sight. Sometimes she went along, and his father would make a big fuss over her, put a cushion in the bow and bait her hooks; she played the helpless girl, though they all knew she could row the boat herself and catch fish on her own. Jack took time off from work, and was there for supper every night, at a little wobbly table in the kitchen or on a back porch. They seemed happy those summers, and close . . . well, they *were* close, the cottages always so small one person could hardly help bumping into another.

He'd never admitted to anyone, himself included, his craving for that closeness, but now he recognized it; he remembered in particular a moment of almost painful craving, as he sat between his parents on a wooden porch glider, his mother leaning past him to kiss his father, and her long hair falling across his own forehead on the way so that he saw through a curtain of gold, he was enveloped in hair, and the rough rub of his father's seersucker trousers next to his thigh, and his own sense (though he could not have been older than seven) that this was what he wanted and that it wasn't enough.

He shifted in his chair and folded his arms. The memory shamed him for some reason. Memory often had that power. He concentrated on what he could see.

This house was not one of the summer cottages. That was one thing he liked about the island, its miscellany, the possibility of turning off the avenue and finding yourself in a real neighborhood of year-round people, of children squabbling like urchins, chained dogs barking, women nagging the gaunt young husbands who came and went from their jobs and on weekends fine-tuned their outboards. When he first moved in, he hadn't given much thought to these people. Their lives did not interest him. But lately, watching them move back into their houses, chop their trees into pieces and clean the rubble from their yards, he thought he noticed something new. Under the squabbling and the sullen, heavy eyes, there was something else, something miraculous, something waiting for discovery.

Next door, a young woman came out of the house with an empty coffee can in her hand. She went to the fence that separated his yard from hers, where his fig tree grew, and not noticing him in his low chair began to pick his figs. Iridescent bugs labored in slow flight around her head. He was as entranced as he had ever been by any rare bird; he dared not move, for fear of frightening her. It occurred to him that a man might learn to be satisfied with what he can see from his lawn chair; that even in the backyard, there may be wonders. He was almost satisfied, but not quite. The woman's reaching arm stirred dissatisfaction in him. The green bugs lit on the figs.

All he had ever really asked for was consolation: those egrets on the golf course, for instance; a remnant of woods; a view of the ocean, preferably from an open boat on its surface. Yet he had the feeling that something else was within reach, close as a ripe fig—something that would render consolation unnecessary. Once, he had thought it would be Louise. But she was rich and married and happy now.

She had sixteen keys on her key chain: three houses (main domicile, country place, mountain cabin), two cars, garage, Hank's office, various safety-deposit boxes and club gates, her bicycle lock, her diary. He had watched her change slowly from enterprising girl-reporter for the *News and Courier* to society matron. Half her day now went to upkeep of possessions, and the other half to charitable projects that never made full use of her talents and her beauty. She was free to do anything in the world. What did she do? Golfed. Shopped. Volunteered to fold towels in the shelter. Painted scenes of historic Charleston onto handbags and lampshades.

He advised her to junk all the keys except the little gold diary key, but he knew it wouldn't happen. Louise was settled; she had equilibrium. Even the sight of someone else—Rob—suddenly losing equilibrium frightened her. She didn't want to think about it. His bungalow had scared her to death.

Because the neighborhood was the last of the unregenerated areas, it was marked for destruction. Albert said a development company had gathered options on all the little houses. By next year, they would be gone. But for the time being, rents were low, attracting a fringe element.

Of which he was now a member.

He had an outboard himself, a thirty-five-horsepower Evinrude, and he had his twelve-year-old boat, now nose up on its trailer in his chain-linked backyard. Other good things: his fig tree had survived, and its fruit had gone overnight from green buds to plump brown bells veined in red; on the windowsill, his old blue globe of the world spun in the breeze; and no ambulances came, always a good sign. At the Fort Sumter House he had heard ambulances night and day, but most regularly at seven in the morning. The heart attack squad. Some wife had given her old man an unsuccessful wake-up shake on the shoulder. Most of his neighbors in the Fort Sumter House had been past their prime. In their midst he had learned to think of himself as past his prime. Ask not for whom the siren howls, he said to himself.

Speedo changed position on the concrete slab. Rob closed his eyes. There were cicadas in the mimosa and gulls crying on the wing. He was better off here on the Isle of Palms than he'd been in the Fort Sumter house. Here he listened not for the ambulance but for the alarm on the water tower. Once you've heard seven blasts (evacuation), you're a little more alert. Not everyone was as alert as Rob. At night the neighborhood hummed with air-conditioners; no one would hear sirens or alarms. He slept with all his windows open, even when the regular midnight thunderstorms swept through; sometimes he woke to a fine spray of rain on his face, blown through the screen to his pillow two feet inside, and he heard the wind and thunder. *No,* he would tell himself, *only a cloudburst, a local disturbance,* and he would lie down again, relieved. But also disappointed. Some part of him missed the big storm, had loved it, was waiting for its return.

Now on the little stoop he sat facing the ocean, though he couldn't see it, and breathed the salt air. He dozed. He didn't hear the pickup truck until it was already past his house; he opened his eyes to see it lurch into reverse, and back up to his mailbox. The horn tooted. Good God, he thought: Billie drives a truck. An old green Ford with an efflorescent patina. She was tiny behind the wheel, but she swung easily into the driveway and came to a stop in front of his chair.

Later he would learn that she didn't need his help at all. But she didn't know that. She didn't know her own strength, and thought, mistakenly, that he was strong. It is a mistake that women often make. But he knew from that moment, when he saw her spin the steering wheel one-handed, waving to him with the other hand, that she was a girl who could take care of herself, whether she knew it or not. He hoped (to his shame) that she did not.

CHAPTER 6

The sun was behind the bulb of the water tower. Four-twenty. A new record in waiting for women.

"I'm late," she said, jumping down from the cab.

"Oh well, what's four hours?"

"I'm sorry. You're angry."

"Not at all. Really. I've been sitting in the sun like an old islander. Me and my dog. It's what I would have done anyway, even if you hadn't been coming."

"You should wear sunscreen, with your fair complexion." She looked at his forehead too closely; he shook his hair to make it cover the incipient desert.

"Anyway," she said, "the reason I'm late is I got a job. Swimming instructor at the Isle of Palms Recreation Department."

"Congratulations."

"Yeah," she said, smiling. Arched her back, posed with her heels together and her toes out. She was wearing a nylon leotard—an extraordinary garment that was like a thin rose-colored skin—and wrapped over it, a black skirt apparently secured only by a bow at the waist. He breathed deeply. Her hair was still damp, a tangled mess. She looked scrubbed clean. Her eyes were red-rimmed. When she passed him on her way in through the door, he caught a whiff of chlorine.

"Swimming instructor," he said.

"In the parent-tot program," she said. "It's babies. Ones that can't even walk yet, but you teach them to swim. They remember how, from before they were born. After a year, they don't remember how, and they're harder to teach, but before that, it's easy for them. The hard part is the mothers. They get scared when their baby goes under."

"I can understand that."

"I used to work in a nursery, near the base. But I quit. I loved my job, but I'm starting all over again now. New job, new place. Hey, this is great. I like it."

"What there is of it," he said, following her through the living room into the kitchen. She inspected his appliances, looked through the window over the sink out into his backyard, and opened the cupboard, recently replenished.

"You weren't lying," she said. "About the beans and rice."

"I never lie to women," he said.

"How about to men?"

"That's different."

"What else have you got? One bedroom, two?"

"Two," he said. "But one is full of junk." He showed her down the hall. "The master bedroom," he said, opening the door to his room.

"Do you have good closet space?"

"Plenty for me." He opened his closet door. "The master wardrobe," he said. "Recently consolidated. Traded my excess lawyer duds for a sofa, over at the Goodwill bin. Figured Goodwill wouldn't mind; the sofa was sitting there waiting for pickup, so I picked it up. They got the good end of the deal. One of my suits was Brooks Brothers."

"You're very neat," she said. "For a man."

"Is that good or bad?"

She didn't answer. "You like everything in its place," she said.

"To a degree, yes. But don't be misled. I'll show you the dark side." He escorted her to the next room. "My den," he said.

"Good grief. How do you ever find anything in here?"

"Some of it I don't want to find."

"Stuff from your old office?"

"Some of that. Some from my old childhood. My parents are moving out of their house and into a full-care residential facility. They saw no reason to carry along my high-school yearbooks"—he held up a copy of the *Clarion*—"or my specimens." He pulled out the top drawer of the desk, where lined in rows were a dozen paper tubes. From the end of each one peeped the cotton eyes and black beak of a small bird. He handed one to Billie.

"A dead bird. A deskful of dead birds. You killed them?"

"No, I only preserved them. This one here's a Canada warbler." He pulled the black bit of thread attached to the beak, and the bird slid out of its tube headfirst. He read the boy's handwritten label on the tube, " 'Found in the garden, October 5, 1970. No sign of injury. Possible window collision.' "

"You were thirteen. This was your hobby? Stuffing little dead birds?"

"My passion."

"How did you do the eyes?"

"That's cotton."

"I mean, how did you get it in there?"

"You go at it from the inside. You clean out the skull with an X-acto knife and Borax, and you stuff it with cotton." he turned the warbler in his palm. "He's held up pretty well," he noted. "No bugs. His color's not so good, but then neither is mine."

She took the bird from him. "Look at his feet."

"Yes, the feet are good. Reptilian."

She reinserted the bird in its tube and laid it carefully in the drawer. She moved on to his jars, set out on the long table he'd built from a not-quite-level sheet of plywood laid across two plastic barrels. A jar of feathers, a jar of shells, a jar of teeth, and on down the line with nuts, seeds, bones, crab claws, the sloughed skins of various snakes.

"You were a collector," she said.

"Well, actually, this is an ongoing project."

"Where do you get it all? Where'd you get these *teeth*?"

"I'd rather not reveal the sources."

She raised the jar to the light. "But there's all different kinds. That's a shark's tooth, and—what, dog teeth?"

"A few dog teeth. Squirrel. Fox, raccoon, possum. Cow."

"They're pretty," Billie said.

"I think of it as rescue work. Something saved from oblivion. Not much, and not saved forever—but temporarily."

He had showed his collections to a few women before, but the reaction had been puzzlement or distaste. Most didn't like the snake skins.

His history with women could have been written two ways. Were he to set down the actual, factual material—verifiable—it would be a slim volume. One summer of Episcopalian necking at Camp Kanuga, various high-school flings of sudden generation and equally sudden mortality, three Yale women, two law students, one law *professor* (tattoo of the scales of justice on her shoulder blade). Nothing, before Louise, lasting more than six months. After Louise, a series of fine but never entirely successful liaisons—a paralegal (not his own), a couple of ex-debutantes, one divorcée (not his client). Some of these romances might go undiscovered altogether by the fact-tracing historian. Even the women involved didn't always realize the extent of their involvement. Louise, evidently, didn't.

But that other history, that rich past of love imagined, undocumented, and wholly unverifiable, would be a rambling tome, a saga of obsession and desire, verging on the visionary. Here was his one talent: imagining women. He was a master at it.

For instance, one of his great loves was a woman whom he knew only by voice. Nina Totenberg, legal affairs correspondent for National Public Radio. Every evening he tuned in, hoping to hear her smart tones reporting on the world of law. Supreme Court, civil rights, legislative news. He had the sensation, when Nina reported, that she was reporting to him. To him alone. She went right to the heart of things, for his sake. He had a pretty good idea of what she must look like: wise fine eyes, a slow disarming smile. Nina knew her stuff, she was all business, but still there was this lovely gentleness in her delivery. An intimacy, of the kind you sense in a woman who trusts you. You rarely get it. Women, like birds, have learned to be wary of men; they pass the wariness on, genetically.

But even when he was imagining other women, he was imagining Louise. She was always in the background. You could say she haunted him, if that is the right term; she was *there*. His private image of Nina looked very much like Louise.

"These things," Billie said, "all these birds and shells and teeth, don't seem like a lawyer's things."

"Aha," he said. "Now you're onto something."

"You wanted to be a scientist."

"Or fireman, pirate, treasure-hunter."

"Then why did you become a lawyer?"

"I lost hope," he said.

He ushered her back into the living room. "Pretend this is an office," he said. "The sofa's the client's chair, and the La-Z-Boy's the lawyer's chair."

Billie nestled on the sofa. Actually bounced, then pulled one leg up under the other thigh.

"Okay," he said. "Let's hear it."

"I've got to get divorced. I want to do it as soon as possible. Carlo doesn't have to give his permission, does he? If one person wants the divorce, does the other one have to want it too?"

"Technically, no; but they should both know about it. There's a separation requirement in this state, and separation assumes a certain consciousness of action. If Carlo doesn't know he's separated from you, then he's not. There's no way you can be legally separated without his knowledge."

"But I've *been* separated from him. He's been in the middle of the Atlantic Ocean. *Under* the Atlantic Ocean. How separated can you get?"

"I know that, but it isn't a legal separation. There's a difference between a true thing and a legal thing. There are conditions that must be met."

"Well, I haven't told you the whole story."

They never do, not at first. But one thing he could count on from women was the whole story, eventually, and sometimes more of it than he wanted to hear.

"See," she said, casting her eyes to her smooth kneecap, "it doesn't have to be a real divorce." She looked up at him.

"No?"

"Because it wasn't a real marriage."

"What was it?"

"I don't know. Carlo said it was real, but there was no wedding, not a regular one. We had gone down to Washington Park— the one next to the courthouse?"

"I used to eat my lunch there."

"We were sitting on a bench. See, I like to feed pigeons, so I'd save bread and then we'd go to the park. This day—it was a year ago—we were sitting there and we saw these people come out of the courthouse, two men and a woman. They went over in the corner under a tree. I didn't know what they were doing, and then all of a sudden it hit me from the way they were standing—the older man holding a book, facing the other two —and I said, 'Carlo, look, it's a wedding!' It was sad. Just them, you know, no flowers or anything. The magistrate, I guess it was, turned and motioned us to come over, asked us to be witnesses. So we did. We kind of stood back, though, behind the bride and groom. When the magistrate said to the groom, 'Do you take this woman to be your lawful wedded wife?' Carlo looked at me and said, 'I do.' And so, I don't know—it was a pretty day. I'm always affected a lot by the weather. There were those big old oak trees, and a lot of pigeons, and little white babies with the black nurses on the benches. I was *lighthearted,* do you know what I mean? Well, anyway, I did it. Said 'I do' when he asked the bride."

Her face turned red, and again she gazed down at her knee.

"Oh, it was a stupid thing to do," she said. She brushed her knee. "Anyway, I knew it wasn't real. But he said it was. The words had been spoken. So I got to sort of believing him, even though I knew better."

"No license?" he said.

"No. But Carlo said it was legal. And he told the navy we were married, so we could get married housing."

"And you, did you tell anyone you were married? Your friends?"

"I only had one friend."

"Did you tell her?"

"It was Carlo. He's always been my only friend." She hesitated, then added, "My life has been odd."

"In what way?" he said.

She stared at him, with what he took to be suspicion. "Are you saying you don't already know?"

He was caught. He couldn't admit to knowing without betraying Louise's confidence. He said nothing.

"Oh, well. It's all right," she said. "Of course she would have told you." She got up and walked to the window. "I don't mind people knowing. I don't hold a grudge against my parents. They did something wrong, but they weren't the kind of people you'd expect the right thing from. I used to blame them. Not for leaving me, just for making my life abnormal. But now I know it would have been more abnormal if they had stayed. They weren't adults. When their trouble got serious, they ran. At least they loved each other. That was their saving grace, the only good thing about them. But that's not much, is it. I don't value love for itself. Like, Hitler loved someone, right?"

"Eva."

"Anyway, I got a little revenge on them, I guess."

"How's that?"

"Stopped thinking about them. I think that's the best revenge, don't you? You just erase them."

"What kind of trouble were they in?" he asked. He didn't want Billie to be the daughter of maniacs.

"Gambling. I mean, they didn't gamble, they were in the business. They owned poker machines, or maybe they didn't own them but they took them around to places and collected the money. I didn't know much about it. Someone came after them for something. They left in a hurry. I just got home from school one day and they were gone. They knew Carlo would take care of me. For a long time I thought they paid him. I didn't find out until last year—that day in the park—that he had paid them. He told me, to prove that he cared for me, but I already knew that. He's been good to me since I was thirteen, paid for music and dancing lessons, YMCA, signed my school permissions. I love him for the way he took care of me."

"You do love him?"

"I don't love him as a man. I love him as a power."

"You, ah, lived together as man and wife?"

"When I was *thirteen?*"

"After that. After the day in the park."

"No." She answered fast. He didn't believe her. He was disappointed that she didn't trust him. It would take time, maybe, to win her trust.

"He's an unusual man," she said.

"Sounds like it."

"But I'm unusual. We got along, all that time. He doesn't want me to leave him, but I don't want to stay with him. He surprises me too much. He thinks different from most people. He says we're married in the eyes of God. But it isn't right, I know it isn't right. I don't want to hurt him, but I have to get away. I thought if I really got a divorce, he'd have to let me go."

"Listen to me, Billie. First of all, there's no marriage. Even under common law. You can walk out the door."

"I know that. But the problem is, Carlo's a good talker. When he's not around, I'm fine, but when I'm with him, I can get confused. If he finds me, I'm afraid I might go back with him."

"Are you afraid of him?" he said.

"He has the force of goodness," she said. She stared out the window. Her little shoulders drooped, her arms hung straight by her sides. He wished he could sweep her up, the way a fireman sweeps up a woman in a burning house and carries her to safety.

"What I was thinking of," she said, turning to him, "was if you could just write up something that looks like a divorce. I would do it myself, only I've never seen one; I don't know what a divorce looks like. But you could make it look legal, and I could just mail it to him."

"I'm afraid I couldn't do that," he said.

"Why not?"

"It wouldn't be legal. It would be illegal, for me to do it."

"How come, if there's no marriage anyway? What difference would it make? And you're not even a lawyer anymore. It couldn't harm you."

"Billie, Billie."

"Come on. Help me. I need your help."

Even the innocent are sometimes savvy. She must have known how she looked, and how her request would go straight to his heart. She must have known he had been waiting all these thirty-two years for a girl to stand before him in rosy splendor and ask for his assistance. He was a goner.

"When is he coming back?" he said.

She frowned. "He was due back today," she said. "They're bringing them in early because of the storm. He knows the apartment was wrecked, but he doesn't know I left. Oh, God, he'll go crazy when he gets the letter. I left a letter saying not to try to find me."

"All right," he said. "We'll figure out something. Let's talk again tomorrow. Come by in the morning."

"What time?" she said.

"I'm an early riser."

"Me too. Seven-thirty?"

He laughed.

"That's too early?" she said.

"No. Seven-thirty is fine. I'll make some strong instant coffee."

He held the door open for her. Outside, the late-afternoon sky was swirling with barn swallows, a loose flock of thousands fleeing

like refugees, with some internal random motion and some strag-
glers—a few lit on the power lines, a few wheeled down onto
the piano in the marsh—but with a general unerring course, en
masse, south by southwest, direct to Albert's house, the inlet,
Jacksonville, and Venezuela.

"What's wrong?" Billie said.

"Oh . . . I'm sorry. Having a fade." He blinked and shook his
head, and put a hand on the door again to steady himself. It was
not exactly a fade, but more of a foreboding, impossible to explain.
Sometimes, when the world looked particularly fair, when the
sky was a certain color and birds wheeled and his chances for
happiness seemed higher than ever, he was overcome by a sense
that it could not last. Failure seemed most imminent when things
looked most promising.

"Do you need to sit down?" she said. She touched his elbow.
"Can I get you a glass of water?"

"I'm fine."

A motorcycle roared off Palm Avenue and onto Tanglewood,
looking like an apparition out of a bad movie. Black-tanked
Harley, black-jacketed, black-masked rider. When it did a double
U-turn and halted in front of his house, Billie gasped and jumped
behind Rob, pulling him into the house and slamming both doors.
Her face was white, and she scrambled backward into the living
room like someone who is not thinking but is driven only by the
command: *flee, hide.* Like Jacqueline Kennedy crawling out over
the trunk of the convertible, one of Rob's earliest TV memories.

He looked out his porthole, a diamond-shaped window in the
door. Billie had retreated all the way to the kitchen.

"It's Ernie," he said. "My brother. That's all." He held his arm
out to her. "Come back. It's just Ernie. He looks like a mass
murderer, but he isn't one. Come back," he coaxed.

When he opened the door, Ernie had his helmet off. His wide
smiling face was one you had to like. The big genius oaf. Rob
flubbed the handshake, a vertical grip with several complicated
and no doubt meaningful shifts.

"Welcome home," he said.

"Jesus, it's worse than I thought," Ernie said.

"Well, it's humble, but my own."

"No, I mean the whole place. The television pictures looked bad, but they didn't touch the real thing. I can't take it all in." He tossed his helmet on the sofa and sat down next to it. "It seems like an elaborate hoax," he said, "like somebody's going to step out and tell me I'm on *Candid Camera,* and the place is really okay, this is just a set they built to fool me. I about cried, coming through town and then getting over to the island. This is the worst."

"It's not that bad," Rob said. "You get used to it."

"You can get used to anything, but meanwhile it breaks your heart."

Billie came back into the living room. Ernie looked up. He stood, trained well by Maude.

Rob introduced them. Ernie nodded. Billie said, "I was just on my way out."

"I don't want to interrupt anything," Ernie said, raising his hands.

"Honestly, I was going. Wasn't I?"

"She was," Rob said. "She was already out the door, and you scared her back inside."

"Me?"

"I thought you were someone else," Billie said.

"I have that trouble a lot," Ernie said. "Everyone thinks I'm someone else. Sometimes I think I'm someone else."

Billie said goodbye, and they watched her go. "I like a woman who drives a pickup," Ernie said.

"Billie's a client," Rob said. "And off-limits to you."

"I'm not in the market. I've got a sort of arrangement in Gainesville. And, well, it's serious. In fact, that's why I'm here. I came to tell Ma. I'm getting married."

"Ah—" Rob tried to be cool. His whole brotherhood was based on the cool style. This time he failed. "Christ, Ernie."

"Yeah. It's even worse than that. Rhonda's not exactly Maude's idea of the girl for me. She's somewhat older. She's thirty. She's divorced." Ernie sat down on the sofa.

Rob had to take a breath. "And, you're actually thinking about marriage?"

"Not thinking about it. It's set; I'm in the chute. She's waiting for me. I felt like I had to come up and let everyone know. Let Maude know."

This would be a real test of Maude. She had never disapproved of anything Ernie had done. She prided herself on being his encourager, his support in every wild endeavor. His *only* support.

"What do you think she'll say?" Ernie said.

"Well—"

"She'll freak out, won't she. I'm not sure I can deal with it, I've got enough to worry about. I mean, it's a major event. It's a big load."

"Ernie, are you sure about this? You've never even had a steady girl before, you're just a kid, there's plenty of time left before you have to—"

"Wait a minute—is this you talking, or are you telling me what Ma's going to say?" Ernie was huffed up, his big shoulders raised. "This is the woman I want. If you could meet her, Rob, you'd see, she's the kind of woman you can't pass up, she's smart and sweet and redheaded—"

"Okay, okay. I'm with you. Here's what you have to do: just tell Ma. *Announce* it, quick and clean, and then clear out. Don't give her a chance to get into the existential implications. Tell her like it's a done deal, unrelated to her."

"Yeah, good idea. And I won't tell her all of it at once. There's more to it, it's a master plan. I'm also going to law school. I doubt she'll like that, either."

"Law school? You don't even have a high-school diploma."

"I'm finessing it. The state of Florida will take me on without one, all I have to do is show up on the Gainesville campus. They want me. I go into an accelerated undergraduate program and then law school; the whole thing takes six years. Rhonda's paying part, and Florida's paying part."

Rob sat down.

"What, you don't like the plan? I thought you'd be all for it. Me following in your footsteps and all."

"Ernie, I'm not practicing law anymore."

"No kidding. You got canned?"

"Of course not. I walked out."

Ernie said, "I'll be damned. Ma will still have the combination, then—a lawyer son and an adventurer son. What are you going to do? I mean, you're looking for something, right?"

He meant a job. Rob said, "I'm looking for something."

"So, no problem."

"No problem."

A problem is a formulated question. Rob didn't have one, not the kind that could be posed to his younger brother and make sense. All he had was a sneaking suspicion that everything was wrong. Could he have said: *Here's the problem, Ernie—my head spins when I see a flock of birds. My heart breaks when I see a bare-armed girl. I am stalked by the fire-girt giant in iron shoes.*

No. The young are different. The young are, to some extent, in some sense, dumb. Healthy and dumb and strong. It is the duty of the rest of us to leave them in that state for as long as possible, Rob reasoned. He could not tell, could not begin to tell, his woes to Ernie.

Ernie put through a phone call to Rhonda. Dialing, he looked like himself; he punched the buttons with a casual, offhand style, his feet still stretched out, his body flung back against the sofa. When she answered, he contracted. His feet came in, his shoulders went forward toward his knees, and he set the phone on the floor between his boots. He mumbled into the receiver with his head dropped low. He *smiled* into the receiver. Sure signs. Momentarily, Rob was envious.

He was inclined to warn Ernie off law school and marriage.

Ernie didn't seem to be aware of the pitfalls. But what good would a warning do? If it were really possible to warn the young, the human race would have shown steady improvement over the ages, and clearly it had not. He would have to let Ernie find his own way. Anyway, Rob could not trust his own motives. Perhaps the old warn the young away from their own failed dreams.

CHAPTER 7

I n the course of his legal career, Rob heard a lot of stories. Women came into his office and laid out narratives that left his head spinning. These were the stories that Louise loved to hear. Lives gone strange. He felt not quite right reporting the details to Louise, as they'd been given in confidence, hesitantly, courageously, even when the information was peripheral to his case. Clients overestimated the amount of truth that he required from them. Even shrinks and priests don't hear the stuff a lawyer hears, because people know the lawyer's on their side. The lawyer's their man, paid to protect, not to cure or judge. They told all. He heard tales he didn't need, didn't want. And the tales had had a cumulative subversive effect over the years.

Now when he walked down the street, he was suspicious. A man might look like an average guy, a woman might look normal, but he suspected untold secrets.

Sometimes he hadn't believed the stories he heard. Or he believed for an instant, but the enormity of the thing proved to be too much for him, and he was tempted to conclude that the woman (it was usually a woman) was spouting fantasy. Freud had reached the same conclusion. But Rob couldn't be sure. The wife of a prominent banker, his own banker as a matter of fact, said the banker liked mashed potatoes. *Really* liked mashed potatoes, "as a medium," she said. It had taken Rob a few minutes to figure out what she meant. Louise had liked that one. He hadn't believed it at first, but the wife stuck to her story. And why would she have made up something so out of the realm of common experience? Lies by their nature have the ring of truth. Every time he walked into First National and saw the vice president behind his glass wall, he pictured scenes he'd rather not have pictured.

And maybe he could have gone on forever hearing the stories, if he hadn't begun to lose perspective. He heard so much that he lost the ability to discriminate between comedy ("Then he gets a bowl of mashed potatoes, sets it on the table, unzips his pants . . .") and tragedy. An important distinction, but one a lawyer can lose sight of.

Billie's story still shocked him. But it wasn't the story itself that drew him in. What drew him was, in Louise's words, "Billie as a person." Billie the person was lovely and unscathed. True, there was Carlo to be reckoned with (the name struck fear in his heart—he saw *Carlo* tattooed across a hairy biceps, *Carlo* embroidered in red script across the pocket of a blue jumpsuit). And there was the bad childhood. He'd seen clients who appeared to have survived horrendous childhoods—but the damage can be hard to see. It can lie low and resurface later.

She looked okay, though. He tried not to think about the dark and deviant Carlo, or about Billie's past, or about Billie's future. These things could be held in abeyance for a time, while he thought only of the girl herself. He lay in bed that night, doing so. Here she was, after all. She wore bracelets woven of Peruvian string. She whistled. She was a swimming instructor. He wanted to watch her swim.

In his dreams, he did. She stretched, reached, fluttered, heels breaking the pool's surface, water dripping from her eyes as she stared straight at him. He dreamed Billie swimming all night long.

He was in some kind of weak phase; he seemed to go through them now and then, turning periodically more vulnerable than usual to music or women. This long thing with Louise, whatever it was, had weakened him. He ought to have latched onto someone else by now. But the fact was, women weren't drawn to him the way he was to them.

They liked him fine. He was their confidant and their buddy, occasionally their sweetheart—temporarily. They tended to move on, or he moved on when he could tell they were about to. He didn't know exactly what the trouble was. Maybe it was his looks, his boyish face, his sloping shoulders. Maybe it was his general attitude, one he thought of as respectful and adoring, *restrained,* but which may have been perceived as indifferent. He came across as the opposite of what he was. Louise thought he had retreated from her!

They had grown up together. There is good reason for that archetypal dream, the girl next door as wife. What more could a man ask for? That girl knows him, knows his world. With that girl, love can seem more than a chance encounter, more than a coincidence; it can take on the proportion of destiny. They found themselves grown and back home together, Rob fresh out of law school, Louise already well into a career at the paper. They gravitated to each other. She had a garden apartment on Church Street, one main room, combination bedroom and living room; her bed was in the corner, disguised as a sofa but clearly a bed. He looked at it first thing, every time he came in; then he looked away and tried not to let his eye fall on it again. He had discovered that Louise was a little jumpy about sex. Not all that crazy about it.

His women before her had been knowledgeable. He preferred them that way, women to whom lovemaking was no momentous event; he was comfortable with a certain casual worldliness that made seduction unnecessary. But Louise was something new. He wasn't sure how to proceed. The result was that he didn't proceed at all. He reverted to the stage of church camp necking. They were a public sort of couple more than a private one. They met for lunch in Washington Park, smoked dope with her newspaper friends, were invited together to late-night parties. By the night of the annual Art Museum Gala, they were seeing each other three or four times a week, and had, he thought, an understanding. She wore a dark green strapless dress with an enormous skirt. They sat at a table with other young couples. The green dress was spectacular. They danced, and he made an unsuccessful bid on a weekend at Hilton Head.

He considered himself, at that moment, married to Louise. They would do the impossible: fit in here, live the Charleston life (a brick house with porches, shrimp for dinner, summers at the Isle of Palms); but they would do it better than it had been done heretofore. They wouldn't fall into the dreamy lassitude and the cocktail parties and the history. He believed that there could be something in the practice of law that would feed the brain. Louise was a good newsgirl. One of her stories had won a prize, a series on the mixed-race population of fake Indians who claimed to be a remnant of the Sewees, living without electricity or running water in a movable town surrounded by cypress swamp. What he fell in love with was that: her ability to look at this old place and see what was interesting in it, and what was more than interesting—what was exciting and what needed doing and what things meant. My God, to marry a woman like that, and have her always by your side, seeing things you have overlooked, and wearing on special occasions an emerald dress that doesn't even begin until four inches below the collarbone . . . He settled into a kind of private comfort at the prospect. Happy union. The stage was set for it.

Wrong. Ah well. The whole time he was savoring his inevitable bliss, she was making other plans. Which did not include him. That was what shocked him most, the fact that he had been duped.

After the auction they had gone back to her place. She was a little drunk; he wasn't, he was sharply sober. He took her in his arms; the green dress rustled, voluminous against his knees. But she pulled away.

"I'm sorry," she said. "I can't."

He acquiesced. Patience was one of his virtues. Maybe now was the time, however, to mention plans for the future. He was searching for the words when she turned and explained that she was interested in someone else, so interested that she thought she would marry him. Hank Camden.

She probably never intended to dupe him. It was his fault, his failure; he ought to have moved more quickly. And maybe he still had a chance, he thought; he could still tell her. But after she said the man was Hank—his *boss,* for Christ's sake—he found that he couldn't propose his plan. The failure left him loose and unanchored, and weak for a long time.

2.

Billie appeared in the morning at 7:25. He was in the shower and called out to her to wait. When he was dressed, he found her out on the porch, lounging in his chair, drinking Ronald McDonald coffee and eating an Egg McMuffin. She passed him a bag of McMuffins.

"I have a good idea," she said. He made a mental note to buy another chair. He sat on the lip of the concrete slab, his feet in the rye grass already sprouting—a thin crop of green pinwheel spokes, radiating from the spot where he'd stood to sling it.

Billie's thin legs were stretched toward him, her feet bare. For such a small girl, with small hands, she had big feet. The soles were white from chlorine.

"You don't want to know what my great idea is?" she said. "I thought of it last night."

"Sure I do."

"This is going to sound funny. But—well, you have an extra room. I need a room. No, wait, let me finish. If you'll rent it to me, I'll cook for you. I'll pay rent, too. It would be perfect. I think we'd get along well, and you could use the rent money, and the pool's only six blocks away—"

"Hold it," he said. "I don't have an extra room."

"You do. I saw it."

"That room is occupied. By my possessions."

"I won't take up a lot of space. I won't touch anything in there. I don't even have to use the dresser drawers, I'll just keep my stuff under the bed and—" She looked at him. "You don't think it's a good idea."

"No. It's not a good idea."

"Why not?"

"It's out of the question."

"Why?" One of her feet curled over the top of the other one, and rubbed it affectionately. Billie had a way of touching herself as if she were her own comfort. She sometimes caressed her face or rubbed her own arm.

"Because I live alone," he said. "And because you don't know me. You can't just move in with someone you don't know. I might be dangerous. I might be a lunatic."

She considered the possibility. "Well, are you?"

"I don't think so, but you never know."

"I could tell if you were," she said. "Anyway, it would be a— a business proposition. I mean, there'd be nothing *between* us. I'd be the tenant. And the cook. That's all."

He knew it was insane. And yet he'd had the thought himself, before she even said it. He had imagined Billie in his house. Cooking for him, filling his bowl. And who would object? Households these days were in disarray. Some were diminished—marriages that were shaky under a sound roof did not improve when the roof vanished. Some were augmented, boarding homeless relatives or construction crews. No one would care, or even notice, if a wacky teenage girl moved in with the failed attorney—no one except Louise.

He said (was it a moment of weakness or a moment of truth?), "All right. Temporarily, though. Until you find a permanent place."

"Really?" she said with surprise.

"I could use some regular meals."

"Right now?"

"I'm on my second McMuffin. I won't need to be fed until evening."

"No, I mean, can I move in now? My stuff's in the truck, all I have is a backpack."

"You're already checked out of the motel?"

"I checked out after one night. I've been sleeping in the truck."

"Christ, Billie. You can't sleep in a pickup truck."

"You can, it's not bad at all, I could almost stretch all the way out. It was pretty comfortable."

Maybe it was the wrong thing to do. His motives were pure, though. The girl was in distress. You can't let a girl sleep in a pickup truck. He got her pack out, brought it in, set it on her bed. There was a moment of awkwardness. Billie said, "Thank you." He backed slowly out of the room, which had become hers.

He sat on the sofa. She wouldn't take up much space, but she would *be* there. Already the house was different, occupied by Billie. And he would have to be different, he'd have to civilize himself—dress decently, eat regular meals. He had the feeling he was about to lose some crucial thing, without which he would not be his old self. The crucial thing was not privacy. It was something more important; it was loneliness—as painful to relinquish as any narcotic. He would miss it and crave it. The thought of doing without it made the hair rise on his neck. How can you give up what has been the habit of your existence?

The answer was, *easily, with joy and gratitude.*

She took up space. She filled the rooms. The change seemed atmospheric: more light, more breeze, more sound. It took him two days to realize there actually was more light and more breeze: Billie had removed the shades, and she had washed the windows—and more sound: she listened to the radio at night, she sometimes talked to herself, she whistled when she was alone in the kitchen. She moved the television from in front of the recliner to in front of the sofa, so that they could both watch the news (they weren't a mismatch, then: they had at least one common interest, the nightly report of global events).

For the next seven days he was slightly out of his head. That was the only explanation he could think of for his extreme happiness. He wasn't the sort of man who often experiences extreme happiness, especially of the ordinary mundane variety. This was definitely mundane. Billie went to the pool in the mornings. He went to the grocery store and bought food. In the evenings they cooked the food and ate it, and watched television and went to bed, she in her little room and he in his. He started the repairs that he'd been meaning to do but hadn't gotten around to before. He painted the living room, he replaced the vinyl flooring in the kitchen. It didn't make much sense to him, that an existence consisting exclusively of food and television and home repair could produce the sensation of bliss. But it did.

Also a surprise to him was the absence of desire. When Billie went to her room at night, he didn't want to follow her. Instead, he lay in the room next door and thought about new ways to improve the bungalow. His most prurient thought was of her toothbrush, child-size and blue, in the bathroom. He thought of the little strawberry magnets that had appeared on the refrigerator door, holding up indecipherable memos from Billie to Billie. Like "Bower: trumpet and grape?" The Billie-brain was a puzzle to him. He studied it.

He was in the grip not of desire but of fascination.

She owned next to nothing. Her clothes took up two drawers in the dresser. She had a few books, a hair dryer, and an answering machine. "It's Carlo's," she said, taking it out of the backpack. "Do you mind if I hook it up?"

"An answering machine? But why—" And then he understood. "Billie, Carlo can't call you here. He doesn't know you're here. No one can call you here. The number isn't even in the phone book."

"Carlo is in communications. You wouldn't believe what they know. He works with radar and microwave transmissions and a lot of secret stuff."

"Radar can't find you, Billie."

"They have this thing at the base that can listen to any phone conversation within a forty-mile radius."

"They don't."

"They *do,* I swear. It's experimental. But they sit around and listen for fun. They can zero in on this big wall map and pick any phone they want, and record the conversation. Don't laugh, it's true."

"Okay. Maybe it's true. That still doesn't mean he can find out where you are."

"I know. But do you mind if I connect the machine anyway? It screens calls. And if it's someone you want to talk to, you just pick up the receiver. You can hear them."

"Go ahead," he said. She seemed grateful. The frown between her eyes vanished.

He couldn't believe that Carlo was the good guy she'd said he was. The way she acted was the way he'd seen women act when they were running from a man for good reason. Not because of mashed potatoes but because of real danger. Billie was wary. She jumped when the phone rang, even though her screening machine was in place. Several times he heard it click into gear and deliver its robotic message; the caller hung up.

In the mornings before going to work, she walked down to the corner and bought a newspaper. But she was always nervous, walking those two blocks, and when she got back into the house she sank onto the sofa in relief. She opened immediately to the weather map.

"I look for a place where the weather is just a background," she said. "Where it won't take over your life."

"You're thinking about moving?" he said.

"I'm always thinking about moving. Aren't you?"

"Not really," he said, and then realized that wasn't true. "Well, I think about it. But I don't want to do it. I moved once, to New Haven, and it was a bad idea." Would she think he was deficient in adventurousness, simply an old Charlestonian who never wanted to leave his hometown?

But that's what he was. He didn't want to leave. He would probably circle around this city the rest of his life, always hoping to settle into it somehow, never succeeding.

3.

He offered to clean off his desk so she'd have a place for her books.

"You don't have to do that," she said.

"I want to." He swept away his old copies of *Audubon Magazine,* his papers, his notebook.

"Can I see that?" she said, reaching for the notebook.

"I don't know," he said, holding it away from her.

"Your little black book," she said.

"Yes, indeed."

"I want to see it."

"Of course you do. They all want to see it. But some things are private, after all. Don't you agree?"

She eyed him, then lunged for the book. He was too quick for her, but she grabbed both his arms with hers.

"Oh no," he said. "Not for Billie's eyes. There's serious stuff in here."

She let go. "Like what?"

"Names, dates. Comments."

"Comments?"

"Yes, ma'am. Even some pictures."

"I don't believe you." She stood back and looked at him. "Not really," she said.

He raised his right hand.

"That's disgusting," she said.

"Disgusting? I don't know. Not necessarily." He laid the book on the desk and stepped back. "Some things a man doesn't want to forget."

He loved the look of seriousness that came over her face. But he felt bad about teasing her. It was so easy. Billie believed him.

"How many—how many have there been?" she said.

"Three hundred and sixteen."

She made a face of horror. "Not really," she said, drawing in her chin and frowning. "You're kidding, aren't you? You said you never lie to women."

"I don't," he said. "Never."

She turned her head to look at him out of one eye. She glanced at the notebook. Then she snatched it from the desk and opened it. Her eyes went down the page.

"These are . . . *birds,*" she said.

"Right," he said.

"You said they were girls!"

"I said no such thing."

She punched him in the stomach.

"You'll break your thumb like that," he said. "You've got your fist wrong. Look, do it like this." He uncurled her fingers and reset the fist with the thumb on the outside. She punched him again.

He said, "Oof," and doubled over, and she smiled.

The fact was, living with Billie was like going back into childhood, into a good childhood, when life does not extend much farther than the fence, or maybe the next street down. That was why desire did not intrude. That was why food and television were such pleasures. They regressed—or he, in her presence, regressed, to that innocent stage in which she still existed. The food was especially good. He had not till now fully appreciated the pleasure of eating.

Not that they were eating gourmet meals. They ate unwisely, according to the whim of Billie's appetite. They barbecued pork ribs on an outdoor cooker. They made a lemon meringue pie from the recipe on the back of a box of vanilla wafers. They grilled hot dogs, fried a batch of chicken wings, baked a tuna-cheese casserole. They ate their hearts out.

Intimacy with a woman is not an easy thing to achieve. By intimacy he meant not lovemaking but what sometimes results from it, the sensation that you and the woman occupy a single world separate from the rest of the population. But you can get

intimacy by other methods. Mutual effort in life-threatening sit-
uations, for instance, like two people lost in a wilderness, or
working together in an office. A third way is to eat food together.
He watched her eat, she watched him eat. A bond was forged,
half comic and half erotic. It was very pleasant. By the end of
the week, he had gained three pounds. Billie had gained none.
Her metabolism was remarkable.

One morning after he had been out for groceries and was
unpacking the bags, he felt suddenly worried. She was at work,
he knew; there was no need to worry about her. But he left the
food on the counter and drove to the playground, parking under
an oak tree among the mothers' station wagons. He hoped no
one would notice him. Leaves dropped onto his windshield, and
sunlight glared from the hood. Near the diving board a rowdy
pack of children dripped and shivered, waiting their turns under
a teacher's eye—not Billie's. She was farther off, standing in the
pool at the four-foot mark, holding something . . . a baby, its
head beneath her chin and its small body centered between her
breasts, its legs drawn up froglike against her stomach. Amid the
mild riot of splashing kids and teachers' voices, she and the child
made a single still figure.

And then together, with no warning but carefully, not even
rippling the water, they sank.

He was not ready. The baby's head went under, then hers,
and he froze, gripping the wheel with his arms straight, pushing
his back against the seat. It lasted too long. He looked around;
in the nearby cars, mothers were reading. He was about to blow
his horn or yell to the lifeguard when suddenly the two close
heads popped up, eyes open. Billie kissed the baby, its hands
moved, and Rob breathed. It was an astonishing event, one he
could not have watched more than once. After it, he could no
longer think of her as a child.

CHAPTER 8

S he stood on the stoop on Sunday morning and surveyed his yard. Their yard. She always got up earlier than he did. Sundays he slept even later than usual, in a futile effort to avoid the day. He had never done well on Sundays. He tried to pretend that it wasn't Sunday, and he could keep up the pretense pretty well until midmorning when the church bells started. Then his old horror of the day returned, Sunday stretching ahead of him with all the burdensome despair of an empty field.

Billie mumbled something in a low voice not directed at him. Few people in this world actually talk to themselves out loud. To do it requires a lack of self-consciousness, and a trust of your own words. He eavesdropped.

"Wisteria," she said. "Or maybe honeysuckle. Wild grape, trumpet vine."

He knew he shouldn't interrupt this conversation, but he couldn't help it.

"Thinking of landscaping?" he asked.

"Oh—well, some vines, maybe. Or a picket fence. I don't know, it's sort of bare. We could do something without spending a lot of money. We could dig up wild plants somewhere and transplant them."

"There's not much point in home improvements. Around here. This place will be gone soon."

"Gone?"

"Developed. Someone's buying up all the houses, going to put in a restricted residential community. By next year, they'll be starting construction on the villas."

"But a year, that's a long time."

He had a vague memory of that point in his life when a year was a long time. On the strength of that memory he said, "Sure, why not?" Generally, that was his response to all of Billie's suggestions.

"Really?" she said.

"Tell me where to start."

A gleam came into her eyes. "We start in the woods," she said. "Take me to the woods, and we'll find the plants. We'll need a shovel."

"Haven't got one," he said. He hadn't been in the woods since July. He didn't want to see the damage. But he was a sucker for that gleam in her eye. And he knew a place where they could find what Billie wanted—in the forest, in the old secret place of his boyhood.

"Let's go," he said. "We'll buy a shovel on the way."

He liked driving with Billie at his side, navigator to his captain. They were in her pickup—or was it Carlo's?—and she settled back next to him, his map of the Francis Marion National Forest spread across her thighs. Heat blew through the windows. They rolled north, side by side, satisfied.

At least he was satisfied. There is much to be said for side-by-sideness. It is, after all, as he realized out on Highway 17, the attitude of marriage. All the frontal thrill in the world will yield eventually to this lateral alignment, this *partnership*. They rode mostly in silence, or if they spoke they did it without turning their heads. He realized he'd like to take Billie to the movies. Ordinarily he didn't like to go to the movies. But he wanted to sit in a theater with her, both of them staring straight ahead, their shoulders touching. That's all, just the shoulders.

Of course, it was false, his sense of marital comfort there in the hot truck. Billie was an accidental girl, in his company only by chance and only temporarily. He knew that. He knew that from the beginning. He had no hopes or intentions of anything more, of anything real.

But there is always the question of what is meant by "real." Real property, legally speaking, is something permanent and unmovable; but he'd have said that the only real things are those that shift and change and can be moved.

They stopped at the do-it-yourself store on the highway, where even the parking lot was stacked high with roofing paper and lumber. Sales were hopping. He could see that the hurricane would turn out to be a boon to business, with all the repairs that would have to be made, added to the thousands of out-of-state workers in town. Billie picked out a heavy garden spade shiny as chrome, its handle clean pine lacquered to a high sheen. He bought some other tools he had no immediate need of—lopping shears, a good rake, a green rubber hose with brass fittings and gun nozzle. In his Fort Sumter condo he'd had no need of tools and garden equipment. But standing there with Billie, surrounded by implements that promised home improvement, he yielded to an acquisitive urge. He would gradually add to his collection until he owned all the necessary tools. He might build a greenhouse or take up cabinetry. In the truck again, he was buoyed by the thought of his new gear, as it rattled in the truck bed behind him.

He was taking her to his country place. Part of the southern dream is the desire for plantation. A man wants as big a chunk of land as he can get and control. Nowadays the old plantations had fallen into subdivision, and the descendants of plantation owners, like Hank, had to be content with what is called a "country place," maybe fifty acres on the waterway or a rice-field hunt club in the Santee Delta. That was more than Rob could hope for, with waterfront property going for fifty thousand dollars an acre and even useless inland swamp out of his price range.

But here was his own quarter of a million acres, only fifteen minutes from town. Most of the time, he never saw another living soul on those white roads, built of sparkling crushed limestone, crisscrossing the swamps of palmetto and cypress, the tracts of planted loblolly and slash pine, the stands of ancient hardwood. The Forest Service did its logging inconspicuously, if not clandestinely; he never saw them at work. Sometimes during hunting season he came across camouflaged hunters out for deer or turkey, and sometimes a Jeepful of boozing teenagers, but most of the time, the place was Rob's. It was his retreat. In its deepest recesses, Hellhole Bay and Wambaw Swamp, there were virgin stands of tupelo and bald cypress. There were salamanders and orchids of endangered varieties.

Well, he knew there had been damage. He'd seen the little woods at the Sewee Club, he'd seen TV footage of trees snapped in the forest. But after all, this was 250,000 acres. It was deep and dense. A whole forest cannot blow away.

He was not prepared.

"You're white," Billie said. "You're sweating."

"I can't seem to get my bearings."

There were no landmarks. The trees appeared to have been *mowed*. He kept driving, hoping that around the next bend they would see an end to the ruin. There had to be an end, a line past which he would see things as they used to be. The Service had cleared most of the roads; he kept taking turns he thought would lead to something untouched, to the original beauty. He pushed the pickup to its limits, driving like a maniac, unable to explain his desperation.

"This part looks a little better," Billie said. "There's a whole oak still standing."

The oak looked familiar. Farther down the road was a concrete bridge, and a black-water creek with banks of papyrus and swamp iris. He slowed down.

"I think I know where I am," he said. "I do. I know exactly where I am." There would be a turnoff just past the bridge . . .

yes. A rut road bumpy with washouts. But the pickup managed well. Here no trees were down, only limbs and branches. He was out of the path of the storm's main force; he was back in the beauty.

Past a small pond and through a piney hollow, the road curved sharply to the right and stopped, just at the crest of an almost unnoticeable hill. He turned off the engine. They were surrounded by heat and silence. Immediately, the cab filled with mosquitoes.

It is risky to take women into the woods. You can't tell how they'll react. It isn't just the discomfort of insects and heat that bothers them; it's the lack of enclosure. Most of the women he knew suffered from fear of forests. Take one out there, and she'll be hoping for a little cabin around the bend, a cottage, a hut. That's why he had chosen this spot for Billie.

First he sprayed her with insect repellent.

"*Cold,*" she said, shrinking from the can.

"Follow me," he said. He carried the shovel. The path was almost impassable. Trees had narrowed in on it, and yet the way was still visible, the hardened ground worn like a shallow ditch. The earth holds man's traces longer than we might expect. This was part of an old Indian trail, and had been used by General Francis Marion, the Swamp Fox, in his successful effort to elude redcoats; the fancy British couldn't or wouldn't follow him into these infested woods. He held the branches back for Billie, and they sprang closed again behind her. He was a little choked up. He had not seen green forest in so long, he had forgotten how it could move him. He felt like Adam readmitted after the eviction. Ahead, he could see what they had come for.

"Where are we going?" she said.

"Right here."

In front of them was an ancient shack, rotting slowly into the ground, almost indistinguishable from the surrounding vegetation. A hunter's shack, maybe; but he'd always thought of it as the home of the last resident of the forest, before the Service moved everyone out. Someone had lived here, once. Growing around the shack were plants that must have been set out by human hands; and hunters don't landscape their shack sites. Wisteria draped the crumbling chimney; trumpet vine and jasmine climbed above the door and under the clapboards.

The door was held up by one hinge and wouldn't open completely. But they squeezed in. He hadn't been here in years. He'd spent the night a few times, fifteen years ago, with a six-pack and a pair of binoculars; but the roof had been intact then. He remembered a dank but tight little cabin. He had not imagined this, the cabin gradually melting back into the earth.

The roof had collapsed inward, leaving a hole six feet square open to the sky. Over the years, both rain and sun had come in, along with enough vegetative litter to form a thin soil across the floor. And the cabin was full of ferns. In the shaft of sunlight they curled and fanned out, pale green. Green moss and lichen covered the floor and parts of the walls.

Billie stared in wonder. "I feel like I'm in a herbarium," she said. She walked carefully among the ferns, then turned to him. "It's beautiful. You knew I'd love it."

He let her think he'd known what they'd find there: he took credit for the ferns. But he was as wonderstruck as she was. You open a cabin door, and you don't expect to find a jungle.

They dug up only a few of the ferns. It was easy—the shovel slid along the floorboards and scooped them up like a spatula. Outside they dug up some small wisteria, chopping the roots with the shovel, and other vines, and clumps that Billie identified as jonquils. In two hours they had half a truckload of plants.

"This is against the law," he said, settling the last bunch of honeysuckle carefully on the pile, covering the roots with dirt.

"We're plant poachers," Billie said.

He didn't mind stealing part of the forest and taking it home. It would be a reminder that somewhere everything was all right.

.   .   .

135

On the way home, she kept looking over her shoulder through the rear window to their cargo. They passed no one on the forest roads; and out on the highway their only worry was the sun.

"The ferns won't make it," he said.

"They will if you drive faster. I know what to do with ferns. I told you, I used to work in a nursery."

"A nursery—I thought you meant a school, with little kids."

"No, a nursery with plants. I have a green thumb. Carlo said I had a magic touch, I can make anything grow. We have to get them in the ground right away, and shade them, water them good."

"An instant garden."

"No, it's not really going to be a garden. It's going to be a bower."

"That sounds good. A bower. What's a bower?"

"It's a hideaway."

2.

As it turned out, it took three days to do the work, with two more trips to the forest (to poach dirt—Billie said his soil was too sandy) and one to the handyman store for fence posts. He spaded out a ditch all along the perimeter of the yard, and filled it with forest soil. At intervals they set in the posts, with a vine at each one. Billie tied up the vines in loops from one post to the next, making a series of arches all around the yard. She divided the jonquils into clusters and planted them under the vines, and behind the jonquils, the ferns.

When they finished, she said, "It's perfect."

They sat, she on the stoop and he in his chair, surveying the completed project. It was not really perfect. Most of the vines looked lifeless, their leaves drooping from the woody stems and curling into cylinders. Billie's archways were not of uniform height.

"It's beautiful. Don't you think?" she said.

"Yes, indeedy," he said, pulling himself up with a hand on the porch pillar. As he rose, he felt something go wrong. A muscle. Or worse: a disk slipped, or the spinal cord snapped? He froze, stung with pain, and tried to breathe slowly. He let himself back down into the chair, and the knife in his back twisted; the air was expelled from his lungs in a loud "Hah!"

"You hurt yourself," she said with concern.

"No, I'm okay."

"You lifted wrong. You pulled a muscle. Where is it?" She came up behind his chair and put her hands on his shoulder blades.

"I wasn't even lifting, I was only standing up. I guess I stood up the wrong way. No, it's lower, it's—hah!"

"Can you get up?"

"Of course I can get up. Not immediately, but I can get up. You think I'm an old man or something?"

"Then get up. Lie down in the grass. I know how to fix it."

"How about if I skip the getting up part and just go from here directly to lying down."

"That's fine. Be careful. Here." She put her shoulder under his arm.

"Hah, hah."

"You're there. Stretch out. That's it."

He lay with his cheek in the green rye grass. His view was of a spindly forest, thin flexible green trees and boulders of sand, and an occasional nervous beast, segmented and antennaed, frantically making its way around the boulders and through the trees on some private but urgent mission.

"There are ants down here," he said.

"Red or black?"

"Black, very large. Gigantic."

"Those are okay. They're not interested in you." She was doing something wonderful to his back, her thumbs pressed on either side of his spine below the waist. "Is it here?"

"Yeah. There."

"The point is to relax. The more you tense up, the worse it gets. I studied muscles in lifesaving. This won't go away immediately, it'll be sore for a few days. You'll have to do leg lifts."

"I don't do leg lifts. Ever."

"You'll have to. Don't talk now. Concentrate on relaxing."

He watched the ants. Acute and close observation of anything will reveal worlds you did not suspect were there. He was down in this one, could not see much above the canopy of the ant forest; his horizon was approximately ten feet away. By and by with the rubbing and the pressing of thumbs and a sort of drumming alternated with a sort of kneading, he felt the pain begin to— well, not disappear but yield to something else, something stronger, which spread through him as effectively as any anesthesia. "This is Chinese, isn't it?" he said in a thickened voice, his breath scattering boulders and bending trees.

"No, I made it up. Is the pain gone?"

"Not yet." He didn't want her to stop what she was doing.

"Think relaxing thoughts," she said.

"Impossible. There are no relaxing thoughts."

"Then think no thoughts."

"Also impossible. I'm always thinking."

"Okay, now I'm going to put solid pressure, right here. It won't hurt." She straddled him and laid both her hands flat on his lower back and pushed.

"Uhh."

"All of my energy is going into you. A great power, flowing from my muscles to yours." She leaned forward, then back, forward, then back. He could see through the forest to her white knee, planted next to his hip. She came forward once more, then suddenly lifted her hands off him and rocked back.

"Do the power flowing again," he said. "I almost felt it but not quite."

He felt something else, a seismic shudder up through the ground: the double thud of something approaching through the forest. Billie scrambled to her feet.

In a low voice, she said, "Hey, Carlo."

"Hey, Billie."

He saw two boots. Steel-toed Sears work boots, scuffed and scarred as if from violent kicking.

"This is, ah, Rob Wyatt," her voice said.

"Hah!"

"He hurt his back."

The boots took a step closer to his face.

"Hah!"

"Can he get up?" said the wearer of the boots. "You're not supposed to move them, back injuries."

"I can get up," Rob said. "It's nothing." He raised himself on one elbow, and the pain bit him. But he leapt through the staggering sharpness of it and achieved an upright position.

Carlo was a kid. Blond, with a thin mustache. Shorter than Rob, verging on the puny.

"You okay? Should we call an ambulance?" Carlo said.

"I'm fine. I bent wrong." He hobbled to his chair but didn't sit. He steadied himself against it. He felt better. Carlo was slope-shouldered. And maybe, slightly, effeminate. Rob felt much better.

"You're living here?" Carlo said to Billie. "With him?"

"I'm renting a room here. I have a job. I'm okay. Did you get my letter?"

"I got it. But I had to look for you anyway."

"How did you find me?"

"The truck," he said, nodding toward the carport, where the pickup was pulled in behind the Toyota. "I just drove around looking for it."

"Drove around looking for it?" she said. "That would take forever."

"I had a map. I eliminated the industrial and business areas, and the empty stretches, and the rich parts. I knew the kind of places you would like. It took me three weeks."

"Oh, Carlo, I didn't want—"

JOSEPHINE HUMPHREYS

"I had to see where you are. I have to make sure you're all right."

"I told you I was all right."

"Excuse me," Rob said, turning toward the house. "I have, ah, phone calls to make."

"Actually, Mr. Wyatt," Carlo said, "it's you I came to see."

"This is none of my business," Rob said. "This is between you and Billie."

"Well," he said, "I wish it was. But I don't think that's so."

Billie's sweatshirt sleeves had fallen down over her hands. She stood to one side, arms straight, a puff of hair over one eye.

Rob hesitated. Then he said, "You're right," returning to his place by the chair.

"I only have a couple of questions to ask," Carlo said. "First is, who are you?"

"Well, I'm, uh, Robert M. Wyatt. Thirty-two years old."

Carlo nodded and waited for more.

"That's about it," Rob said.

"You have a job? A family?"

Rob sighed. "I have two parents, a brother, a dog, no job."

Carlo thought that over. "I might be able to give you some leads," he said. "The shipyard is hiring. Most of it is skilled, but with the storm damage, they're taking on whoever they can get. I know the foreman, I can put you in touch with him. I can't promise anything, but it's a possibility." He took a pencil and pad from his shirt pocket and wrote down a name and number.

"No, I—well, thank you," Rob said, taking the paper.

"Carlo, Rob's a—"

"This is good," Rob said. "I appreciate it."

"A man can fall on hard times," Carlo said. "I've been there myself. Quit the service once, thinking I'd find something better, but come to find out it was mostly fast food. A man can't put on a hat and suit like that and serve french fries."

"No," Rob said.

They stood there looking at each other. The situation was

140

complicated. Billie seemed dazed; her eyes were directed to a point in midair somewhere beyond both men.

Carlo shifted his weight from one boot to the other. "And then, the second thing was—I don't know how to put this—but with regard to her."

"Yes."

"I got to be sure nobody does her harm."

"You can rest assured—"

"I've been looking after her, you see, a long time. I've done a good job, too. She means a lot to me. She means the world to me."

"I can understand that," Rob said.

Carlo wanted something more. "I don't mean to pry, but I have to ask your intentions."

"He doesn't have any intentions, Carlo. I'm renting a room here. That's it."

Carlo, to his credit, did not mention the power flow in the grass. He said, "You know you can come back, Billie. Anytime, day or night." His wiry body seemed to lean in her direction.

"We talked about this, Carlo. We talked about it so many times."

"All right, I just want to make myself clear. If you change your mind. You know Carlo will be there."

"I know. Thank you."

He turned to Rob. "If I can help you out, until you find something . . ." He was reaching for his wallet.

"No," Rob said.

"Give that guy a call. Tell him I said for you to contact him. And just in case . . ." He wrote another number and an address on the pad, ripped it off and handed it to Billie. "That's where I am. We're in port for three months. I'll be available."

"Thank you," she said. She wasn't looking at him. She put the paper in her pocket.

"Day or night," Carlo said.

He couldn't see her face, but Rob could. Her eyes had sprung tears along the bottom lid, but they didn't fall. She blinked them away.

"Okay," Carlo said, clasping his hands. "I guess that's it." Turning to Rob, he said, "Just take good care of her."

"The truck—" she said.

"Keep it. I got new wheels. The car of my dreams. You can see it there, down at the corner? 'Eighty-two Trans Am, loaded."

She smiled. "What you always wanted."

"Listen, I can pay you for the truck," Rob said. "I'm not broke. I can write you a check."

"That truck's not worth fifty dollars. When you get back on your feet, we can work something out." He started for the street, then stopped. Rob wanted him gone. Billie had a funny look on her face. Of pain, of love.

"Want to take a look at the car?" Carlo said to her.

She hesitated and cast a quick look at Rob. "Sure," she said.

They walked down the path together. Rob could not have run after them. He felt for his car keys. Carlo could have been planning all along to get her to the car and lure her in. Rob had the Toyota keys in his pocket, but the truck was blocking the Toyota. He took a couple of steps after them, but they were already nearing the Trans Am. Carlo opened the car door and she looked in. He got in, put his hands on the wheel, motioned her over to the passenger door. She walked slowly around the front of the car, her hand grazing the hood—she looked back at Rob once— then opened the door and got in and closed the door.

"Fuck," Rob said. He looked wildly at the Toyota and tried to gauge the gap between its rear bumper and the front bumper of the truck. There might be room to back out over the lawn.

The horn of the Trans Am tooted. The antenna went down, then up, the wipers took two dry slaps across the windshield, the windows opened and closed again. From inside the car came the deep bass rumble of a two-megaton audio system. Then it quit. A few seconds passed, and Billie got out. She leaned down and spoke into the car, then closed the door. The Trans Am pulled slowly out and away. She stood there alone on the sidewalk.

He didn't go after her. Instead, he went inside and waited. She came back into the yard and sat in the lawn chair awhile and seemed to be listening to the wind in the oleanders, her head cocked, her arms on the chair and her feet together. When he went out, tears were running down her face. He didn't know what to say.

"You see what I mean now," she said. "He was my only friend. We were—we were—"

"It's okay," he said. He didn't have a handkerchief to give her, so he wiped her face with his hands, forgetting the dirt from the plants and making muddy stains on her cheeks.

"—we were crazy, it was crazy. He doesn't have anyone. All he has now is the navy and the car. But what else could I have done? We weren't a real couple. He wanted to—to please me, but it didn't work—"

"Why don't you come in," he said. "Come inside."

"But I was right, what I said. He's good, isn't he?"

"He seems to be, yes, good."

"He wanted to help you get a job. He thought you were laid off. He tried to give you *money*. Oh, God."

"It doesn't matter," he said. "You can't worry about it."

She tried to catch her breath, wiping her face with her own hands, which were as dirty as Rob's. "The only thing that matters in this world," she said, "is how you treat the people who've been good to you."

"How about a shower," he said. "You come take a hot shower. You're tired. I'll fix something to eat."

"I can't eat anything. I don't want to eat anything."

She was not hysterical, but she was shaken. He got her inside and started the shower for her. "Please," he said. "Take the shower. Here's your shampoo. Okay? Here's your towel." He left her in the bathroom and closed the door.

While she showered, he reconnoitered. Washed his face and hands in the kitchen sink, threw away the name of the shipyard foreman. It was uncomfortable to win and be bested at the same time. He was humbled. Carlo had handed over to him the care of his beloved. What sort of love theirs might have been, Rob couldn't venture to guess, but he didn't doubt that it was love. That's what she had been hiding from: love itself, of some impossible kind. Carlo didn't look older than twenty-three, at the most . . . making him seventeen, eighteen, when he took in the abandoned girl.

When Rob was seventeen, he was still goofing around in the pup tent and flushing cherry bombs down the school toilets. Responsibility came to him late; some would say it had not really ever come. While in other parts of the inhabited planet, heroic children were saving each other. Christ, the kid had tried to give him money. If Rob had been Carlo, he would not have entrusted Billie to his care.

He actually said out loud, "I won't fail you, Carlo."

When she had been in the shower for twenty minutes, he knocked on the door. "Billie?" She didn't answer. He knocked again, then opened it. She was in the stall, leaning close to the frosty glass of the shower door, letting hot water flow down the back of her head, over her shoulders and the length of her back.

"Do you need anything?" he said stupidly.

"No." She moved deeper into the stall. He couldn't see her.

"You'll shrivel up if you stay too long in there."

"I'm coming out."

"Towel's on the tank here." He backed out, but waited outside the closed door until he heard the water stop. In a minute the door opened, and she came out wrapped in the towel, her wet hair hanging over her eyes.

"Want me to dry your hair?" he said.

She stopped. "I think I'll sleep for a while. I'm going to just sleep. What time is it?"

"Three-thirty," he said. "But you've been working hard."

"I thought it was nighttime. I'm just going to bed. I think that's what I need to do."

She walked down to her room, leaving a trail of wet footprints in the hall. He felt useless. He was failing already, in the first hour of his duty.

3.

It doesn't sound like a hard task, taking care of a woman. But it was harder than he'd thought; it was more than feeding and guarding. Billie stayed in her room all afternoon and didn't come out for the supper he fixed. For days she was morose, and he could do nothing to cheer her up. There is nothing sadder than a sad girl, especially when you may be the cause of the sadness.

Speedo tried to cheer her up too, with more success because he was persistent. He dogged her, begged for the dance, learned to nose open the door of her room. In the mornings when he heard the truck start, he leapt into the back and rode to work with her. When she watched television, he whined until she got down on her knees and tussled with him.

"This dog is starved for affection," she said one night, sitting cross-legged on the floor.

"He's not, I pat him plenty." From the sofa Rob watched her stroke the dog's bony skull, the coarse bristles on his nose, and the knots of his ears. She laid her own cheek against the golden hide. Rob envied them both.

"And he has fleas. Come on, boy, that's it, lie down." She ruffled the soft hair on Speedo's belly. His hind leg jerked back and forth in the air.

"A dog is meant to have fleas," Rob said. "He's a real dog, a hunter and a fisher, an outdoorsman."

"Poor old thing. Look, Rob, he's *crawling* with fleas. He needs a dip."

"He wouldn't stand for it—unless you did it. He seems to have lost his heart to you."

"He knows I like him," she said.

Behind her head the television lost its vertical hold and the picture scrolled slowly upward. Billie inspected Speedo's teeth, and then suddenly looked up. "Rob, I need to tell you something," she said.

He steeled himself. She was going back to Carlo, he knew it; but he said, "Sure."

"I'm grateful to you." She dropped her head again and seemed intent on massaging the dog's ears while she talked, her voice low. "If I hadn't been here—if I hadn't had this place—I might have gone back to Carlo. I had a strong attachment to him. You can have that, even when you're not attracted physically. I've missed him. But I think I'll be all right now."

"Of course you will."

"And I hope you'll let me stay."

"You can stay as long as you want to."

She looked up, pleased. "But also," she said, "if you want to go out sometime, you should. You don't have to watch over me. You haven't seen any other people this whole time."

"What other people?"

"Your friends and family. You've been cooped up with me, avoiding the rest of the world."

"Ah," he said. "Maybe I understand: maybe *you* feel cooped up. I'll take you out. We can hike in the forest, go to the movies, hop a flight to Brazil—anything."

"I was wondering," she said, "are you keeping me a secret?"

"Of course not. Why would I do that?"

"Because they'll think it's strange, my being here."

"No one cares, Billie. You can do what you want to do. Come watch the news." He adjusted the television set and she sat on the sofa beside him. But he heard none of the news; he was smiling against his will, his face turned so that she couldn't see the smile. He thought it best that she not know his great delight. She wanted to stay, she wasn't leaving.

"Rob, do you have any money?"

"Some. How much do you need?" He was surprised; but he knew that he would give her his whole twelve thousand if she asked.

"Fifty dollars, I think. I was looking at the house yesterday, and it needs something, some kind of *adornment*. I thought of grape ivy in baskets, to hang from the porch. And some wind-chimes. And some birdfeeders. I've never had a birdfeeder, but

I thought you would like one, the kind that looks like a little house. What do you think?"

"An interesting idea," he said. "We'd have a little house with little houses hanging from it."

"I'm pretty good at thinking up ideas," she said. "But this is the first time I've had a chance to do them." She drummed her fingers on her knees, and turned back to the news. He stole a look at her face. It was, for the first time since he had been looking at it, serene. She had her own smile, small but real. Thinking up more ideas, probably. Rob couldn't have been happier.

CHAPTER 9

I t wasn't true that he was avoiding the rest of the world. The rest of the world simply hadn't occurred to him, since Billie's arrival. He didn't even notice that his phone hadn't rung once in the last ten days, and when it did ring the next afternoon, he jumped. Billie was in the yard, giving Speedo a bath with the hose. From the kitchen, Rob heard the ringing stop and an in-human voice speak—the answering machine was still hooked up. Then he heard the voice of Louise.

"If this is your number, Rob, I want to talk to you." He raced for the phone. "If it's not"—she hesitated, and he went sliding across the floor, lunging—"then, um, forget it." He snatched the receiver off the hook. She was gone.

He called her house. No answer. Maybe she had called from the club. Billie came in, spattered with water.

"He shook on me," she said. "I've never seen such a filthy dog. The water ran black. Don't you ever wash him?"

"Annually," he said.

"Who was on the phone?"

"They hung up."

As he spoke, the phone rang again.

"Rob?" said Jack in an unnecessarily loud voice. Was Jack getting deaf? "Rob, how are you?"

"I'm fine."

"Well, sure, if you want to. When?"

"What are you talking about?"

"Fifteen minutes? Hold on. Maude, Rob wants to drop by. He wants to know if we'll be around in the next fifteen minutes."

He could hear Maude's voice in the distance. Then Jack again: "Yes, we'll be here. Mother and I were planning to go for a drive, out to Gracewood, but we'll wait for you. You'll have to come right away, though, if you want to catch us."

"What is this, Doc?"

"No, we don't mind. I understand. I'll tell her you just want a few words with her." He hung up.

"What is it?" Billie said.

He looked at the receiver in his hand. "I don't know what it is. I'll have to go over there."

"Can I go?"

"It won't be a pleasure trip. I'm delegated to ask my mother if she's secretly planning to abandon my father. He thinks she's trying to get him into the old folks' home and leave him there. He wants me to find out. Does that sound like a normal family?"

"I don't know," Billie said. "I've never seen a normal family."

"I've been putting him off. Maude can be hard to talk to."

"I could go with you and wait outside. I don't want to stay here alone."

"You aren't afraid Carlo might come back, are you?"

"No, he won't. Just the same . . . if he did, I don't want to be here. Let me go with you."

He said what he always said when she made a request. Yes.

They took the pickup, down the island and across the bridge. Some houses were still cordoned off with yellow plastic banners that said "Unsafe for Occupancy." Others had been jacked and buttressed. Along the roadside was the incongruous scenery to which they had become accustomed, but an occasional object still shocked the rational mind: a bathtub in a parking lot; on the shoulder, an open suitcase and a trail of clothing, flat and caked with mud. There was something embarrassing in the public display of these domestic things, as if the private, intimate detail of lives had been suddenly brought to light. It made Rob nervous.

The county was nearly a month into cleanup and relief, and though much had been cleaned and relieved, it was clear that the job was bigger than the authorities had surmised. Companies that had contracted to clean the streets couldn't meet their deadlines. Landfills had filled, and there was nowhere to dump the dump trucks. Lawsuits were being filed. Rob thought of the old lawyer's line, applicable on any number of disastrous occasions: "What a mess. What a gold mine."

Uptown was still in bad shape. He would have said, in fact, hopeless shape. People were at work with hammers on jobs that looked to him to require dozers and cranes. The little wooden houses and barbershops and churches, which had not looked sturdy even before the storm, now appeared to be ready to tumble in a heavy breeze.

Downtown was looking better. In the historic district tourists were already returning. A house tour was on, and packs of sightseers walked down Church and Tradd Streets, consulting their maps. A clump of them had gathered in front of his parents' house. He parked and waited for them to move on. He liked having tourists around: it was like being a patient with an exotic disease, and the medical students come to see what you have, fascinated by what you thought was only sickness. Tourists gave him a temporary sense of importance. But this house was not what they thought it was.

From the outside, maybe it suggested the possibility of drama and romance. It was old, and that made the tourists think of accumulated lives, "the stories this house could tell!" And it was charming, small and cozy-looking, sunburnt pink stucco with a second-floor balcony overlooking the narrow street. Behind an iron gate the walkway led back into the small garden.

"You lived here?" Billie said. "You must have loved it."

"I grew up here," he said. "But I can't say I loved it." He had no regrets as his parents prepared to leave. Inside, the house was dark and uncomfortable. No closets, cramped kitchen, obsolete dining room with a long gloomy table. Though he had trouble imagining his parents at Gracewood Hall, he was glad they were going. Forty years is too long in one house.

They weren't the only ones going. For some years now, the old Charleston families had been gradually disappearing into the suburbs. "I don't know where they've all got to," Jack had said. "I think there must be some secret place, like where elephants gather to die. The Pringles are gone, the Pinckneys are gone, where are all those Hugers who used to be everywhere you looked? I knew when Louise and Hank Camden moved into that island house that the end was near. It's the death of the aristocracy."

Jack looked on any change as decline. Rob wished he could think of a way to cheer him; but what can you do to cheer an old man? Everything he thought of to say seemed, upon reflection, untrue.

2.

"I don't have to come in with you," Billie said. "I want you to, but I warn you—it could be a circus."

He hoped that no questions would arise. He didn't want to get into an explanation of Billie. What would he say? "She's sort of a client but not really. She's living with me but not really: we don't touch, she uses the bathroom before I even wake up . . ."

In the hall the floorboards creaked, and the walls were damp. The house had never been comfortable. Part of the problem had been Maude, who put little effort into making it comfortable. But part was the fault of the house itself. Smells never cleared out of the rooms. Maude hadn't owned a cat in two years, but in the front hall Rob could smell cats. He could smell fried fish, though for the sake of Jack's heart she no longer fried anything. The house kept things in. He couldn't go into it without being sideswiped by history.

He didn't mind history if it was recent and relevant. What he disliked was pluperfect history, a double shift into the past, into the dead and gone. The world would be better off if history were limited to the range of memory alone, and better still if the range of memory were fairly short. He had read of people who after a sharp blow to the head had memory spans of only two to three minutes, approximately the span of Speedo's memory. He envied Speedo's lack of history. Speedo might recall (dimly) that he had hidden a bone somewhere, five minutes ago; but beyond that, his past was blank. History was only a faint bell tolling in his doggy brain, enough to make him stir in the sun but certainly no burden to him. And the past past, the pluperfect, cannot have existed for him at all.

Maude, on the other hand, had gone deep into the pluperfect, eleven generations of it. He hoped he would not find her in the dining room with those damned papers. It was a second-floor dining room, with French doors onto the balcony for the harbor breeze. He called up the stairs; she hollered in answer. She was a good hollerer—a good fisherman, a good hunter. She'd have made a good man.

Bending over the table, penciling in some newly found ancestor, she did look different, as Jack had said. Rob couldn't put his finger on what it was, but she looked younger, she looked hopeful.

"Ma?" he said.

Without looking up, she said, "Hello, Rob. Your father's out on the balcony. I wish you'd talk to him, he's acting funny."

"Ma, I want you to meet someone. This is Billie."

She straightened. "Hello, Billie," she said, and then, "Good Lord, how old is she?"

Billie laughed.

"Twenty-three," he said.

"And does she have a last name?"

"Poe. Like Edgar Allan," he said.

"Billie Poe. I like that." Maude held her hand out to Billie, who took it. "And does she talk?" Maude said.

"My mother is direct," he said.

"I should hope so," Maude said. "The alternative is a waste

of time. I haven't got much time to waste. Come and sit down, Billie—oh, we can't. My chairs are all gone. I can offer you some sherry, though. I wouldn't let them pack up the sherry."

"You're already packed?" he said. "When's the closing?"

"It's been," she said. "Luckily, a cottage at Gracewood became available unexpectedly. I shouldn't say *luckily*. It wasn't so lucky for the poor old gentleman. But they called and said if we wanted it we could have it. We're striking while the iron is hot. I was surprised at how easy it is to sell a house. It's simple! I called the realtor, and he brought over a rich dentist from Philadelphia, and it was *done*. The movers came yesterday, packed up what we'll need and put the rest in storage. In case you need it, Rob. I'm sure Ernie has no use for it. You haven't heard from him, I don't guess."

"You know Ernie, Ma."

"Well—" She looked around as if she'd lost her train of thought. "Well, tomorrow we'll be in the cottage. Today I am finishing up the last of the Project."

"What is it?" Billie said, taking a look at the papers on the table.

"It's history," Maude said. "Rob does not approve. But he doesn't really understand. Maybe when he's older he'll appreciate it."

"I'm older now," he said. "The appreciation hasn't hit me yet." He changed his mind about the sherry and poured himself a glass from the decanter on the table. All the familiar objects of the room were gone; only the sherry and the genealogy remained, necessary right to the last minute. He leaned against the wall and lit a cigarette. The room looked neat for the first time in his memory.

"If you've gone back eleven generations, Ma, you ought to have a couple of thousand ancestors by now."

"I'm not doing all the lines," she said. "Since when did you smoke cigarettes? Billie, do you have any influence on this man? I certainly hope so. He hasn't been himself lately. No one has.

His father's been grouchy all week. Sometimes I think I'm the only sane person around here, and that comes as quite a surprise. But it goes to show you. The only thing that counts is stamina. If you hold on long enough, you'll be victorious. But I wish you wouldn't smoke in here, Rob. I can smell it for a week."

"You won't be here in a week."

"Well, the Yankees will smell it."

He stepped closer to the table for a look at his ancestors. If he showed a spark of interest in them, Maude would be happy for the day. But he couldn't bring himself to do it, because he had no spark of interest. He couldn't bear to see her stooping to record another dead Bonnette.

He said, "When you move, why don't you leave this material with the dentist? As part of the history of the house. He might like to have it."

She peered at him and said nothing.

"Eleven generations, that's hard to believe," Billie said. "It must be a very old family. I don't know the names of my grandparents."

"Every family goes back the same distance," Maude said. "I'll tell you something Rob doesn't know, Billie. I'm not doing this for the reason he thinks I'm doing it. I'm looking for something interesting."

He pushed on. "But doesn't this stuff occasionally—like when you wake up in the dead of night—strike you as somewhat pointless? Somewhat a waste of time?"

She straightened and put her pencil behind her ear. "Now, what would strike me as pointless would be if I had no obligations, no dependents, the chance of a lifetime staring me in the face, and I was doing nothing at all. That would strike me as pointless. Or if I was past thirty years old and had never been outside the state of South Carolina, except to school, which doesn't count. That would be a waste of time. Don't you agree, Billie?"

"I can never tell when I'm wasting time and when I'm not,"

Billie said, polite as ever. Maude seemed to like her answer; she took a closer look at her.

He started to remind Maude that she herself was past thirty and had never been anywhere—but maybe that was the main point. So he made no comment. He was always afraid that if the conversation proceeded into a danger zone, she might bring up things he didn't want to talk about, their own sad pluperfect. His history with her. So he would grant her this genealogical obsession. It was harmless enough, as was the sherry. There were worse possible obsessions and beverages. These two kept her on an even keel.

He didn't want to think about the times when she hadn't been on one. He said, "You've done a lot of work. A lot of research."

"Yes," she said, and smiled. "Look here, Billie, I'll explain some of this to you."

"I'll smoke outside," he said.

He sidled through the French doors onto the balcony, where Jack sat in a hunch, his straw hat on his knees. "Meditating, Doc?" Rob said, taking a seat next to him on the bench. Below them, Tradd Street was empty. No tourists. It was lunchtime, and hot. They had gone back to their inns.

"Did you ask her?" Jack said.

"Not yet."

"It's worse," he said. "Did you see the living room? Everything's gone! Some of it, she gave to the movers. She gave them my desk and my old *National Geographics*. I'm been saving the *Geographics* for years, I had them all indexed, so if I wanted to read about Tierra del Fuego, I could turn right to it. Gone."

"But did you ever actually do it?"

"Do what?"

"Read about Tierra del Fuego."

"That's not the point. But yes, I've looked things up from time to time. I don't think you're taking me seriously. I don't think you mean to talk to her about this at all."

"I do, I promise. I'm going to. The time wasn't right just now. I've got—someone with me."

Jack turned and looked through the glass doors. "Who is that— Louise? I want to talk to Louise. She'll do it. She has a way with Maude."

"It's not Louise. It's Billie. She's sort of a client."

"Client? You've gone back to work—"

"No. I'm just helping her out. She's got some trouble, and I agreed to help."

"Ah," Jack said. "I know what you mean. When they come to you, it's hard to turn them down. It's the hardest thing in the world. But you can't help them all, and maybe it's better just to concentrate on one. I wish I'd known that sooner. See, I didn't set out to be the kind of man I've turned into, which is a failure of a man."

"You're no failure, you're—"

"No, I know what I am. I'm a man who made a dozen women happy for a short time and one woman unhappy for forty-five years."

"That's not true," Rob said.

But Jack ignored him, talking on. "And at our age, there's an urge to tell all. Your mother's been hiding something from me, and now I think she's getting ready to tell."

"And just what is it she's been hiding?" Rob tried not to sound annoyed, but hadn't Jack done some hiding himself?

"What she thinks of me. And I don't want to hear it, Rob."

"I thought you wanted me to ask her—"

"I do and I don't. I'm— I'm scared, to tell you the truth. Right now all I want to do is sit here alone for a while. It's my last day in this house. All I want to do is sit and look at the harbor. I've always liked this balcony, I like the view and—it's just the place I'm used to. I've always been comfortable here."

Rob stood behind him for a minute while Jack leaned forward, his face toward the sea, already thinking of himself as alone.

"I'll be inside," Rob said.

3.

Maude and Billie were sitting on the floor together, their backs against the wainscoting, Maude with a glass of sherry in one hand and part of her family map in another, explaining parts of it to Billie. Maude looked up at Rob. "Oh, don't take her away yet," she said. "I haven't finished with her. Can't you go do something, like say goodbye to your old room? We're having a grand time. Without Ernie, I've been out of touch with the younger generation." To Billie she added, "Rob doesn't count. He's out of touch with it too."

"There's nothing in my room to say goodbye to, is there?"

"How about the walls and windows? Go sit in the window like you used to."

He glanced at Billie, and she nodded. So he left them alone together and went up to the third floor, to his empty room with sloping walls, a single window at each end. Through one he had been able to see rooftops and spires; through the other a part of the harbor, and the ships coming in, so close that when one passed at the end of the street it looked like a moving building. The air was musty; he opened the seaward window.

Maude had kept the room intact for years, the way a mother keeps the room of a lost child—books on the shelf, globe on the desk, pencils and sharks' teeth and Sunday school attendance pins in the drawer; but one day last month she had called him to say she was throwing everything away and if he wanted anything he had to come get it. He retrieved his birds, the globe, the teeth, a few books. Everything else disappeared overnight.

She had a right to do it, of course.

("You, Robert, would you say that your mother needs help?" And his answer, while Maude watched: "Yes," and the stenographer look-ing up in surprise, and Maude still watching.)

He sat on the windowsill. If at age thirty-two you stop and see that your life so far has been a pitiful performance, what is there to do? The stage is set, the action proceeds headlong in directions you have chosen. Midlife, there is a little death, and we inherit our selves as we have made them.

When he went downstairs, the tête-à-tête of Maude and Billie had broken up. Jack was standing between them in the dining room, and Maude had her pocketbook in hand, one that Louise had given her. The scene painted on it included this house.

"Daddy and I are going for a little ride," she said to him.

Jack shot him a questioning look.

"Ma, I was hoping to get a word with you—"

"But it's not necessary, son. I've had a wonderful talk with Billie here. She'll tell you. I'm glad you brought her over. But I want Daddy to drive me over to Gracewood so we can drop some things off. It won't take long, Jack, and we don't have to talk to a soul there if you don't want to. Daddy wasn't wild about some of the other gentlemen over at Gracewood."

"Old fogies," Jack said. "Walk with their legs apart."

"That's what's good about the place, though: we have our own cottage. It's not a commune. Come on now, let's go. Rob, you lock up before you leave. And I hope I'll see you again, Billie. I know I will."

From the balcony he watched them get into the car. Jack held the door open for her, but he might as well have been a chauffeur; she sat, tucked her dress around her knees, and never once looked at Jack.

"I'm sorry," Rob said to Billie. "Did you have to hear the whole eleven generations?"

"No, I asked her about the other thing. You said your dad wanted you to ask her if she was planning to leave—"

"*You* asked her? But you don't even know her!"

"That made it easier."

"But . . . what did you say exactly?"

"I said he was scared she was getting him into that home so that she could leave him there. She laughed and said there was some truth in that, but not the way he thought. He's too dependent on her, and he needs independence. Did you know that he has never fixed his own lunch? If she doesn't fix it, he doesn't eat. It might be good for him to learn to make a sandwich. She said the home is an adult community. 'We'll be adults,' she said. It all made sense to me."

"You're something else, Billie."

"Was it wrong? I thought I might as well just ask her . . ."

"No, it was right. What else did she say?"

Billie hesitated. "Well, she said she'd always known you would see the light someday, and finally you have, and she's glad."

"She never liked the idea of me being a lawyer."

"It wasn't that. It was your love life. She said you'd been in love with someone for too long, and she was pleased to see you with me. I had to explain that you *weren't* with me, not in the way she thought."

Women don't waste time, he thought. Those two had been alone together for ten minutes, but that was enough to cover all the major points. Maude had always been like that. He was surprised, though, that she had mentioned the "someone." Surprised that she *knew*. But then, it was probably clear to everyone.

"So who is it?" Billie said. "Oh, never mind, I'm sorry. It's none of my business."

He knew that if she asked outright, he would tell her. Searching for a distraction, he said, "We have time to go get those hanging baskets you want. There's a place we can stop on the way home."

She lowered her chin and looked up at him. He should have remembered the first thing he'd noticed about her, that night at Louise's; she wasn't easily fooled. But she said, "All right."

4.

They bought six hanging baskets, three bird feeders, three wind chimes, plus the chains and hooks. In the yard he stood on his chair to attach everything, while she gave directions. "I'm sorry it cost so much," she said. "It was twice as much as I thought it would be. I'll pay you back." She was holding the chair steady for him; he could see only the top of her head. "But it's going to look great," she said. "I don't know why people don't decorate their houses more. A house should be a work of art, more than just walls and doors. I like those houses that people cover with license plates and bottle caps. One time I saw one covered with toys."

"I draw the line at wind chimes," he said.

She said, "Oh, your mother said something else, I forgot to tell you. She told me what she was looking for in the genealogy— some kind of outlaw, I think. She's funny. I think a lighthearted person like that makes the best kind of mother—"

"What outlaw?"

"I don't know—she said it in passing. Maybe it was a robber, I can't remember. His name was a little different."

Rob stepped down from the chair. "A pirate?" he said.

"That was it. She said nobody would admit there was a family connection, but she thinks she can find it."

"But why didn't she say so? I'm the one who always wanted Stede Bonnet for an ancestor."

"Maybe she wanted to surprise you. She's the type that likes surprises."

"Billie, how do you know that?"

"Well, doesn't she?"

"Yes, she does."

Billie backed into the grass, tilting her head to judge his work. "Come see," she said, her hand out to him—but she dropped it when he came close. He turned to look with her. In the light breeze, all of the hanging things danced, baskets and feeders and chimes. One set of chimes, made of pink seashells, could hardly be said to chime; its sound was more like a thin clatter. Another, of metal rods, gave out clinks and clanks; and the third, an iron triangle swinging inside a ring, bonged like a dinner bell.

"What do you think?" she said.

"It looks like Gypsy headquarters."

"Perfect," she said. "That's what I wanted."

CHAPTER 10

While Billie took a shower he got out a cookbook Louise had given him at a time when she'd been worried about his eating habits. In the refrigerator he had some good apples and some pecans; he worked away, chopping fruit and nuts and thinking about nutrition; also thinking about the sounds of the shower, how she must be turning, soaping up, rinsing; then washing her hair, with the herbal shampoo he would smell when he went in later for his own shower; and then just standing, letting the water run full in her face . . . When the shower stopped he was mixing the salad. While she dressed he spooned it onto a bed of lettuce in a yellow bowl and covered it with plastic.

She came to the door in her leotard and thin skirt, a towel on her head, a pair of scissors in her hand.

"Will you cut my hair? It's not hard. Just trim an inch off all around." She pulled a chair into the middle of the kitchen, draped the towel over her shoulders, and handed him the scissors. "What's the matter?" she said.

"I can't do this," he said. "I'll buy you a haircut at the beauty parlor, how about that?" He tried to return the scissors.

"I've never been to a beauty parlor," she said. "Carlo always cut my hair."

So he had to do it. She sat erect, holding her chin high, waiting. He began slowly, afraid he was going to do it all wrong. He cut a tiny lock in the back and watched it fall to the towel. He was careful not to let the scissors—or his hand—touch her neck.

"Don't be afraid," she said. "You can cut more than five hairs at a time."

But he was afraid—of ruining her hair and also of standing too close to her, of seeing the curve of her neck. She bent forward and he lifted her hair; the neck was white and smooth. He cut with a steady hand, but his heart was racing. "My hair grows fast," she said, talking toward her lap. "I have to keep it short because otherwise it's out of control. I don't like long hair anyway. Long hair makes women act funny, like they're something special. I don't mean your mother, of course; she wears her hair up—that's different."

He came around to the left side; he had to lean close and angle the scissors along her jaw. Accidentally his thumb brushed her chin. Immediately she stiffened. He kept working as if nothing had happened, but she fell silent. Outside there were evening cicadas, and the sounds of children in the street. He saw that her eyes were closed.

He bent in front of her to even the sides, and when she opened her eyes she was looking directly at him, closer to him than she had ever been.

"I think that's it," he said.

He had expected she would run to a mirror, but she sat still, looking at him. "Have I cut too much?" he said. "Is it all right? You'd better go look."

"It's fine," she said. "I know it's fine."

She folded the towel carefully, took it to the door and shook it into the yard, then stood there a minute looking out. It was his fault; he hadn't meant to touch her but he had wanted to, so the accidental nature of it was not absolute. Now she was afraid of him.

"I made you a Waldorf salad," he said.

"What is that?"

"Apples and nuts in a mayonnaise sauce." He pointed to the bowl. She lifted the plastic wrap and made a face.

"No? The only other food in the house is limes and Pop-Tarts. Tell you what, I'll take you out to eat, how about that? Unless you're tired. You don't want to go out?" He ran ahead of himself, trying to read the little frowns that came and went on her face, trying to guess what she wanted. "The Conch serves a great seafood platter. Fried shrimp, scallops, fish. Hush puppies."

Her face lit up. He'd hit on the right thing. He would reestablish himself as trustworthy, and she would relax in his company, and everything would be good. She was smiling again.

"Let's go," he said.

He left all the lights on. He didn't lock his door. He stepped into the evening air with Billie at his side.

And saw Albert coming up the path. Albert's head was down at its usual angle, as if he did not need or want to see where he was going. When he did look up, he missed a step.

"Aw," said Albert, taken aback and not finding the right word for the moment. He didn't do too well with new people. Rob introduced Billie, and Albert went into the bartender shuffle, with a grin and a nod that continued past logical limits.

"Don't I know you?" Billie said.

"From the Camdens' party," Albert said.

"You're in time," Rob said. "We're going to the Conch. How about a seafood platter and some old songs?"

"No, I was just stopping by, I'm on my way home."

It was impossible to talk Albert into something he didn't want to do. Rob didn't try hard; this friendship was based on an understanding of its limits.

Billie turned to Albert. "I've never been to this place Rob's talking about. Can we eat outside?"

Albert said, "Outside is the only place you can eat. It hasn't got much of an inside."

"Please come with us," she said.

Who could resist her? She looked at Albert the way she always looked at people, as if they were interesting, as if she had important questions to ask and could hardly wait for the answers.

"Well . . ."

"We won't stay late. I'm not much of a night person."

"I guess I could, for a while," Albert said.

"Good," she said, looking pleased, stepping between them and taking both their elbows.

They made an odd threesome, Rob thought, walking down to the car—a trio of misfits. But misfits may suit one another. They might have been a family of some new sort, joined not by blood or sex but by pure shared loneliness, which makes strong bonds.

2.

The Conch had once been a gas station. Two years ago the Vietnamese had moved in and taken it over. Now it sold gas, live bait, shear pins, and, at four small tables on the deck, a seafood platter somewhere between southern fried and tempura, along with a nightly special that was actually Anna and Huong's own meal but could be shared. Huong would also rent you a jet ski or paint your beach house. Spattered tarpaulins and paint cans were stacked in a corner. A herd of hybrid mallards wandered loose along the mudbank by day and roosted under the deck, waging an evenly matched battle with the resident marsh rats. The Conch gave Rob a good deal of pleasure, his home away from home. Anna was tiny and square-faced. Huong's front tooth was outlined in gold. No golfers dined here.

He stuck his head in the kitchen, where Anna was lifting two buckets off the stove.

"What's the special tonight, Anna? Something new?"

Anna spoke good if phonetically flawed English. She pointed to the buckets.

"Duck paw vein," she said.

Rob nodded. "Sounds good to me."

"Count me out," Albert said. "I'll have the flounder."

"That's the trouble with you, Albert," he said. "Tradition-bound." They took a table near the railing, the dark water of the Intracoastal Waterway lapping at the mudbank not ten yards off their shoulders. "Scared of a little ethnic cuisine. What's the trouble, you don't want to eat the duckies?"

"That isn't what she said."

"Well, I'll admit I didn't get every word. With Anna, you have to settle for the general concept."

"You settled for a bowl of paint. You ordered the Dutch Boy Paint."

"Did I?" he asked Anna. She nodded and hid her smile.

Huong was already threading his machine. He knew to put on his old tapes when Albert and Rob walked in. Rob had never asked where the tapes came from, whether they were gift or booty. Huong had never spoken about the war. No indication of which *side* he was on. And Rob didn't want to know. The tapes and the obsolete reel-to-reel seemed to date from approximately 1968, classic tunes, the favorites of someone with a taste for fine music. The kind of carefully selected and ordered medley that you'd put together if you knew you were embarking for hell— and knew, in addition, that if anything was going to see you through and get you home again, it would not be your Saint Christopher's medal. It would be Marvin Gaye, the Temptations, Sam Cooke.

Huong and Hank were the only two men Rob knew who were bona fide Vietnam veterans. He had never asked either one of them the thing he really wanted to know: What are the birds of Vietnam? He wouldn't have made much of a soldier, in a place like that; he'd have been distracted by the birds. They must have been beautiful and exotic. Parrots, maybe.

Albert put his feet on the railing. He was feeling easier. The feet didn't jiggle. "Smell that night air," he said.

"This is perfect," Billie said. The moon was out, or at least half of it was. Waves lapped, stars shone. In the distance across the water, the electrified city was a spit floating between layers of night. Above it rose a hazy glow, like a faraway fire. Billie set her elbows on the table, her chin in her hands.

They ordered seafood and the beverage special, which was available to favored customers. Huong was licensed only for beer and wine. Rob had helped him get the license, having once negotiated a handsome settlement for a lady commissioner. Huong, however, kept a locked cupboard of Chinese vodka behind the jet skis. There were no other patrons in the Conch tonight. Tuesdays were slow. On the weekends a ragged crew gathered to shoot rats from the deck, but tonight no one else was likely to show up. On slow nights Huong would unlock the cupboard for them.

Anna came back with glasses and an iced-tea pitcher full of vodka. Rob filled his glass. Half-filled Billie's glass. Huong's old Sony hissed, and the music began. But it wasn't what he had expected.

"What is that?" Billie said.

"Saxophone," Albert said, leaning back in his chair. "Albert Swan himself, sound wizard."

"How'd you do that?" Rob said. "How'd you get it on a reel?"

"Sound wizardry," Albert said. "Involves inserting a jack in a hole. Thought Huong needed a wider range of material."

"But what is it?" Billie said. "What's the song?"

" 'Blue Moon.' "

Billie cocked her head and squinted her eyes, as if she could hear better that way. " 'Blue Moon'?" she said. "You mean *the* 'Blue Moon'?"

"Right, but—see, 'Blue Moon' is what was playing in my head while I was playing the horn."

Music was a mystery to Rob. He could be moved by it to an extent that frightened him, but he didn't understand how it was made. He certainly didn't recognize "Blue Moon" anywhere in the long wild tumble of notes that Albert had put together. What he heard was sorrow.

"I can't hear the 'Blue Moon' part," he said.

"I can hear it," Billie said, nodding.

"You play an instrument?" Albert asked her.

"Piano, a little. Mostly I listen; I have a good ear. Because I dance."

A dancing Billie! Why hadn't he thought of that? There had been plenty of evidence. The leotards and wraparound skirts, the stance that had first attracted him. He wondered if there was a modern-dance class on the base, for wives whose husbands were at sea. The navy probably had to provide all sorts of entertainment for these women. Would he see Billie dance? The thought energized him.

"Do you have a band?" Billie asked Albert.

"Nah."

"What do you do? For a living, I mean."

"Ah," Rob said. "Her favorite question. Listen, Billie. You can't tell anything about a man from what he does for a living. There's no correlation between job and soul. You couldn't guess Albert's profession. I'll give you fifty dollars if you can guess it." He poured more vodka into his glass and into Albert's. Skipped Billie's.

"Not a musician," she said.

"Nope," Rob said.

"It's something weird. Something I wouldn't think of."

"No hints."

"I was going to say a teacher," she said.

"Teacher!" Albert laughed. "I look like a teacher?"

"Sort of," Billie said.

"This isn't fair, making her guess," Albert said. "Tell you what, Rob. You guess, too. You guess right and I'll give you two hundred dollars. Got it right here." He laid two hundreds on the table, set them under the pitcher. Rob stared. Albert never had more than ten dollars cash on him.

"Where'd you get that?"

"Doesn't matter, does it? It's yours if you say what I do for a living."

"I don't want to take your hard-earned money, Albert."

"You smell a trick, you mean. Lawyering is what you're doing.

Sidestepping. You worried about taking this money? This money I didn't earn. This here is *severance*. And now the bet's off. See, you waited too long. Made me get my money wet." He wiped the bills on his shirt and pocketed them.

Rob stared at him.

"You got fired?" Billie said with a look of concern.

"*Resigned,*" Albert said.

"I don't believe you," Rob said.

"Because you think you're the only one can do it. Think only Rob Wyatt can walk off a job. I will admit, it was you made me think of it. Planted the seed."

"What was the job?" Billie said.

"Get up in the morning, clean the parish house kitchen from what the auxiliary cooked the night before. Mop. Check the graveyard for beer cans and butts from the teenagers. Unlock the church, clear out the dead flowers, if any. Take the robes to the cleaners. Meet the funeral director or the wedding lady and set up for whichever one is on the schedule. On days when it's neither one of them, I could spray out the garbage cans or polish the narthex floor. I had a lot of freedom on the job when there wasn't a sacrament called for."

"No wonder you quit," Billie said. "I've had jobs like that, where you do everything and nobody notices and you might as well be invisible."

"I only told you the good parts."

"But what are you going to do?" Rob said.

"God's work," Albert said.

"Not door-to-door with the Witnesses."

"No," Albert said. "It's music. Full-time music. Band instructor at Charleston High School. Going to shape that band *up*. Start a quintet. Maybe a jazz combo, too."

"I guessed right," Billie said. "You owe me fifty dollars."

"I'll take it out of the rent," Rob said.

Albert said, "What rent?"

Rob hesitated. Billie looked at him. He didn't answer. Instead, he drank.

"Well," Billie said. "I'm renting a room. His back bedroom."

"You don't say."

"Temporarily," Billie said.

"I see." Albert grinned.

"You don't," Rob said. "Explain, Billie."

"I'm in this sort of complicated situation. I made him rent me the room, until I can get on my feet. I forced him into it. He said okay, to help me. But he's not happy about it."

There was silence. Albert was not one to probe, especially if he thought there was something there to probe. "Hey," he said. "Like she said, it's a beautiful night. We are here for a celebration. Three beautiful people, all free, white, and twenty-one, except for one."

"Except for two," Rob said with a sort of groan. "Billie is not exactly twenty-one."

Albert rubbed his chin. "But—over eighteen. Surely."

"Just," Rob said.

"Hmm," Albert said. "Still, it's a good night. Boats going by, ducks tucking their head under their wing, evening sky. And we have prospects."

"To our good prospects," Rob said, raising his glass. "Here's to what comes next." He felt that he spoke the truth. With his left arm he gave Billie a clumsy and rather inebriated embrace, and tipped his glass to Albert.

In the tipping, he saw the headlights of a car pulling up under the canopy out front. Huong waved with both hands in Vietnamese gestures that Rob translated to mean, stow the pitcher and glasses. He noticed Albert's feet jiggle, sure sign of trouble. Was it cops? He looked at Albert, who nodded his head slightly toward the front door. A man and a woman came in. Formally attired, obviously new to the Conch. Lost, maybe; looking for a country club.

"Friends of yours," Albert muttered.

169

Rob was blank.

"Your ex-boss, I believe. And his wife."

For an instant Rob considered leaping the railing into the inlet, even though there was a sign warning of treacherous currents that had swept away three swimmers in the past year. Instead, he removed his arm from around Billie's neck, took a deep breath, and called out a hello.

handsome couple, Mr. and Mrs. Charleston. Hank tuxed, cummerbunded; Louise dolled up in black, gold on her arms, diamonds in her ears, a knockout. But the look was a little eerie: too much accoutrement, too much blue on the eyelids. Sometimes she went overboard. Jewelry and makeup were a mistake on Louise. When she was decorated, she looked older; and that was the opposite of the effect she was after. Rob didn't mind the little crinkles at the corners of her eyes. In fact, he thought Louise looked better at thirty-two than she had at twenty, she looked delicious. But she minded. Minded to the point of grief.

Now and then she mounted a short-lived campaign to achieve a new look. One summer she frizzed her hair and took to wearing designer-ripped jeans. Another time it was a blond streak and shoulder pads. But these were only forays. She always came back to herself. Tonight's ensemble wouldn't endure. The bangles, the dress (short in the hem, low in the neck), the shoes (high-heeled, backless, toeless), were a masquerade. Walking across the deck, she wobbled on the heels.

Maybe she'd already had some drinks at whatever downtown winging they'd attended. Hank, too, looked to have had a few, not a common occurrence; Hank wasn't much of a drinker. And the Conch was a place Hank wouldn't have entered in his usual sober and prudent state of mind. Louise might have suggested it. She knew it was Rob's latest hangout. She knew that on any given night, chances were good he'd be here.

But she seemed surprised when she saw him. She stopped halfway across the deck, as if she might turn around and leave. Then Hank ushered her forward.

Greetings all around. Won't-you-join-us back and forth, with the Camdens finally pulling up two more chairs. Rob wished he weren't wearing Ernie's old Led Zeppelin T-shirt. He looked like a rat-shooter. Hank looked like a gubernatorial candidate.

Rob was not a belligerent man. He prided himself on his lack of belligerence. Had never picked a fight in his life. But at the moment, he could feel belligerence rising. On the belligerometer he was measuring in the danger zone.

And for no reason. The tuxedo? The friendly suntanned face, full of goodwill? The affable shaking of Albert's hand, the charming hello to Billie? Still not enough to justify this desire to reach across the table and deliver a hard right to the gubernatorial chin. Something Rob had never done before, something he had seen only in movies. It was good in the movies, a long arm flashing out, the fist connecting, the satisfying crunch of knuckles on jawbone.

Louise's tan had faded; she looked a little under the weather.

"I've just heard some surprising news, Albert," the jawbone said. "Is it true that you've embarked on a new career?"

Albert nodded. "News moves fast in the church," he said.

"Of course it does, when the news is we're losing our mainstay. But frankly I think it's a solid decision on your part. You've always loved music. You'll be a great teacher. Charleston High, is it? They're lucky to be getting you. But still, it's a surprise. We'll have a hard time finding a replacement."

Albert laughed. "That's right," he said. "You will. Have to find someone *unique*."

"I don't suppose you have any suggestions."

"Huong," Albert said. "Huong will do anything."

"That's an idea," Hank said. "But isn't he pretty well tied up in this enterprise?"

The man was on another wavelength. That's what it was, that's what made Rob's blood boil. No sense of humor. No sense of irony. No sense of absurdity or tragedy or mortality. Hank was a candidate for a kick in the ass. Only it would not likely do much good. That kind of innocence and honor is genetic. At one time, Rob had admired it. Now he hated it. Hank had never fucked up in his life and was not likely to do so in the future. Never an unwise investment, never stone-roaring drunk, never a pass at a secretary. No doubts as to the beneficent workings of the universe. And why should he have such doubts? His universe worked as smoothly as his Mercedes. The only thing Rob could think up as a possible Hank Camden failure was the likelihood of a low sperm count. And there was only a fifty-fifty chance of that.

Louise was sitting between Billie and Hank. So far she had said nothing. She hadn't looked at Rob. He didn't want her to start asking questions, so he took the bull by the horns.

"Billie and I have had discussions of her legal situation," he said.

"Oh, really?" Louise said. "And has he been helpful, Billie?"

"Well, yes, he's letting me—"

"We're drawing up papers," Rob said. "Moving in the right direction."

Food came, but then there was the question of whether they should wait until the Camdens were served too. "I'm sorry," he said, digging in. He spoke with an oyster in his mouth. "But I'm starving. Billie's starving. Albert I don't know about. He's probably starving too, but he has good manners."

"Please, go ahead," Hank said, gesturing at the food. "By the way, Rob, we hired a new man today. Law Review at Virginia."

"Mmmp," Rob said.

"I think he's going to work out fine."

"Does that mean Rob can't go back to his old job?" Billie said.

"Rob can always come back," Hank said. "He knows that. And I believe he'll come around. He's just taking a breather. Everyone needs a breather."

173

"You need one yourself, Hank," Rob said. "And you need to take off your coat. Need also a couple of quick glasses of Huong's special spirits. Four dollars a fifth. Out of the inscrutable East." He poured vodka for Hank. "And Mrs. Camden," he said. "Mr. Swan. Ms. Poe." But he didn't pour one for Billie. He ordered a Coke for her.

"I don't know," Hank said, looking at the glass. "I'm over my limit already. This stuff looks like it might do some damage."

"That is the general idea," Rob said.

"We do have to get the ladies home tonight."

"Not necessarily," he said. "We can always sleep on the duck deck."

"It's been done," Albert said. "In recent memory."

"That night," Rob said, "what we were doing can't accurately be called sleeping. There's a difference between sleep and deep coma. I prefer coma. No dreams to distract you from the basic experience of death. See, Hank, I've been thinking about what you need, and I think it's death. I mean, an awareness thereof."

Hank smiled handsomely. "Another Wyatt insight," he said, turning to Billie. "Rob is a theoretician. Full of theories. That may be what I miss most around the office, now that he's gone. He was good at law, but his real talent was making up new laws. Wyatt's Rule of Revenge, I liked that one, 'Time wounds all heels.' And there was another one, what was it? The Law of Decreasing Desire? 'Desire varies in inverse proportion to possibility'?"

"Not original work. I pilfered them all. 'Dear Abby.' Ecclesiastes. The Unitarians—they put up a new one every week on their sign. But the law at hand, the one for you, Hank, is *Memento mori*. That's what we're talking about now. The trouble with you is you live every day as if it were your first. A man aware of his own mortality does not, for example, wear a tuxedo in the Conch."

Hank took the coat off and hung it over the back of his chair. "How's that?"

"Better. Now you're ready. Personally, I think you have a golden opportunity before you. You're among friends. Nobody else is coming in this place tonight. I say you should go for it."

"For what?"

"Deep coma. One of life's few opportunities for revelation. A view of the other side. I'd like to see you give it a shot. Hell, it's easy, with this stuff. Three more, maybe, and you'll be there. The big black nothing."

"That's funny," Albert said. "Me, I see white when I pass out. The big white nothing."

The music had stopped. No one spoke.

"Dave cough," Anna called out to Huong. "Foot on you, Dave."

"What was that?" Rob asked Albert.

"The tape stopped. She told him to put on a new one."

This time it was the Temptations and "My Girl." He'd like to meet a Temptation someday, get him into the Conch and arm-wrestle him, thank him for the songs.

"We could dance," Billie said.

No one responded. Rob cleared his throat and said, "The last time I danced was . . . as a matter of fact, it was—"

"1984," Louise said.

"Precisely."

"I don't think that's a bad idea," Hank said. "I'm game."

"No, not me," Louise said. But he was already up and taking her hand, leading her out to the middle of the deck. Very gallant.

"Okay. Okay, Billie. Let's do it," Rob said.

He must be drunk. It was true, he hadn't danced since the Art Museum Gala in 1984, and his partner had been Louise. He was not a good dancer. Men who dance—and Hank was one—are men in harmony with the universe.

He experienced a moment of panic when he took Billie's hand. What the hell was he going to do? Which steps? Hank was holding Louise in an old-fashioned embrace, as if for waltzing, but they moved smoothly to the song. They looked as if they'd been dancing together for years.

Idiot, he said to himself, they *have* been dancing together for years; 1984 was not *her* last dance.

"I'm not good at this," he said to Billie.

But when she was there, in his arms, somehow it was not so difficult to hold her and sway some, and move his feet in imitation of a dance step. He got into it. He made up his own dance, and she came along.

"You're good, Billie. You're excellent. I should have recognized you as a dancer right away."

"Well, I only really dance by myself," she said.

He pulled her closer and went into a higher dance gear, a sort of tango shag. He twirled her. She liked it. They bypassed the Camdens.

"*You're* good," Billie said.

"It's highly unethical, you know. Dancing with your attorney. Against the rules altogether."

"Is it really?"

"Indeed it is. Doesn't it feel unethical?" He let her go as the music stopped.

"No, it felt good."

"That's what I mean. Let's do it again," he said.

Drink and music and dance and a bare-armed girl in hand—a man is not to be held accountable, under these conditions. His sense of the present moment heightened, and his sense of history and context diminished. To the point of zero. He was approaching a state of exhilaration, a state which can be achieved only by human beings blinded to context. A dangerous and delusive condition. He found himself thinking, Why not? Why not Rob and Billie, dancing through this world? They danced four more songs. He wanted to tell her that this was one of the high points in his life, but he didn't think she would believe him. It was true, though. This was a moment of breakthrough. No reason why such a moment cannot occur in a ramshackle creekside restaurant, with the smell of mud in the night air and old songs playing. He danced. Billie was so small in his arms, his heart broke for

her smallness. He gathered her in. He dipped her, catching her
by surprise, letting her drop backwards. She was light as a child.
He could have lifted her above his head.

But exhilaration is like any other high, a tease, a trick. You
can only dance so long. In the middle of a spin his eye caught
the table where his friends were sitting. Hank and Louise had
quit; had re-seated themselves and were watching him. Albert,
normally poker-faced, wore a look of pure dismay. Was he making a fool of himself? When he saw Louise's eyes, he came to a
halt, in the middle of "Just My Imagination." Yes. He had revealed his true self: clown, and worse. Evildoer. He led Billie
back to the table.

"Well, that's a side of Robert Wyatt I never saw before," Hank
said.

"Me neither," Albert said.

Then a big silence. Billie was out of breath. Rob regretted
himself. He loved all the people at this table, plus Anna and
Huong, God bless them, and he wanted the best for every one
of them, and yet he was the taint here. He was the danger. He
ought to lock himself away from them. Hands off Billie. Trust
Albert to direct his own life, he's a grown damned man. And
how could anyone turn against Hank—worse, desire to corrupt
him, for that's what he'd wanted to do. Poor Hank was now
sinking if not already sunk, tongue-tied and generally incapacitated, and Louise sitting the way a woman sits when she's ready
to go home, arms folded, spine stiff, mouth set. Oh no, don't go,
please, he thought. More drink, more music? What could he do
to hold them all together in fine friendship? She was mad at him
for egging Hank on. He had to redeem himself; but even as he
thought of atonement, he felt a spike of pleasure at the sight of
old Hank there, wrecked.

Hank tried to talk. "Time for me," he said. "Me and Weezy
to go."

"Weezy?" Rob said.

"My wife. To get her home."

"He calls you that?" he said to Louise. "Do you call him Hanky?"

"He's right, it's time for us to go," she said. She got up and tried to right Hank's upper body, which had listed thirty degrees east. "All right, Rob," she said, stepping aside. "This is your problem. Get him to the car."

"He's okay. He only sleeps."

Albert did the job. He ducked his head under Hank's arm and hoisted him to a standing position. Hank's eyes opened. "Thank you very much," he said. Louise was about to cry.

"Keys," Albert said, holding out his palm to Rob.

"Mine?"

"You drive the Camdens' car, and I'll drop Billie off."

Rob handed over the Toyota keys. Together they maneuvered Hank out to the Mercedes and into the backseat. He sat straight, eyes open, gave Rob his car keys, then keeled over, curled up on his side like a kid. Heartrending, Rob thought; he could hardly bear to look. The hero felled. Also, simultaneously, extremely satisfying. Billie and Albert took off in the Toyota.

"I'm driving," Louise said.

"Oh, no. I insist." He wouldn't give her the keys. He got in and started the car. For a minute she stood outside. He waited. She got in.

"Anger is not good for you," he said. "You'll thank me for this someday." She said nothing. "Listen, the man's forty-five years old. If he'd gone to his grave without this night, he'd have felt like a failure. Believe me. This is a necessary accomplishment. Now he can run for governor knowing he's one of the people."

"You're sick," she said.

"We knew that already, didn't we? Boy, I've never had the opportunity to drive one of these babies. Hank told me this car was a good investment. I don't know, sixty thousand for automotive equipment. I mean, it's nice and all, a fine machine, but—"

"Shut up, Rob."

"Oh," he said.

He drove slowly. This good feeling he had—he wondered

what it was. He felt charged with power. Ah, yes: this was what it felt like to be a rich man. Carried along by something very large and smooth, which will go faster if you choose to accelerate, but you don't choose to, you hold back; and your life itself is very large and smooth and immune to breakdown, and you are in the driver's seat of it.

"Look, Weezy, I apologize."

"Don't call me that."

"I kind of like it, to be honest. After the initial shock. I mean, how long have I known you, twenty-two years, and I didn't even find out your *name* until tonight."

"Life is full of surprises, Rob," she said in the flat voice of one who is no longer surprised by anything.

"It is, it truly is. Now I'm being sincere when I say don't worry about Hank. He's absolutely okay."

No response. She stared at the road. She was stewing, thinking hard, hating his guts, worrying about Hank.

"I promise," he said, and reached over to touch her knee, which moved away. "Come on."

"Come on, what?"

"I didn't mean no harm."

"You said that just right. That is grammatically correct."

"Okay, don't believe me. Work yourself up into a lather," he said.

"What did he mean, he would drop her off?"

"Come again?"

"Albert. What was he talking about when he said he'd drop Billie off?"

"Just that. Drop her off, take her home." The Mercedes balked, and he downshifted. "This car's not accustomed to twenty miles an hour," he said. "But I'm driving like this to demonstrate my sincerity and remorse. I'm going to get you home safely."

"Is she still in the same motel? It's all the way into town. Albert's house is a four-minute drive. I don't call that dropping her off."

He didn't speak.

"Has she moved?" she said.

"She has."

Louise waited a couple of seconds. Then she said, "And her new address is a secret?"

"Maybe we should discuss this tomorrow."

"She's *not* at your place." Her voice dropped at the end of the sentence.

"Louise, it's a long story. Very complex. It was probably a mistake, but it's temporary, you said yourself that she needed somewhere to go, and—"

She put her hands over her face.

"But it's not a tragedy, for Christ's sake. What are you afraid of, that I'll ruin her? I have my scruples, measly as they may be. I'm not out to ruin anybody, not Billie, not Hank."

"You're doing it, aren't you," she said.

"Doing what?"

"Getting involved with her."

"I'm not. I swear. Nothing. She goes to her room, I go to mine. She uses the bathroom before I even get up in the morning."

"Sure."

"Louise, I give you my word. She's a kid. She's . . . not my type." He was pretty drunk. "How could I fall for Billie when I've got you?" he said, trying to keep his eye on the dark, humped shapes on the side of the road, hoping they were trash piles. He had driven drunk only twice before: after Louise's wedding, and more recently after a long night at Huong's, when he got home without mishap and fell into bed and then bolted awake with fear: How could he be so sure it had been without mishap? What if he'd hit something . . . a dog, a pedestrian . . . and been too drunk to notice? He had gotten out of bed, dressed, and walked all the way back to Huong's, checking for corpses.

"But you let her move *in* with you!" The accusation came out in a high wail.

"Louise, I absolutely promise you, I haven't touched the girl and have no intentions of doing so. What else can I tell you?"

His voice rose to a desperate pitch. "Why won't you believe me?"

"Don't yell," she said. "Okay, I believe you. I'm sorry. The trouble is that I haven't seen you for weeks, Rob. I didn't know what was going on."

"I know, I've been—"

"I called you and got that stupid machine. I need to talk to you." She turned to look at Hank, then turned the other way, to look out her window. "I can't do it now," she said.

It was dark. Still, he saw in her face, when it turned toward Hank and back, a weariness. He'd seen it before, on clients who were tired of their husbands—had nothing against them, no complaint that would stand up as grounds for divorce, but only a great fatigue.

"I'll make this up to you," he said.

"Make what up?"

"This whole evening. I'll take you fishing tomorrow. We'll discuss all the great questions facing the world. You like that. We'll catch a bluefish and settle everything."

"Some questions are too hard to settle."

"Not for you and me, right? We've settled the Middle East several times, remember? We figured out whales and abortion. Nothing's too hard for us."

Hank stirred.

"You're home," Rob said over his shoulder. "Wake up now." He pulled into the Camdens' driveway, up to the back steps. He off-loaded Hank, who was able to take the new steps with some assistance from Louise.

"Don't worry about me," he called to her. "I don't need a ride home, I'm going to jog it. I'll pick you up in the morning. We'll have to get an early start, around seven-thirty, set your alarm—" She wasn't even turning to look at him. "*Louise!*"

"What?"

He stood there at the bottom of her stairs with his hands at his sides. He raised them slowly to her, palms out.

"Go home, Rob," she said.

2.

S he would come around, he was fairly sure. She would get up in the morning and feel good and put on her fishing shorts. He would prove his good faith, his irreproachable character, once in the boat and on the waves. Out in a boat every man looks good. Captainly. Maybe he would wear his yachting cap, even though his boat was more like a dinghy than a yacht, an old flat-bottom with two slat seats. But she had always liked his boat. She liked to fish with him; it was a contest, who would catch the first fish, the most fish, the biggest fish. Louise got pleasure from besting him in contests of various sorts. He would make sure she bested him tomorrow, and then everything would be okay.

He did jog, or at least ran in imitation of the joggers he'd seen. Maybe there was more technique to it than he realized. But he only ran. He ran his heart out, down the glistening straight stretch of Palm Avenue.

You run from danger or toward safety, or you run a message to the army on the plain, or in pursuit of your next meal, with your spear held high; but here on Palm Avenue with the half-moon ahead and the shadowy houses hulking, he ran for purposes he did not know. The thing he ran from seemed to sit on the back of his neck, he could not put any distance between him and it. He was running parallel with the shoreline, and he could hear the ocean, and he could hear his own heart and his own breath. When cars came he veered to the shoulder. People who saw him must have thought him nuts, loping along in his jeans and canvas shoes and Led Zeppelin T-shirt, in his baldness and in his despair.

After a mile on Palm he made the turn at Tanglewood and slowed. The street was narrower and the trees closer. He seemed to have left the thing behind. He was coming home. Tanglewood, a Tolkien sort of name. His house under the hill, dangling with magic charms, surrounded by looping vines. Okay, he was okay. The Toyota was in the carport, hunkered down, sleeping. He would sleep now too.

The thing at the back of his neck, that he could not shake off, was a dim and prickly memory of something he had told Louise and could not quite (or would rather not) recall. Something not exactly true, but to which he had sworn.

No need to worry. Everything under control. Nothing seriously wrong, nothing that can't be fixed. He turned and jogged a wide circle in the street before heading through the viny archway and up the path; into the bower. He would see his girl, his innocent and peach-haired waif, his (he understood) true love. *True,* he thought, does not mean *only.* May not the heart, even an average, a below-average, heart, accommodate as much true love as falls in its way? And love the first (my God, he couldn't *not*) and love the second, too?

CHAPTER 12

B illie had already gone to bed. He thought of calling for her, but maybe she was asleep by now. He stood forlorn outside her closed door, listening to her radio: a weather forecast, line of thunderstorms moving through the state toward the coast. It was two A.M. How many people could be listening to the weather at two A.M.?

More, probably, than might be expected. One night in late July, a fireball had shot across the sky at just this hour, a meteor of unusual size and brilliance; and hundreds of people saw it. Some had been out in boats, *fishing*. One bunch, for reasons unexplained, had been in the Burnside Dodge parking lot. It was a mammalian instinct, to prowl the night. Rob liked the night himself. At times when he was in danger of starting to think of life as mercantile and rational, he could always go sit in the dark outside his door, and see that there was something else.

He did it now, dragged his chair out under the leafy fig tree, beyond the glow of the porch light. He sat and lifted his head the way a dog does, for evidence. Smell of fig bark and fruit, sound of the sea, chill of the moving air, and then the nameless thing, describable only by simile. Like hunger, like fear, like desire, something to do with god (unmodified; not *the* god, or *a* god, but like them both). It was the closest he could come to religion: this sense of something in the backyard at night.

For which he had no words. It could have been Jehovah himself; it could have been weather. The effect was the same. He was inspired, humbled, grateful, guilty. In that state (whether it was the state of a mystic or of a porcupine, he didn't know) he fell asleep. The fig trunk held his head. He dreamed that he stood in a court of law, charged with some wrongdoing and sentenced to make reparations. He was willing; *give me the job,* he pleaded, *show me the task, I will attend to it.* But not knowing the crime, he could make no atonement.

It was past three when he woke. He was disoriented, what with the fig leaves framing his view and the light burning yellow under the pediment of his porch. His back hurt, and he walked to the house bent like some fine old lawyer (for all the fine ones bend). Maybe he had a fever. He pulled off his damp shirt. Maybe he had caught something, as it is said one may, sleeping under the moon, breathing the vapor of swampy marsh.

He had left Billie unattended—the doors open, the windows open; any maniac could have sneaked in while he dozed. He locked both doors. He checked to make sure the stove was off. He checked the doors again. And Billie, he should check on Billie. He turned the doorknob slowly so that it would make no noise, opened the door a crack and peeked in, just to make sure she was all right . . . then he closed it quickly.

There was someone in bed with her.

His first instinct was to pad on back to his room. His second instinct was for attack; this was his house, he had trusted Carlo. He opened the door again, and saw the two sleeping bodies, Billie's white arm flung over the shoulders of the darker form next to her. The darker form lifted its head from the pillow and looked at Rob.

"Bad dog," Rob whispered. "Get out of there." But Speedo was already on the floor, slinking past Rob into the hallway.

Billie hadn't moved. She was curled up, her arm still outstretched, the sheet crumpled at the foot of the bed. He watched her for awhile. The room was hot; no breeze came through the window behind her head. Maybe he should buy her an air conditioner. He didn't go into the room, he only looked, and there was nothing wrong with that, he was only seeing to her needs. An air conditioner or at least a fan . . .

But then he realized he had been standing there for quite some time, long enough to feel dim-witted or deviant, watching like that—and long enough for the weather to change. The curtains moved. Faraway lightning lit the room briefly, and its low thunder followed. She was wearing a T-shirt that came down to her drawn-up knees.

He took two steps into the room. He could see her hair on the pillow, her hand raised to her mouth, maybe touching her lips; he could see the soles of her feet, which he had seen before and which were therefore dear and familiar. She didn't move, and he didn't move.

A very simple and beautiful thing, a girl asleep in a room, but also a heartbreaker: in his house in his bed but not his. And all he could do was look. The room blinked on and off with lightning. He could hear the clang of the iron wind chimes, like a last-minute warning, and then only the rush of hard rain.

Is it possible for any man not to imagine? If Billie were ten years older, if his heart were free of Louise . . . and if he himself were a fine, upstanding man . . . But certainly men have loved young women in the history of this world, and he wasn't such a bad fellow, not a criminal at least. And what had he promised Louise, anyway? She was the one who had married someone else. He had no contract with Louise.

He knew that when he started thinking in those terms, legal terms, he wasn't thinking straight. He was making a case. The truth was, he had to find Billie another place, a safer place, as far away from him as she could get.

Those were his thoughts, when, still unmoving, she said, "I can see you."

"Me?"

"Yeah. When the lightning strikes."

"I'm sorry." He stepped back.

"It's okay," she said. "Don't go. I'm always a little afraid of lightning."

He stepped forward.

"Come sit here," she said. He did it, but kept his feet on the floor, his back to her. He didn't even look at her face.

"What is it?" she said.

"You can't stay." He hadn't planned to say that, but it was what had to be said. He stared at the bedroom wall.

After a second she said, "I know. I figured it out. I'm not blind."

"What do you mean?"

"It's her. You don't want her to know I'm here."

"No, it isn't her. It has nothing to do with her."

"You're not in love with her?"

"No, no." His voice came out in a kind of wail.

"What is it then?"

"I don't know." He still faced away from her. "It's a sort of mess," he said.

"You don't have to worry about me, you know," she said.

"Yes, I do."

"No, really you don't. I can take care of myself. I'm not worried about Carlo anymore. I don't think he's coming back."

"It's not Carlo you're in danger from. It's me," Rob said.

She lay there. He felt the mattress shift. He turned to look; she had lifted herself up on one elbow. She was smiling. "I can take care of myself," she said again, and held out her arms.

It was dark. His excuse wasn't Jack's old one—courtesy— though if he'd thought of it, he might have made it. He thought of nothing and made no excuse. He only sank, in somber gratitude. Billie noticed the somberness. She put her hands on his chest and held him off. She said, "We don't have to do this if it's not what you want."

"It's what I want."

It was what he'd wanted for a long time. The guard he'd kept fell instantly, as if it had never existed. But he had not suspected that this was what she wanted, too. She had never given him reason to suspect. He was still not sure exactly what she did want. So he lay on his back next to her, his head on the other pillow.

She was still. He could smell the clean cotton of her shirt, the swimming-pool hair.

"You're a little bit afraid of me," she said.

"I am, am I?"

"Yeah."

"What would I be afraid of?"

"I don't know. You said a person shouldn't move in with a stranger. The stranger might be a lunatic."

"I meant *me,* Billie. Not you."

"Still. You're afraid."

"Yes. I am."

"Of me."

"Oh, I guess so."

"You don't have to be," she said. She sat up and drew the T-shirt over her head. The sudden appearance of her bare back made him cough. Narrow, long-spined, white as the bed. She held the T-shirt in her hands in front of her chest and lay back down, facing him. "I think this will be all right," she said. "I don't think it will cause you trouble."

He didn't know what she meant; but he found it hard to concentrate on an interpretation. He still didn't move. Maybe he could just lie here and let this happen and not be responsible for it. And if nothing happened, still this gentleness and comfort was beyond what he'd hoped for. The smell of her hair, the surprising bareness of her shoulders . . . It was also more than he deserved.

But then her hands moved toward him, with the shirt, and he took it. He dropped it behind him onto the floor.

She leaned into him, set herself against him. Lightly though, only grazing him. She didn't close her eyes. He touched her slowly, ready to stop if she seemed reluctant. He didn't want to scare her. He still had on his jeans. But she didn't seem scared. She only took a breath, as if in surprise. Her breasts were small, her hips were small; he'd known that before, but now all the smallness was in his hands, measurable. Rib cage, thigh, mouth, ear, neck, knee. He knew he was welcome, that she was lone and starved. She stretched and curled, and breathed in shallow puffs. Her hands held the back of his neck, then loosened, and she turned onto her stomach but not in retreat. She spread her arms across the bed. Her back was the most beautiful back he'd ever seen, and he stroked it the way a child strokes silk, amazed by the smoothness, laying his cheek against it. She turned again, and once more held him around the neck, and he couldn't help thinking, Louise was right about her, *she is dangerously lonely.* Her skin was electric with loneliness, sparking with it. The sparking leapt to his fingertips, and he was in her trance, his own skin alert to hers. But then he must have done something wrong.

"Oh-oh," she said. Her eyes widened. He stopped, his fingers touching the bony place between her breasts.

She tensed and arched her back; her arms flew from his neck and back to the headboard, and she gasped. She stopped breathing. But still stared at him, wild-eyed. Then her body shook and fell, and her arms dropped limp to the sheet, and she laughed.

"Oh, I'm sorry," she said. "Oh, my Lord."

Then long rips of laughter. She hid her face in her hands. "I'm so sorry. I wasn't supposed to do that."

"Well, it must be something of a record," he said.

She was in loose-limbed collapse, still trying to catch her breath. He was, as a matter of fact, surprised. He hadn't known a woman to come with so little encouragement. But he was pleased. He let her lie still, and he listened to the rain. He was half hovering over her, not resting his weight on her but still keeping her between his arms. She might fall asleep, but that was all right too. Love is strange, and true love is strange but true. He felt that he had stumbled upon something he had not anticipated, even though he had been looking for it for years.

She stirred, turned her face to his, and yawned. "I'm embarrassed. Can we—start all over again?"

"Do you want to?"

"Let me just, um, catch my breath."

He lifted away from her. Her chest glistened, and rose and

fell with her breathing. She pulled the pillow up over her mouth.

"Don't hide," he said.

"I didn't think it would be like that. I'm ashamed."

"You should be proud. You have a talent."

"No, because it's so rude." She squirmed out from under him and out of bed, walked back and forth across the room six or seven times, arms folded. Standing, she looked less childlike, more womanly—long-waisted, deep-naveled. She was unabashed. He got the feeling that she folded her arms not to hide herself but as a natural aid to thinking. She was thinking hard.

Then she raised her arms like a victorious swimmer, stretched toward the ceiling, and came back. She climbed in and sat with the sheet pulled up around her hips.

"Are you asleep?" she said.

"No. My eyes are open." He couldn't have closed them. He didn't even want to blink, and lose for an instant the view of Billie, naked in his bed and full of talk, as if energized by the lightning still flashing and the great rain blowing in sheets through the oleanders outside.

"It brings back memories," she said. "The sound of the wind like that." She shivered and leaned forward. "It won't come again, will it? The TV said it wouldn't come again for two hundred years."

"No. It won't. Not one like that. Were you afraid?"

"Not then. Sometimes now. If I hear the wind. And then sometimes I get the feeling something was hurt but we can't see it, like an internal injury, and it's worse than it looks. I saw some rats at the pool today in broad daylight, three of them."

"They're homeless. Give them time and they'll find new holes, new dark spots to inhabit."

"Like me."

"This is a dark spot? My house is a hole?"

"I didn't mean that. Only that I've found a new place." She touched his forehead.

"I'm losing hair," he said.

"You are not." She swept the hair back from his forehead and bent down to look.

"You can't tell in the dark," he said. "We're in the darkest hour. What time is it, four o'clock? You can't tell anything at four o'clock."

"I can tell," she said. "It looks like plenty of hair to me."

"It is not what it once was. I am not the man I used to be."

"I didn't know that man. I only know this one. Do you think I'm too young for you?"

"That's not the question. The question is, am I too old for you? and the answer is yes. Here it is almost daybreak, and you're wide awake. You're wired. Your synapses are snapping and firing off, and mine are barely wiggling."

"You can sleep if you want to."

"Don't want to." He reached for her, but she leaned back again. He didn't mind. She was cross-legged, bare-breasted, her hair around her head like a nimbus. He touched it, drew one strand out and let it spring back.

"See, I don't think I'm too young," she said. "There are advantages. Like, I don't know that other guy you were talking about, the man you were. You're the only one. Also, we're a lot alike. I know it seems like we're not, because you have a good education and a good family"—he raised a hand to object, but she went on—"but those are accidents. Your heart is like mine."

"And how's that?"

"Sad."

"You think my heart is sad?"

"I know it is. I knew it was when I first saw you and you were standing all by yourself."

"You saw me before I—"

"Before you came over. You were next to the table, hiding behind those big leaves."

"I was not hiding."

"You were, and looking sad, and then she came over and you lit up."

"I lit up when I saw you."

"And you put your arm around her, and then she dragged you over to meet me."

"That's not how it happened. I spotted you. I made Louise introduce me."

"It was your idea?"

"Sure, it was my idea." He tried to recall the exact sequence of events, and he was pretty sure it had been his idea, but maybe Louise had actually been the one to suggest an introduction. . . . "It doesn't matter anyway, does it?"

"In a way it does."

"How?"

"I don't know. She kept telling me you were the one to help me out. She spoke so highly of you, even before I met you. She kept saying I had to meet you, and she gave me a lot of details, personal things about you."

"Like what?"

"That you were different from most men. That you were a thinker and sort of a loner and self-destructive."

"All of which was misinformation."

"She didn't mean any of it in a bad way. She meant it all good. She wasn't even telling it to me, not like talking behind your back. It was funny, she was sort of talking to herself. She has that way, you know? Of talking with a faraway look in her eye? And you can't tell what she really has in mind. I'm grateful to her. She befriended me."

"Hey, I befriended you too."

"But you want me to move out."

"Move out, no. Why move out?"

"You said so, thirty minutes ago."

"That was in another life. That was before this." He touched her shoulder, and her upper arm, and the inside of her elbow. Her eyes closed, her chin lifted.

"Do you want to talk some more?" he said.

"No."

It was as if he had caught her in a net, a light and silken net that fell around her and cast her into hunger. As he touched, her upper body leaned toward him. He watched in fascination.

"I'll do better this time," she whispered. "I'll wait."

She didn't. She was alive to the slightest touch; he had never seen anything like it. She tried to hold back, he could tell, but the trying itself seemed counterproductive. The second time was like the first, except that afterward instead of laughing, she cried.

"I wanted to do it right," she said.

"Billie, you did it right. Boy, you did it right, you couldn't have done it righter."

"But now you're disappointed, and you probably won't try again, and—"

"How about if I promise I'll try again?"

"You will?"

"Word of honor."

She pulled herself close to him, one knee over his, her neck under his arm. Under his wing.

He said, "Anyway, I doubt that you can keep this up. It's not physically possible."

The rain stopped. It moved out across the island to open water, a fast heavy storm. She fell asleep. Head fallen, mouth open, arm slack as a doll's across his thigh.

It is no coincidence that acts of love and crime occur mostly at night. By day we're governed and law-abiding. But the nocturnal soul is weak and lorn, hungry for the thing it needs and driven to it without reason. Reason is a solar-powered device. Its little light wavers and fails by night.

He got up and went to the bathroom, took a shower. Avoided the mirror. Went back to the bedroom.

He shook her to wake her. It was difficult, she was deep in sleep.

"What?" she said. "What is it?"

"Fulfilling a promise," he said, gathering her to him. He didn't touch her with his hands but held her easy, kissed her good mouth and her eyes and hair, but suddenly she tensed and pulled away. He let her go.

"I don't think—" she said, up on an elbow and looking at him.

"What is it?" he said.

"I don't know."

"Here, lie down. Lie down. You're not even awake. I shouldn't have tried to wake you."

"It's just that—I've never done this before."

"I'm sorry, I didn't understand."

"I told you," she said. "You didn't believe me?"

"Sleep," he said.

In the dark outside, frogs sang. He could see through the window all the yards silver with standing water, and the houses like so many boats on a glassy sea. And theirs, the blue boat, was strung with chimes and madly ringing—pealing, bonging—in the wind.

She slept.

CHAPTER 13

He was still half sleeping when he heard the sounds of conversation from the kitchen. He was so tired his bones ached; but he crawled out of bed, put on his pants and watch. It was 7:15—he'd had three hours of sleep.

Ernie was sitting at the kitchen table, eating Waldorf salad and Pop-Tarts. "We saved two Pop-Tarts for you," he said, but Rob could tell Ernie had his eye on them.

"You eat them," he said. "You're a growing boy." He watched Ernie pour a greenish-yellow liquid into his glass. "What is that?" Rob said.

"Limeade," Billie said. She looked straight at him as if nothing had happened in the night. He was annoyed by Ernie's presence. He ought to have been able to sleep late and wake up with Billie by his side.

Ernie was nervous. He ate another tart and stared into the limeade. "I'm going to see Ma," he said. "Billie says I ought to get it over with."

"Well, I just don't think a man can get married without telling his mother," she said.

"Okay," Ernie said. "I'll do it straight, I won't make a big deal out of it, I'll just say, look, this is the way it is. If she thinks it's a *fait accompli,* maybe she won't fight it. I'll be calm and quick. You're right, Rob, that's the best approach."

"So go do it," Rob said. "What are you waiting for?"

Ernie looked glum. "She's going to give me hell."

"Why?" Billie said. "What does she want you to do?"

"Roam the seven seas," Ernie said. "Be an adventurer. I tried it. I'm not up to it. Rhonda's got a little cabin and a horse pasture, horses . . . I admit, marriage is a big step. I wasn't all for it right away. But I've thought it all out and made the decision. To tell you the truth, I don't want to hear Ma's arguments against it. She's a pretty good arguer. And what can I say? I'm in love?"

"I don't see why you can't say that," Billie said.

"You don't know her," Rob said absently. He was thinking, *a pasture, a cabin! Rhonda waiting at the cabin door in her faded jeans, the Florida greenery flashing, scrub jays in the piney woods . . .*

"She's against marriage," Ernie said. "Also church, the armed forces, lawyers and doctors, the Boy Scouts." He laughed. "Not your ordinary mother. But then, you can understand why."

"Why?" said Billie.

"Well, a number of those institutions failed her, at one point." He glanced at Rob. But Rob was not about to explain. "There was a fake hearing," Ernie said, "with a fake judge, and they committed her to a psychiatric institution."

Rob had never talked at length with Ernie about that event. They had only alluded to it in the most indirect ways. "It wasn't a fake judge," Rob said. "You weren't there. You only heard her version."

"True," Ernie said. "But you were only a kid. And you never heard her version. Did you?"

"No."

"But what's it about?" Billie said. "What happened?"

"My father was screwing around with other women, and she found out, and he denies it and says she's crazy, and he has her locked up and zapped."

"Wait a minute," Rob said, getting out of his chair. "It wasn't like that. He didn't deny it. She needed help, and what do you mean, *zapped?*"

"Shock therapy. You knew that."

"No, I didn't know that. I don't think it happened. I never heard that."

"She probably didn't want to scare you. She told me it wasn't so bad, not like Sylvia Plath or anything. She thought it helped."

"Goddamnit, Ernie—" But he stopped. What was it he wanted God to damn? He realized the story must be true. Of course she wouldn't have told him. He remembered the day she came home, and how she ran to him and beckoned him from his hiding spot behind the gate, and smiled and folded him in her arms. There was no word of his part in the thing, his blame. She had not wanted him to blame himself.

Billie poured him a glass of limeade, and then stood behind him, where Ernie could not see her hand touch his back. "Well, anyway," she said. "It turned out all right."

The telephone rang; Billie picked it up without hesitation, and with only a trace of her old anxiety in the tentative hello. Like a secretary, politely formal, she said, "Yes, one minute please." She handed Rob the receiver.

"Fishing trip," Louise said. "You forgot?"

"I'm running a little late," he said, panicked. "Five minutes."

"That's exactly how much longer I'm going to wait."

Five minutes. She meant that.

"Give me a hand with the trailer, Ernie," he said on the run. "Hitch it up for me, all right?" He collected his rods and tackle out of the closet. Billie sat at the table, watching him scramble. "My cap," he said, "where's my yachting cap, it was on this hook by the door—"

"Top of the refrigerator," she said.

"Sorry. I forgot, I had this fishing expedition planned. I'll be back this afternoon."

"Want me to go with you?"

He stopped short. "You want to?"

"No." She was smiling. "I can't. I have a lesson at ten."

"Another time," he said.

"Okay."

"It's something that was set up, before." He looked at Ernie. "And I forgot all about it."

"Really," she said, "it's okay."

He backed the car to the gate and Ernie locked the trailer on. Rob raised his hand out the window. "Hey," he said to Ernie. "Don't worry."

"Thanks," said Ernie, without enthusiasm.

Rob pulled into the street, taking out more rye grass on the way, forgetting to allow for the drift of the trailer; but he didn't care. He had two minutes left, and a mile and a half of Palm Avenue between him and Louise. Luckily there was no traffic on the straightaway. Louise was probably changing into her shopping clothes, or already getting into her car, and he would miss her.

He had promised to take her fishing. If he didn't, it might be the last straw.

In the final approach, half a block from her house, he began blowing his horn, and when he pulled into the driveway he was yelling out the window. No need. There she was, sitting on the bottom step. He closed his eyes in relief. She got in without a word. They made it to the marina, got launched and out the inlet without discussion.

2.

Afloat. One of those miracles of the world, one of those surprises: that a man may float upon the sea. Below him, full fathom five; above, infinity. Louise lounged in the bow before him looking gorgeous in fishing shorts and a halter top, propped against a mildewed flotation device with her long legs toward him, his father's antique Shakespeare rod, golden split bamboo with brass fittings, nestled in her crotch.

And yet he found it hard to look at her, for all the gorgeousness. He knew he was going to lie to her. He didn't know exactly how it would occur, or what kind of lie it would have to be.

She had on dark glasses. She dangled a hand in the water. Her tone so far was breezy, no mention of his behavior at the

Conch. She appeared to be, as he'd hoped and predicted, back to her old self.

He threw the bow anchor toward the rocks of the jetties, and it caught on the first try. Luck was with him. She would see how good he was at this. The stern anchor slipped into the water and the rope played out twenty feet, went slack; he set it with one quick tug. They were out of the channel, but a freighter coming through would send out swells that might throw the boat against the rocks if the anchors weren't secure. Wind and tide were good: dead calm, dead low.

He baited her hooks with some seven-dollar shrimp. Not an efficient exchange, those shrimp for a few fifty-cent whiting and maybe a two-dollar bluefish. But profit was not the point. The point was for Louise to land a fish. He dropped her line overboard. Louise couldn't cast worth a damn, but out here one place was as good as another, as long as you didn't get fouled in the rocks. He baited his own hooks and cast near the jetty, felt the sinker drop, scrape, snag. Good. The other point was for him not to catch anything.

She sunned herself, chin to the sky.

"Hangovers this morning in the Camden household?" he said.

"One. But you were right. He's proud of himself."

"Course I'm right." He wished she didn't have on the Ray-Bans. He couldn't say whether her eyes were open or shut, couldn't get a good reading on her state of mind, whether the breeziness was genuine or sham. They fished for a while in silence.

"I apologize for last night," she said.

"You apologize?"

"Yes. I was in a bad frame of mind. I'm better now. I shouldn't have suspected you. You're only trying to help that girl. I thought about it all night. I'm seeing clearly now."

"Good. Pass me a beer if you don't mind."

She bent up and forward, reaching between her knees toward the cooler. The rod dropped. She threw him a can.

"Hold on to that rod," he said. "It's an heirloom."

He wanted a big fish to take her bait. He imagined its slow approach, its dumb search along the sandy bottom among seaweed and snails and crabs. These warm waters were cloudy with plankton and protozoa and all manner of organic murk. It was on its way, he knew—the big one, twenty inches of silver muscle, propelled by destiny toward the hidden steel barb. Thinking about it made Rob nervous. On the surface everything was smooth and quiet. Terns circled in the air. Any second now. His skin prickled.

"This is what I wanted," she said. "Peace. I've been having a hard time. I've been needing to talk to you. But I couldn't *get* you, and then to see you with her last night—I panicked."

"I'm here now. No need for panic."

The rocks of the jetties had an odor that was both pleasant and unpleasant, salty and fishy. He and Louise had been out here before in this boat, on this sea. Whenever they went, a comfort settled over them. They usually didn't talk much. They were lulled. He started to be lulled now, when the rod sprang out of her loose grip, clattering to the gunwale, lodging under the oarlock. They both grabbed for it. Her sunglasses fell to the bottom of the boat, his cap into the water.

"I've got it," she said.

"Ease the tension, you've only got five-pound test," he said, reaching for the reel.

"I can do it."

She was up and fighting, one leg on either side of the seat, her heels against the boat. She played the fish, gave it some slack and let it run till it hesitated, then slowly drew it back. Her hands were steady. The muscles worked across her bare back.

"What is it?" she said. "It feels big."

"Don't horse it now. Let it take its time. I'm ready with the net. Bring it up to the boat, but don't lift it out of the water."

"I know how to do this, Rob," she said.

The fish ran twice, but it didn't have a prayer. When she finally got it in close, it wasn't fighting. It let itself be pulled in, just under the surface. Rob saw the dark, blank eye.

"It's a blue," he said.

"Oh, boy."

He couldn't help smiling. Whenever she said "Oh, boy," she was really happy. It took a fish or par on the ninth, victory of some kind. He reached down and netted the fish. In the green mesh it curled and snapped, but it was caught. He deposited it in the cooler.

"Good one?" she said.

"A prize. A trophy fish," he said. He patted the top of her head, and she looked up at him.

"I'm in love with you," she said.

He tried not to miss a beat. He said, "Of course you are. We've been in love forever. We'll be in love forever. This is the big love. Eternal love." He sat down again and hauled in the bait bucket. He got out a shrimp, felt it twitch between his fingers.

She hadn't taken her eyes off him. "I'm kind of tired of eternal love. I want today's."

"Eternity includes today, I think," he said.

"Not really. If you make it big enough, it doesn't mean anything."

He busied himself with the shrimp and the hook, not looking up.

She said, "I don't know how to say this. Can you look at me? I'm— I'm serious, I mean I'm not joking and also I'm serious about you." When he did look at her, she hung her head in embarrassment. "I'm making a sort of declaration," she said. "What I mean is, I think we should get married."

He sat with the line in his hand, the baited hook dangling.

"This surprises you?" she said.

"You're already married, Louise."

"But I love you. And you love me. Don't you?"

"You know the answer to that."

"So. It makes sense, doesn't it? I thought for a long time that we could just go on . . . the way we've been. We've spent so much time together we were more or less married. But when you took up with this girl—I couldn't bear it. I can't bear it."

"But I've had girls before."

"Yes, but they were—*harmless*." She tried to smile. "This one's different. But I'm not reacting out of jealousy. I've thought this out very carefully. I know what I want."

"Louise, I—"

"Wait, I know what you're worried about. The time I said you couldn't afford me. I regretted that when I said it, right away. It wasn't true. Hank will give me the house, I'm sure, and enough money to live on for a while, until we get settled. You don't have to worry about the money part."

He sat there blinking in the sunlight, on the flat water, while what he'd imagined for years was coming true before him. She was shy in the telling. He saw her hands shake. She was brave, but he knew she was not brave enough for this, and he didn't know if he was, either.

"What do you mean, until we get settled?" he said.

"Until you go back to work. Meanwhile, you have *some* money. Don't you? And I can live simply, Rob. None of that means anything to me. I don't care about it, I absolutely don't."

"You told Hank?"

"No, but I will. Don't think about that. That part of it's my problem. There aren't any real obstacles, Rob. I finally realized, you think something's impossible so you give it up, but really anything is possible if you want it bad enough. I feel so calm about this. I feel very clear. We can do what we've always wanted to do. Run away like you said. Out to sea. We can do anything. Don't you think? Do you love me?"

"I love you," he said. It was not a lie.

"Oh, God, I'm so glad."

"But we can't do this."

She stiffened. "We can. It will be all right, I promise. Unless you— Which do you mean, we can't because it's impractical, or we can't because you don't want to?"

"I don't know."

She shook her head. "You have to know. You can't just say you don't know."

The sun was hurting his forehead. He couldn't think of what to say. He said, "You wouldn't be happy with me."

"I would."

"This kind of thing isn't what you're cut out for."

"What kind of thing? Love?"

"Divorce, a mess. No money. No future. I'm living hand to mouth."

"I said I know that. I said it doesn't matter."

"It would, though. I'm fine for you in limited doses, but not permanently. I'm not the man for you. You knew that five years ago. You were right to marry Hank. He's good for you." He could see that it was true; at the mention of Hank's name her eyes teared up. He wished he had left her alone, had not played golf with her or joked or gone fishing. Without his interference she could have stayed as happy as she'd been at her wedding.

"That's crap," she said. "You never liked Hank. There's some other reason."

He had never seen Louise cry. It scared him. Her face shivered and seemed to break. He tried to reach her, but she pulled back from him and brought her knees up, so he embraced the knees, and she slugged him in the shoulder.

"Leave me alone," she cried. "You've been lying to me for years."

"I haven't, I've never lied to you."

"You said all those things! That we would go to Brazil, that we'd known each other in an earlier existence, that we could read each other's thoughts. You said we were *meant* for each other. I believed you!"

"No, you didn't, we were joking around, you joked around too—"

She looked at him wildly.

"Honey, please calm down," he said. "Please be careful, that rod is my—"

She threw the rod overboard. Then she threw the beer.

"Louise, stop."

The bluefish flopped in the Styrofoam cooler. She made a move toward it.

"Hey," he said, but she had her arms around it already, hefted it to the gunwale and tipped it over. He saw the fish slip into the sea, rest momentarily near the surface, then streak out. They both stared after it. The cooler bobbed away on the tide.

"How about the motor?" he said. "All you have to do is unscrew these two clamps."

She put her head in her hands. "Jesus Christ," she said. "What's happening to me?"

He tried again to hold her.

"No. I want to go home," she said. "In a minute. Give me a minute."

So they sat in the boat, facing each other, not talking. He was looking at her, but she wasn't looking at him; she stared at a spot on the horizon. Gradually her face settled into what looked like serenity, with a hint of trouble in the eyes. They were red. He felt like a bum, Rob the Worthless. But he had told no outright lies. He had come as close to the truth as possible, hadn't he, under the circumstances, and to the degree that he knew what the truth was?

"Have you slept with her?" she said.

"No."

She nodded. "I needed to know that, just to make sure that it's strictly a question of you and me here. That you're turning me down straight, without complications. It's just me and you we're talking about."

"I'm not turning you down."

"I don't know what else you could call it."

He couldn't think of anything. His brain was very slow, still hung up on her last question and his answer to it. Not a lie. But not truth.

For the first time he realized that truth and lies were not

opposites because they were not equals. Truth was much stronger. He saw it as if it were a clear and open path, one that he had never really taken. Always he had been sidestepping, choosing irony and imagination instead, both forms of falsehood. But to choose truth was difficult. He wanted to choose it, but it was so hard.

"Louise—excuse me, I— What exactly did you mean by that last question?"

"What question? Have you slept with her?"

"Yes, that one."

"Oh, Rob."

He closed his eyes. He wouldn't blame her if she knocked him into the sea. But after a minute he felt her hand touch his, cover it. She leaned toward him.

"You should have told me," she said. "I wouldn't have complicated it for you. I tried to get you to tell me."

"I know," he said. "But I do love you, and I've always wanted you, and if you'd come to me a year ago, or even a month ago—"

"No, don't say that. I don't want to think of it like that, as if we just barely missed each other. I'd rather . . . I don't know . . ."

"If I'd known how you felt, I wouldn't have let her move in. I wouldn't have spoken to her, that first night. I wouldn't have noticed her."

"That may be true," she said. "But you should have known. You should have— Hell, this is pointless. I knew it was going to happen. Let me just . . . ask you one question. How much— that is, how long do you think this will last, with her?"

"I don't know."

"But it isn't minor."

"I guess not."

She took a breath; she nodded. "But I don't have to—stop *seeing* you, do I?"

"No, never," he said.

"We can still talk on the phone? We can still do things?"

"Of course," he said. He leaned over to reach for something

in the tackle box between his knees, anything, the bait knife or the leaders, because he was close to crying and did not want to do it.

"Maybe we'll go to the firemen's fair on Sunday," she said, "and it will be like it used to be. I was always happy at the fair."

Motoring home, all he could hear was the big hum of the Evinrude and the regular whap of the bow against the water, now picked up into choppy wavelets by an afternoon breeze. With each whap, Louise was sprayed with a fine salt mist. She turned into it, and let it hit. He could see only her back and shoulders, her wet hair. She was cold. He couldn't take his eyes from her bare back, her shoulder blades. Goose bumps rose on her skin.

In every life is there one large error, the one misstep that makes you realize all previous mistakes have been mere deviations, negligible? And was this his? They were past the protection of the jetties now, crossing the open water. The waves were bigger. He followed the shoreline toward the inlet. He could see people on the beach, and behind them the gabled houses with dormer windows.

Rounding the sandbar, making for the inlet, he pretended for a while that he hadn't turned her down, that he was taking her back to a gabled house, to live the life he had long imagined. He would go to work for Legal Aid. Louise would . . . Louise would what? The imagined life faded. He could no longer see it. Louise, in his bow like a brave masthead, was soaked to the skin.

They puttered over to the landing. She, good girl, slid over the bow and into the shallows with the line. She looked strong and—almost happy. For an instant he thought maybe this was nothing important, after all. Only a small blip in the big picture. Maybe they would go on as they had before, golfing and joking.

But he saw her standing in the mud, feet apart, rope in hand. She smiled at him, and it wasn't her usual smile, it was a different smile altogether, the kind he had seen on clients who head out into the world alone as if nothing has gone wrong: a brave smile, masking unspeakable fear.

"What do we do now?" she said.

"Hang on to the rope a minute. That's good. I'll get the trailer."

He took her home. He was sunburned above his forehead. The Toyota was sluggish and balky. It stalled at an intersection, and he was afraid it would die right there, with the traffic streaming around it, and she would see that he was a man for whom things did not work—even though, now, it didn't matter how she saw him. And would he always see himself as if she were watching? Would he always be seeing the world as if she were there, in it, with him?

"What are you thinking?" she said, touching his shoulder. "Are you thinking about me?"

"Yes."

She settled back in the seat. "I'm thinking about you."

They sat in her driveway, in the Toyota with the boat and trailer attached, and she said again she loved him, and he said he loved her, again and again, until it seemed enough, and it seemed over.

CHAPTER 14

A imless gulls crisscrossed the sky. Rob drove with his fingers tight on the wheel—as if under a looser hand the
car might leave the road. *Keep your grip,* he said, *you
have been here before.* To abandon hope should be a one-
shot deal; a man should not have to do it twice. But he saw that
in fact he would have to do it not only once again but daily from
now on, and maybe hourly, fending off hope as one fends off
pride, sloth, avarice, and the other sins. Yet the more he steeled
himself, the more daring and frequent were hope's sallies against
him.

He would not see her again.

He would see her again.

Okay: the thing to do was to move forward. Cast away imagination, take on the habits of scrutiny (an eye on the here and
now) and endeavor (a foot in the here and now). Time to make
up for lost time. At the thought, he felt his right front tire slip
from the pavement onto the soft shoulder.

Louise, Louise.

Resolved to scrutiny, he hardly saw the road he drove or the
trees and houses he passed, finding himself suddenly at a halt in
his carport, where everything was bathed in green, the sunlight
filtered through fiberglass. Green in the chrome of the Harley,
in the beach towel hung on a peg. Music in the air: a child's
piano-playing, stop and start. Overhead, a black patch of pine
needles caught in the troughs of the milky green roof. Desperate

for endeavor, he thought of sweeping them off. But he seemed stuck in the car. He didn't move until he saw Ernie in the rearview mirror, standing in the glaring white driveway. Ernie didn't look good.

"What is it?" Rob said, getting out and slamming the door so as to appear resolved and deliberate.

"It's them. When I got there, Dad was *crying*. He's supposed to make some kind of speech at the fair, and he was writing it and weeping at the same time. Ma didn't know what to do with him. And then I made things worse. I think you better go over there."

"You told her?"

"It set her back more than I thought it would." He rubbed his forehead, a look of dismay on his face that Rob had never seen there before. The young can be flabbergasted by the old. Ernie was smart, but there was still a lot he didn't know. "When I left, they were both crying. It might be a good idea for you to go over there. I'm scared I screwed things up, Rob."

"I'll go now. Is Billie inside?"

"No, she came out to fill the feeders. She's around somewhere. Listen, do you think I screwed it up? Maybe it was the wrong time to tell her. Maybe she isn't as steady as I thought. Maybe *he* isn't, either. I've never seen him like that."

"Don't worry about it. I'll go see. They have their ups and downs."

But he wanted Billie with him. He looked in the backyard. She filled the feeders every afternoon. He saw the bag of birdseed on the ground, the feeders filled. He warned himself: do not panic, she's here, she hasn't gone. The sky was clear and still. A dog barked, and the distant piano-player missed a note in the practice scales. Speedo lay in his spot on the concrete. No signs of trouble. Rob walked around the side of the house. Billie knew he had gone fishing with Louise, she had answered the phone when Louise called. But she had said it was all right. She hadn't seemed angry.

She wasn't in the front yard either. He gazed down the empty street, and then across it to the marsh, and saw her. In the mud and reeds she was bending, in short cutoffs and a pair of Rob's white fishing boots planted wide, at the keyboard of the white piano.

He had to laugh. Ernie had seen her too, and stood shaking his head. "That's some girl you've got," he said. "If you've got her. What's the story, anyway?"

"Hard to tell," Rob said. They watched her for a minute in silence.

"Well, if I were you I'd put some effort into it." He went inside.

Rob called out to her. She looked up and saw him and called back, "Hey! It works," raising an arm in victory. She played "Heart and Soul," her face turned to him for approval. He beckoned, and she came back through the marsh, striding. Oh, my playful girl, he thought, my little one. Seeing her like that, at some distance, he felt as if he were looking not at the real Billie but at a photograph chanced upon in a magazine ad—the kind that catches a guileless girl at a private moment, laughing or smoking a cigarette, far more erotic than any centerfold. He fell into a momentary swoon. Old-fashioned expressions of harmless tenderness popped into his head, the phrases that girls used to write in his high-school yearbook. Stay as sweet as you are. Love ya. Don't ever change.

"I found these funny boots," she said.

"Found them in my closet, you mean. And they're not funny boots. They're oysterman boots. They look lovely on you."

"Sure."

"No, they do. I'm surprised they fit."

"I have big feet," she said.

"I've noticed."

"You think they're too big?" She pulled off a boot and a sock and showed her foot. "Size eight. That's not abnormal, is it?"

He hugged her, catching her off balance and one-booted. "Are you okay?" he said. She nodded. He was a lucky man, in many respects. He had to focus on the luckiness, focus on Billie now.

"Did you talk to Ernie?" she said.

He nodded. "I'm heading over to the retirement home now. Come with me. Get some shoes first. And maybe put on a skirt?"

"But I want to wear the boots, they make me feel sort of swaggery. I can just rinse the mud off with the hose. You don't like the shorts?"

"They're my favorite shorts. But you go like that to the home, and the old fellows will drop in their tracks."

She put on her dancer skirt while he hosed off the boots. He liked a swaggering Billie.

2.

He had never seen Gracewood Hall before, but the place looked familiar . . . that veranda, white with a blue ceiling, those rocking chairs, and the sound of a woodpecker in the oak limbs . . . It reminded him of the hospital (or whatever it was) where he'd sent his mother twenty years before. Another scaled-down plantation replica. A maid pushed her cleaning cart down the path toward the cottages out back. A breeze sifted through the azaleas along the asphalt path and up the slope of a small hill. Next spring the whole place would turn purple; there were azaleas everywhere. Recently a botanist on the news had predicted a profusion of spring flowers: plants respond to stress, the botanist said, by redoubling their efforts. After a major hurricane we may expect bigger acorns, more peaches, azalea blossoms twice their normal size.

"What do you think?" Rob said to Billie.

"The cottages look sort of bare. They could use a little decoration."

"Bird feeders and wind chimes?"

"Maybe, or potted plants, some benches out front."

His parents' cottage was so tiny he couldn't imagine Maude

and Jack coexisting within it. In the old house downtown they had been able to pass whole afternoons without seeing each other.

"Anyone home?" Billie said as they went in.

"I'm not home, I'm here," Jack said. "My home has been sold out from under me." He was sunk back in a ruffled flowery chair. Through a door Rob could see Maude in the bedroom, on the edge of the bed. It was the sight of her that alarmed Rob most. He recognized the look in her eyes, a look of fury mixed with defeat. Worse, her hair was down. He didn't know what to do, which of them to go to first. He leaned over and said to Jack, "Hey, Doc." But there was no response.

He saw his mother pull her legs onto the bed and curl up on her side.

"Billie," he said, "could you—" but she was already on her way into the bedroom.

He said, "Got your speech all ready, Dad?"

Nothing.

"I guess you could use last year's speech. Nothing changes much with the Volunteers. All you have to do is say the fried fish are better than ever; me and Albert are going to do the frying. You could add something about the hurricane, I guess. Make a plea for increased donations." He pulled up a wooden chair and sat next to Jack. "I don't recognize this furniture," Rob said. "Did Ma buy all new stuff?"

Jack blinked.

"That chair you're sitting in there," Rob said. "That's the ugliest chair I've ever seen. Why'd she go and buy something like that?"

"It's worse," Jack said.

"What do you mean?"

"It's worse than a new chair. It's my old chair." He lifted the ruffled skirt. "She had it recovered, she made my chair into a woman's chair!"

"I'll be damned," Rob said. "It *is* your old chair. I see the leather there."

"You see what it means. It's a woman's chair. And I'm going to sit in it, if that's what she wants. I'm sitting in it forever. If she wants me stuck here, I'm stuck here."

"You, ah, saw Ernie this morning?"

Jack sighed. "You know how those two are," he said. "They shut themselves up in the kitchen, and I sat here. They didn't want to talk to me, they have their little secrets."

"Ernie's getting married," Rob said. "He's going back to Florida, and he's marrying a thirty-year-old woman named Rhonda. That's what he came to tell Ma."

Jack sat up. "No," he said, and glanced toward the bedroom. Billie was sitting next to Maude on the bed, swinging her booted feet, her hand on Maude's. Jack's glance meant he was thinking straight; he understood that if Maude lost Ernie she could lose the balance of her heart.

"I imagine she's not taking it well," Rob said. This was their old way, the father-son cahoots to which Jack was accustomed; in this mode they used to ally themselves, not against her but in well-meaning if bumbling concern for her. He hoped Jack would spring back into it.

"She's going to need your help, Doc. She'll be scared. It was you and me before, but this time it's Ernie, and it could be much worse."

"I don't know what to do," Jack said.

"Neither do I."

As if by agreement they both turned toward the bedroom— not meaning to eavesdrop, but Billie's voice was strong, she'd taken a commanding tone with Maude, and they listened.

"Well, I personally talked to him this morning," Billie said. "You must have misunderstood. Here, sit up and I'll tell you what he said. And just turn your head, I'll pin up your hair."

"I didn't misunderstand a thing," Maude said. "He came in and announced he's getting married. He said and I quote, 'This is something I'm doing on my own. You aren't part of it.' Those were his exact words."

"You know—if I can speak freely—it seems to me that sometimes the people in this family don't always say what they mean. Sometimes they maybe even say the opposite of what they mean. That makes it hard to tell what's really going on."

Maude turned to Billie in surprise. "You're absolutely right," she said.

"I can't hear what she's saying," Jack whispered. Quietly he stood up from his chair and moved closer to the door; Rob followed.

"I wouldn't mind telling you what's really going on, Billie," Maude said. "I've never confessed it to anyone. Should I tell you?"

Rob felt his father's hand on his elbow.

"If you want to," Billie said.

Maude put her hands over her face. Even in her worst moments, Rob had never seen her do that. With her head bent forward she rocked back and forth. "Ernie . . ." she said, then looked at Billie with her hands dropped to her cheeks so that only her eyes showed. "Ernie's all I have."

Billie must have expected more; she hesitated, but only for an instant. "And when someone's all you have, you're afraid of losing them," she said.

"Yes, oh yes."

"I don't think you'll lose him," Billie said. "I think he hasn't quite understood what it is you want. And women can't wait for men to understand; there isn't time. Women have to announce themselves. Did you tell him you wanted to go to the wedding? Did you say you wanted to help?"

"How could I, he didn't give me a chance! He stormed in and talked like someone I didn't know."

"You see, he hasn't thought it out. Imagine Ernie trying to plan a wedding. You're going to have to help, whether you want to or not."

"Oh, I could plan a wedding. I have very strong ideas about weddings. They should be held out of doors, and the couple should write their own vows—it means so much more that way."

"You know, maybe Ernie's even a little bit scared of marriage."

"Jack was." Maude laughed. "He was so scared his hands shook and he dropped the ring. Jack," she said, "is still scared of marriage."

Rob heard a small cough of surprise from his father. Maude turned and saw them in the doorway. She stood and straightened her sweater. "Well, come on in, you two," she said. "Don't just stand there and eavesdrop."

"We weren't—" Jack began.

"Billie says, in case you didn't hear, that I should help out with Ernie's wedding. I think we'll have to go down there, Jack. We'll go down and meet—"

"Rhonda," Billie said.

"Yes, and have a grand time along the way. We'll make a trip out of it."

"I'd like that, Maude," Jack said, with a kind of shy gratitude, as if he were accepting a date with someone he'd never thought would ask him. And Rob could see what was coming.

"No, I meant me and Billie," Maude said. "You don't have to go, Jack, there's no need for you to go." She went to the dressing table and checked her hair in the mirror. "You'll have everything you need right here," she said.

Billie widened her eyes at Rob. Jack, crestfallen, moved toward the door.

"We should all go," Billie said. "I think we should all go, the four of us. It would be fun." She looked around from face to face.

Maude had a hairpin in her mouth. "Mmm," she said, and put in the last pin. "Maybe so."

"Sounds like a good idea to me," Rob said.

"But not unless we get some things straight around here," Maude said. "I have three main things to say—just so you'll know."

"All right, Maude," Jack said.

"First, I'm not crazy. I never was. The doctor explained that to you, Jack, I was sitting next to you when he said it. Still, you've both clung to the notion, as if *you liked it*! I don't understand that. For a while I found life difficult, yes, but I got over it, I adjusted. Secondly, I am not a heathen. Just because I don't go to church, you think I'm not religious. I am. Yes! That surprises you. But you two jump to conclusions about me, and then you discuss me, and I don't like it."

"Well, I think we understand all that, Maude," Jack said.

"And I'm not leaving," she said in a lower voice. "I've never thought of leaving. I don't know where you came up with that idea. As if I were some sort of flighty actress! I know who I am. I know who you are, Jack. And it's all right. Why can't we just settle down now? I thought we could be happy here; I thought, finally—" She broke off and looked around the room.

"We can," Jack said. "I like the place. I like it, Maude. It was the chair more than anything."

"What chair?"

"My old chair. I miss my old chair."

"But it's here. You mean the slipcover. But that comes off, Jack. You can just take it off."

"You can?" he said.

"Look," she said. They all followed her into the living room, where she tugged at the back of the chair. Snaps popped, and the ruffled dress dropped away, leaving Jack's old cracked-leather brown chair.

"Well, then, everything is fine," Jack said.

"It's time for us to eat supper, Rob," Maude said. "I'm glad to see you and Billie, but if your father and I don't go on in to supper, they'll be calling us to see if we've fallen and broken our hips. But we won't fall," she said, "will we, Jack?"

"No, we won't fall."

They left the house four abreast, Maude and Billie chatting. "Is Disneyworld near Gainesville?" Billie said.

"Oh, it won't make a piece of difference," Maude said. "We'll go wherever we want to go."

The path narrowed, and Maude moved out in front, humming a tune Rob recognized. *With my eyes wide open, I'm dreaming . . .* one of her favorites. Rob had never been sure of that song's meaning: it could mean that life is an illusion, or it could mean that dreams come true—two opposite messages. He did not know which his mother would be choosing as she hummed. She strode ahead in her new white slacks, arms across her chest, holding her own elbows the way women do when the air at night is chilly and they are alone.

"I had been thinking of taking her on a trip myself," Jack said, watching her go into the dining room. "But I guess that's out."

"Where to?" Billie said.

"It wouldn't have worked. She'd have laughed at the idea, I'm afraid. It was this place near Myrtle Beach—"

"But that would be great," Billie said. "A vacation."

"It wouldn't have been exactly a vacation, it would have been . . . something more. It's a place people our age go—there's a chapel, and . . . well, there's no use talking about it, she'd have said it was ridiculous anyway." He opened the screen door of the dining room and looked around for Maude.

"She might like it," Billie said. "Don't jump to conclusions."

Jack cocked his head at Billie. "You're right," he said. But Rob knew Maude wouldn't want to go to a church retreat, no matter what she had said about being religious.

"He's going to get his hopes up again," he said after Jack had gone in.

"What's wrong with that?" Billie said.

That night she lounged on the sofa next to him, her feet in his lap, her pink-nailed toes in his hand. On television a psychiatrist was talking about posttraumatic stress, predicting an increase in depression, divorce, and crime. "Folks might not even realize they're under stress," the shrink said. "They might say they're doing just fine, but we have to realize that some storm damage, the strain it's put on our community, is invisible at this point. We may not know the full extent of it for quite some time."

"That's what I was thinking," Billie said.

Her foot moved. She was able to take his finger between her first and second toes.

"My mother loves you," he said.

"Well, I love her."

He couldn't proceed, though clearly there was another thing to say here. He saw the newspaper next to him on the sofa cushion, and picked it up. Billie turned back to the television. After a minute she withdrew her feet. As soon as they left his lap, he regretted his failure to say more. He was trying to think how to get the toes back in his hand when the phone rang, and he answered automatically.

"Do you have time to talk to me?" Louise said. His heart nearly stopped. Billie had pulled her knees up under her chin and was concentrating on the television screen.

"Not exactly," he said.

"I left home."

"You what?"

"I left. Packed my bag, ran away. No, I didn't run away, I mean I talked to Hank, he and I sat down and had a long talk, and then I left. Moved out. It's done. I guess I figured if you and I can't do it together, I'll do it alone."

He couldn't say anything.

"Um, is she there with you?" Louise said.

"Correct."

"Hell. Well, anyway. Thought you would want to know."

"Yes, that's true."

"It's a step in the right direction. But the thing is, I'm a little shaky. A little bit afraid. I think I'll be all right if I can talk to you. Maybe you could come over."

"I don't think that would be a good idea."

"Thirty minutes is all I'll need. I want your advice."

"I'm finding it difficult to understand the situation. This is something final?"

"Yes, but— Look, could we please not do this on the phone, if she's right there? Couldn't you come over here?"

"Where?" he said.

"At the club. I rented a villa. Take a right on Sewee Court, third house on the left. Will you leave right away?"

"More or less."

"I know you don't want to do it."

"No trouble at all," he said. He hung up. Billie looked curious. "That was Albert," he said. "He wants me to come over and look at the contract the school board offered him. I said I'd help him out. I won't be gone long."

"Okay," she said.

So much for the path of truth. He would get on it, though, pretty soon, after this minor detour.

3.

He made his case in the car, driving the dark road. This was the right thing to do. He had an obligation to Louise, to see her through. He couldn't just abandon her. Their parting had been abrupt, leaving a sense of something unfinished. That was why he lacked resolve, because the thing with Louise was not yet finally cleared. If he could meet her and clear it, then he could get on with his life; he'd be able to move ahead.

The club entrance was dark; there was no guard in the sentry box, and the gate was open. Great. They guard the place when there's no danger at all and nothing to protect, then leave it wide open when hard times come, when a defenseless and not entirely rational woman is inside. Anyone could get in. Along the road, the lamps were out. He had to aim his headlights at the street signs to find the right one. Three driveways down, the only lit house. He climbed the wooden steps and looked for the bell, but she must have been waiting just behind the door. It opened immediately.

She looked bedraggled. She wasn't dressed, had on a bathrobe, no shoes.

"I didn't really think you would show up," she said.

"Tell me what happened. What have you done?"

"I just left. That's all."

"What did you tell him?"

"Don't worry. Your name was not mentioned. Why should it be? You don't figure in this."

"I didn't mean that. What are you going to do now?"

"With my life, you mean? This is the question I used to ask you, isn't it? You said you were going to wait and see. That's what I'll do. Not that I'm in the same position you're in. He gave me a lot of money. Look."

On the coffee table was a stack of bills. "Four thousand dollars in cash," she said. "That's for immediate expenses. Oh, God. Why don't you take some of it? No, you wouldn't, of course. You're so pure."

"I'm not pure."

"You are, in your way."

"Louise, you shouldn't have that much cash here. There's no security, the place is wide open. I don't think you ought to be staying out here."

"This is all so familiar! I'm saying what you said and you're saying what I said. But I think you were right, a while back. You told me to get rid of my earthly possessions. See, that's what I'm doing. I'm following your lead."

"I never suggested that you leave home."

She looked at him. "Well, as a matter of fact, you did, but as you say, that was just joking around. Anyway, it's all different now. I'm doing what I can. It's not much. It's so *dark*. I can't see very far into the future, I can only see a few hours. What will I do? I don't know. I don't think the paper will take me back. I've lost my credibility. I used to be a reporter, then I got married. I thought I was still a smart person, still even a reporter, just not doing the reporting. But I've come to find out I was nothing. I've been nothing for five years. I wasn't a mother, I wasn't a wife."

"You were a wife. You are a wife."

She ignored him. "So what I think I'll become is a divorcée. That's not a bad job. I'll get some new clothes and I'll buy a crafts shop and sell découpage."

"Louise, I'm not here to listen to you talk nonsense. If you want help, I'll give it. I don't know what I can do, but if there's anything—"

"Yes. There is."

"Good. I'll do it."

"I want something very specific from you. I'm going to tell you the truth: you've ruined me. No, don't turn away. I'm not trying to make you feel bad, I just think you ought to know. I don't think you did it on purpose."

"How can I have ruined you? I've done nothing to you. I have only adored you."

"That's how. That's what did it. When I was with you I felt pretty and smart."

"You *are* pretty and smart."

"What I'm trying to say is, we are out of all that now. And I'll be fine eventually. But meanwhile—until I can get myself steady—I feel this tremendous loss, like my soul has shrunk to a little stone. I've tried to think what to do, and I can only think of one thing."

"What?"

"We should make love."

"Jesus, Louise. That wouldn't help."

"It would help me."

"I can't."

"No one will know," she said. "Then we'll be free."

"It wouldn't work that way. You're not in the most lucid state of mind. It would tangle things up further. It would be bad for you."

She smiled. "I know very well that I'm not lucid. I'm the

opposite of lucid. My head is solid darkness. But I want you to do this for me. Look at it this way: you've never done anything for me. I never asked you to, until now. This is what I want, the only thing."

He walked back and forth across the room. The carpet was white, thick; his footsteps made no noise.

"Look at me," she said. "I'm just your old friend."

She sat in a chair across the coffee table from him. He was off balance, among all the resort furniture, chrome and glass gleaming despite the low light of the room. She was thinner, her cheekbones visible, her wrists knobby. Her eyes were bright but circled below with dark rings. She wore no makeup, her skin was pale. He felt the old, immense, sad desire. They stared at each other. Maybe she thought he was thinking it over, but he was not; there was nothing to think over, no path by which rational thought might lead him out of this. There was only the room, and the woman he had loved and ruined, and the chance that she was right, and the certainty that he would do as she asked, whether she was right or not.

The force that drew him was one that he could not have described in words. She was not just his old friend. She was not just a lost love, or a found love either. He crossed the carpet and stood in front of her, drawn as if to his sister self.

In the villa bedroom, they made love and, she said, unmade it too.

But he learned from the way she held him, from the way she cried out, that nothing made can be truly unmade. He learned from her arms and legs, from her mouth and wet hair and hunger, that she was as caught in it as he was, and equally afraid. They could not see each other and they didn't speak. Even after he had dropped away from her, she lay quiet on the enormous bed next to the wide window, beyond which the desert of the fairway stretched dying to the marsh. He was consumed by sorrow; boats came lit like lanterns up the inland creek, moving from one side of the window to the other; she said nothing. After a while she reached to the bedside table and turned on the light.

"I think I'll go home," she said. She pulled the sheet from the bed and wrapped herself in it. "Where's my robe? I thought I—"

"It's in the living room. I'll get it for you. Can't you wait a minute? You don't mean that you're going home now, do you? Tonight?"

She walked, still wrapped in the sheet, into the living room. He got up and dressed, and found her waiting on the sofa, robed, silent, staring at her hands. She tried to laugh. "That was a little— dangerous, I think." Her shoulders shivered. "We might have killed each other."

"Are you all right?" He sat down next to her, and tried to stop her shaking.

"No, it's okay. Don't say anything." She pulled the robe tighter and folded her arms around herself. "Well, anyway, it was what I wanted. Thank you."

He winced.

"I do think I'll go home, though," she said.

"Do you want me to take you? I don't think you should drive."

"I'll call him. He'll come for me."

"All right."

"We'll see each other," she said. "We'll run into each other now and then, and we'll say hello, right? It will be fine."

"Louise, listen—you said, didn't you say, that no one will know about this?"

"Of course not," she said.

He didn't want to leave. With her hair tangled and her lips pale she looked beautiful, and he said so, but that made her cry. She seemed to hold her breath, then let it out. "Is this *normal*?" she said. "Do all people suffer this much in their ordinary, normal lives?"

"Some do, I guess."

There wasn't much left for him to do but to say goodbye. She watched from the doorway as he went down the steps, and he heard the door close when he reached the driveway. He made it through the darkness to his car and fumbled for the keys.

No planets were visible in the sky. There was a high cloud

cover. Mist lifted thin over the creek, and animals moved in the underbrush. He heard a closer noise, a rustle in the bushes next to the driveway, and he turned, expecting a deer; but he turned too late. Someone came out of the shadows, caught him around the neck and held him. The catcher seemed peculiarly gentle, the headlock one Rob could have sprung out of in an instant, but he didn't. He offered no resistance; didn't even think, *Who?* He was finally caught, and it hardly mattered who had caught him.

But when he saw who it was, he was scared. Of all the people who might have found him out, this was the one he would not have chosen.

CHAPTER 15

H e sat dumb in the Toyota, having followed directions—
driven down to the corner, pulled over, turned off the
lights. The catcher sat beside him, looking gloomy.

"What did you have in mind here?" Rob said.

"Rescue," Albert said. "Getting you out of trouble again. She
called me, and I thought you'd want to know." He got out of
the car and slammed the door.

Rob followed. "Wait," he said. "*Who* called you?"

"Billie. She asked me to tell you to call her when you got to
my house. I knew you weren't coming to my house, so I ran out
to try and catch you somewhere on the road. I figured you might
be going to the Conch, but saw your taillights turn in at the club
gate. By the time I got here you were inside that house. I saw
who's in there. Next time you use me as alibi, it would be a good
idea to let me know."

"You waited outside all that time?"

"How was I supposed to know how long it would be? I don't
know what you're up to. It's not my idea of a good time to wait
in the bushes while you finish your business. Excuse me, my car's
down the road."

"Why'd you jump me, for Christ's sake?"

Albert shrugged. "Spur of the moment. Thought you deserved
it. I don't too much like what it looks like you're doing, and then
on top of that I don't appreciate being treated like some kind of
fool."

225

"Wait a minute. You're talking about you and me now? I treat you like a fool?"

"That's right."

Rob stared at him.

"Saying how good a friend you are," Albert went on. "Never asked me once what I thought. I have a thought sometimes, every once in a while. Shit, you never even invited me inside your house."

"I invited you inside my goddam house."

"Never. You said, we'll sit outside."

"But you *could* have come in. You knew that."

"That's not the point, is it? Point is, you never said it."

"Well, I—"

"That's right, not one time. You need a errand, someone to get you a generator, call up Albert. You need someone to listen to your philosophies, figure out your mess with women, that's when you come to Albert."

"That generator was your idea. That *generator,* you offered to me."

"Because you said *before* that, if I run across one, call *you!* You been acting like a spoiled white kid who don't see nothing, don't know how to treat women right, like to pretend you got a nigger friend."

"Bullshit."

"How come you never asked me about my family?"

Rob frowned.

Albert was moving around him in circles. "How much I know about your family? Everything. Your mama's troubles, your daddy's troubles, your brother—I know it all. What you know about mine?"

"You haven't got a damn family!"

Albert nodded.

"Well, do you?" Rob said.

"You think I sprung from dirt?"

"Where are they?"

"Well, I'm not starting now, telling you."

"You're lying," Rob said. "You came to the church because you had nowhere else to go. You said you had no family, that's why you were there."

"You got everything figured out," Albert said. He started walking down the road.

"Hold it," Rob said. "You're going to have to tell me."

Albert didn't stop. Rob ran after him and leapt onto his back. Albert shook him off with one powerful shudder, then turned and landed a punch above Rob's left ear that made the dark night go yellow and sent him staggering backward. But he went at Albert again. "Tell me," he said, grabbing Albert's shirt.

Albert hit him again and watched him fall. On his way down Rob saw broken pines and the whole white moon fly up around him, and then he was on his back in the roadside weeds. He could not think of a reason to get up. Lying still, almost comfortable under the unmoving sky, he wasn't sure how he had got there but it seemed like the right place to be. For long minutes there was no sound but the whisper of underbrush and the creak of pines.

"That's enough," Albert said. He lifted Rob to a sitting position. "I think you're right," he said. "You want to know so bad, I'll tell you. The state hospital and the state penitentiary, places you never thought of, that's where my family is. Edwina Swan, James Swan, schizophrenia and murder one. Been there twenty years and not likely to see the light of day again, either one of them."

Rob closed his eyes.

"Maybe that's too much for you? I thought so," Albert said.

"I had no idea—but what can we do, we can do something—"

"Nothing. I go see them, Wednesdays. One week to the hospital, one to the prison. I was supposed to look after her, he had asked me to do that, but he didn't know how bad off she was."

"Did he have a lawyer?"

"Court-appointed. Never heard from the man again. My father shot a white man, see. He was guilty."

"But maybe he's eligible for parole. We can contact the parole board and—"

"No," Albert said. "I don't want any favors."

"I'll charge you. You're making a decent wage, and I need the work."

"Forget it," Albert said. "Straighten out your own mess."

"I'm straight," Rob said.

"Hope so. But leave me out of it. Say what you want to, but don't make me part of it." He turned and walked down the road to his car.

Rob made his way back to the Toyota and did not look up at the darkened villa. For a while he drove the winding club roads, past the wrecked tennis courts, the empty swimming pool. He needed time to think; everything had become complicated. But time did not help, no solutions occurred. He turned toward home.

And when he neared the Camdens' house, he saw the Mercedes pull out and swing to face him, the two cars the only lights on the empty road, their beams meeting. At the moment when they passed, he thought he saw Hank's face above the steering wheel, gaunt with worry, staring straight ahead, not even noticing Rob's car but only intent on her, speeding to rescue her.

Once (it seemed years ago), Louise had called Rob a good guy. But he was now in the other camp. You know when you are in that camp, but you don't know where you fall along the line that shades from ordinary human failure to serious offender: troublemaker–miscreant–criminal–sinner. If he were to be arraigned, the judgment would no doubt be harsh. And yet he had not *acted,* had he?—but had fallen, without plotting, into a tangle of trouble rising to meet him. There must be men who wouldn't be quick to judge, who had got tangled themselves and might recognize him as kin and fellow.

On the other hand, he may have been kin to no man.

It was after midnight when he sneaked into the house. Billie was asleep, curled up in her T-shirt in his bed. When he saw her, he was relieved. He wondered if a man who is ill with a disease, as the disease progresses, begins to feel himself regaining health, feels health gaining a hold. And can he tell which one will win?

He slept beside her without touching her.

2.

In the morning she was already gone when he woke up, and there was a note on the pillow: "You are a lazy bum. I made some coffee for you."

It was 10:15. He was exhausted; muscles ached in his back and thighs. He showered and shaved, drank Billie's coffee, and sat outside in the sun with Speedo, a memo pad on his knee, a pen shaking in his hand. This would be the list that mattered.

One, James and Edwina Swan. "Get them out," he wrote. Maybe it wouldn't be hard; he couldn't tell until he had the facts. And then he'd spring them, he knew he could do it. He was a lawyer, he ought to be able to outwit the law.

Two, Maude and Jack. Could they be sprung as well? The mysterious phenomenon of long marriage baffled him. But maybe the solution was something he knew how to do. Next to the names he wrote "Divorce." A divorce was what Jack feared most, and it would shake him to his soul, it might even be his end; but it might free Maude. Rob had never liked to take cases like this one; you couldn't be sure whether the people had enough time left to make a recovery and a new start. And there was something grotesque about suggesting a divorce to your own parents. But he couldn't help thinking of it: Maude free.

And last, Billie. He didn't write her name, he wrote only the B, and then filled in the loops, drew a circle around the B, underlined it twice. If he'd had the money he'd have bought two tickets to Brazil. Well, he had the money. But he realized it was now money that he thought of as necessary to the future, because . . . he wanted to buy this house. The developer must have scrapped his plans by now, as it was not a good time for new

golf villas. And he wanted to buy the house because . . . Billie
liked it. Which meant that she would be in it. He ran his pen
over the *B* again, and then he wrote "Marry her" and stared at
the words.

He called Albert.

"I decided," he said. "I'm going to marry her."

"Which one?"

"Give me a break. Billie. I want you to do it, the ceremony.
Will you? You got ordained somewhere along the line, didn't
you? She'll want a preacher."

"She'll want a real one, then. If you're going to do this you
got to get a real one. That girl won't settle for borderline mat-
rimony."

"Neither will I," Rob said. "That's why I'm asking you. There's
no one else I'd let do it."

"I don't know . . ."

He knew when Albert said "I don't know" that he'd do it.

"Hey," Albert said. "You asked the girl yet?"

"No."

"*That* might be a good idea. You ask her tonight, then call
me. I'm making no plans until then."

"Okay. I'll do it."

When Billie came home, he was waiting in the driveway. She
had walked to the pool and walked home, and he saw her coming
down the sidewalk. She didn't see him; she was whistling. When
she passed his neighbor's picket fence, she stuck out her hand
and ran it bumping over the pickets.

"What are you doing out here?" she said.

"Waiting for you."

"What time did you get in last night? I didn't even wake up."
Her eyes did not meet his. She batted at the string of shell chimes,
setting off a stiff clatter.

"Late, too late. Listen, I've got something I want to ask you."
He followed her inside.

She threw her bag on the kitchen table and began making a

peanut-butter sandwich. "I did twenty laps after the class," she said. "I'm starving. Want me to make you one?" She held up the knife with a gob of peanut butter on it.

"No, no. Sit down. This is something serious."

"What?" She sat and chewed.

"I have a proposal to make."

"What is it?"

"The usual kind. A proposal. I propose. I think we should get married."

She put the sandwich down. There was still a bite of it in her mouth, but she didn't chew.

"Swallow, so you can give me an answer," he said. "Yes or no?"

"This is for real?"

"For real."

"Yeah, but you're joking."

"No. I'm dead serious. I think we should drive in to the courthouse right now and get a license."

"What's this all about, really now? Tell me."

"That's it. I'm in love with you."

"You are?"

"Very. You're the light of my life."

She picked up the sandwich. "And you're serious?" He saw it as a good sign that she took another bite from the sandwich.

"Yes, but what about you? What do you think?"

"I think you're a lunatic."

"That's no answer. Yes or no?"

"Where did you get the idea? From Ernie, because he's getting married? Or from Albert?"

"It's my own idea. You don't have to track it down, all you have to do is say one word. One of two words. Here's yes"—he held up his left fist—"and here's no"—the right fist. He held them both out. "Which one?"

She was swinging the foot of her crossed leg. She reached out and touched his left hand.

"Yes?" He picked her up out of the chair and swung her

around to the countertop. She sat there smiling, but worried.

"It's too quick," she said. "I'm afraid you don't know what you're doing. You haven't thought it through. You're supposed to think it through."

"I have. What's there to think? We're a perfect match."

"Not hardly. We don't match at all. Seriously. What about the physical part?"

"The physical part is a good part, an important part. I'm all in favor of the physical part."

"You know what I mean."

"You need practice, that's all."

"What if it doesn't change? Then you'll be married to—a freak."

He laid his forearms alongside her thighs. "I'm not worried about it," he said. "I've read up on it. It's nothing to worry about."

"You *read up on it?* It's in a book? What, a book of sexual freaks?"

"There's nothing freakish about you, Billie."

"And what about the other problems?"

"I plan to go back to work. There are no other problems."

She wriggled out of his grasp and off the counter. "I don't want to pry into your personal life—"

"You are my personal life."

"—but if you're really serious, I have to ask you something. What about Louise Camden? I don't need the details. I just need, like you said, yes or no, because I think she's in love with you. I don't want to mess things up. I mean, if there's something going on, and it was going on before I got here, you have to be free to work it out. I like her. She was good to me. Not that many people have been good to me. I don't want to—"

"Stop," he said. "There's nothing there. Nothing between me and Louise."

"But . . . last night." Billie dropped her face and hid behind her hair. "I called Albert's house and you weren't there. I thought maybe you had gone to see her."

"I did not," he said. His head buzzed, the kitchen seemed close and hot; he wanted to be alone in the forest, with his dog, with his birds. He heard himself saying, "I went shopping. I went, as a matter of fact, to the jewelry store. Looking for a ring. Then I decided I had better ask you first."

She was silent for a few seconds. Then she said, "If two people love each other, they shouldn't give it up. No matter what the problems are, even if everything seems too complicated."

"That's what I'm saying," he said. "That's why I'm asking. Say yes, and we'll go get a ring and a license and live happily ever after."

She looked at him. "Okay," she said. "Then, yes."

"Yes? For the rest of your days? For better or worse?"

"Yes, yes. You didn't hear me?"

"I heard. I just want to make sure."

"Rob, are you all right? Your hands are shaking."

He hung on to her for another minute or so. She let him hold her, swaying, in the kitchen.

"Okay," he said, releasing her. "We have to go get the license. After you finish your sandwich."

3.

He took her to a tiny jewelry shop on King Street, where dust flew jewel-like in the afternoon sun and settled on the velvet boxes of rings the jeweler had set before them. Rob watched her try them on. In his heart he was dancing the thin line between joy and fear, and fighting off the sensation that none of this was really happening. She turned to him for advice, but he stayed where he was, leaning against the door, letting her choose; he was afraid that if he entered into the event, his presence might bring it all to a halt. He said to the jeweler, who looked like a jeweler, pale and bald, "The sky's the limit," and the man's faded eyes lit up. "Don't tell her any of the prices," Rob added. "Just let her choose."

She leaned over the glass counter with her hands clasped behind her back. She studied the rings in the first case and then moved to the second. When she had seen them all, she raised her eyes to the jeweler. "I'm afraid these are all too thick," she said.

"Thick?"

"Yes, sir—chunky. Do you have something fine-looking? Delicate?"

"These are all my wedding bands."

"What is that one behind you on the shelf?"

The jeweler turned to look. "This? This isn't a wedding band."

"What is it?"

"Well, it's a sweetheart ring. We carry them for Valentine's Day. It's just a wire, as you can see, with the heart there."

"That's what I want. If it's real gold."

The man sighed. "It's real gold."

"Perfect," she said. She tried it on and smiled, and raised her hand to Rob. In the dusty light it seemed to him that she was waving from across a great distance. When they left, he took the outside of the sidewalk to protect her from the cars that seemed to be driving dangerously fast down the narrow street.

They walked down King Street, past the antique shops, past the library with its golden ginkgo trees. He could see no signs of storm damage anywhere. Not since his childhood had he felt so comfortable in the heart of the city, as if now he had finally entered it and could be one of its citizens. He might see the mayor, he might hail him with a snappy greeting to show that, at last, he was at ease here, about to settle in.

In the courthouse lobby a sign directed citizens to the various offices, for tax payment or deed registration or marriage licensing. Behind a window the license clerk took one look at Billie and asked for proof of age. But that was all. Rob was surprised by how easy it was to get a marriage license. They didn't ask his age. No blood tests, no background check for criminality or bigamy or deception. The only requirement was to wait at least twenty-four hours. He signed his name. Billie signed hers, "Elizabeth Poe."

"Elizabeth!" he said, peering over her shoulder.

The clerk glanced at his face.

"I didn't know her first name," he explained. "It's been a whirlwind courtship."

On the steps of the courthouse, license in hand, Billie said, "You're going to be hard to be married to. Where are we going to do it, anyway?"

"Everywhere. On the kitchen counter, in the National Forest—"

"Please." She looked across the street into Washington Park, where the brick paths and the benches were all vacant. It was five o'clock, and the business district was closing down for the day. "Not in the park," she said. "Not like that sad couple I saw."

"In the church," he said.

"With a preacher?"

"With a preacher. The Reverend Albert Swan. If that's all right with you."

She said, "It's perfect." She was wiser than anyone seeing her would have guessed; she was no child. She called perfect the things that to most eyes were obviously imperfect, as if imperfection were not something to be settled for but something to be sought. Someone else might have seen flaws, in the ring and the preacher and the love—in the man himself—but if she saw them she didn't let on.

All around them the city looked quick and sharp, charged with clarity and purity. The humid haze under which it usually slept had lifted. At the intersection of Broad and Meeting, the "Four Corners of Law" rose clear and pure themselves, the buildings representing each of the four regimes under which Charlestonians live: city hall, county courthouse, federal post office, Episcopal church. From the Four Corners of Law, Rob walked back through the autumn afternoon, licensed to marry, dazzled by the bright clean edges of the buildings, the clean street just washed and swept, the clean bride-to-be at his side. He thought of stopping in at the French restaurant and feeding Billie; some sort of celebration or ritual was called for. But food didn't seem

235

right. It might be more proper not to eat at all but to fast. On the brink of a right and good life, a man should prepare himself.

"We're engaged, Billie," he said. He liked the sound of the word.

"Until when?" she asked. "You didn't mention a date."

"Any day now," he said. The date hardly mattered, he thought; he was happy with engagement. She was promised to him, she was his future bride, and he was a lucky man.

CHAPTER 16

E ven a sideliner, even the most peripheral of citizens, may become on fair night one of the folk. A boy could run wild on fair night; a boy who ordinarily kept to himself could whoop and holler with the rest of them. Even back in his early days he understood that the firemen's fair was more than a fund-raising event. It was a celebration—of what, he couldn't say precisely. Some people came for the fish, some for music or fireworks, but there seemed to be another, unvoiced purpose in the gathering. Everyone came: the well-to-do and the marginal, islanders, golfers, renters, rat-shooters—and, this year, Alabamans—everyone who had $4.50 for the flounder supper, at the fairgrounds near the recreation center, a patch of field mowed annually for the occasion, stiff with the milky cut stalks of weeds seeping their sharp, vegetable smell.

He felt the same shiver of anticipation that he had felt as a boy, entering the fairgrounds as the sun sank, watching the cars arrive and peel off into parking spaces at the end of the field, directed by a Volunteer with a two-foot flashlight whose beam would not become visible for another couple of hours; and then the people tramping through stubble to the ticket gate . . . he remembered as a boy being spellbound by the sight of those families, making their way through the weeds, coming and coming until the crowd was a throng and the throng was a multitude, and the music and eating began.

At one end of the field was a small bandstand and a makeshift plywood dance floor; then a dozen rows of folding chairs labeled with the name of the funeral home that had lent them. At the other end was the fry shack, a low white block hut on the front of which a plywood panel opened downward to reveal the serving counter. Along one edge of the field, booths had been set up for contests and raffles and miscellaneous entertainment: palmreading, dunk-the-fireman, ring-the-bottle. There was the old Ferris wheel, next to an exhibit of firefighting equipment, and the department's new yellow engine, upon which children swarmed, wearing fireman hats. Teenagers disappeared into the bushes, on paths teenagers had disappeared down for decades, leading into the myrtle thicket and out onto the beach. He had gone down those paths himself, long ago.

The fair, like all fairs, had its ceremonial aspects; but it was also a night of lawlessness. All the town's lawkeeping authority was assembled there, and no real crime was done. But children ran free, and beer was consumed, and people danced on the little platform in front of the bandstand, with partners they would not ordinarily have been allowed to choose: husbands with other men's wives, wives with teenage boys, girls with girls, blacks with whites, islanders with millionaires. On the night of the fireman's fair, rules were relaxed. Rob felt relaxed himself, as if he had been cut loose from his weight of private trouble.

With Billie and Albert he unloaded the first batches of raw fish from the refrigerator truck. Their frying shift was the last, at nine o'clock. Albert was in good spirits. He had already started teaching, and he, too, seemed cut loose, free at last. Billie had never looked prettier. Rob couldn't keep his eyes off her strong arms, swimmer's arms, as she stood in the truck and relayed to him the flat boxes of fish. She wore new blue jeans, tight across her canted hips, and a short white shirt that lifted, when she reached for a new box, to reveal a bare strip of midriff. He felt free to look, every time she reached.

He didn't want to see Louise. In past summers they had sat together, he and Louise and Hank, sometimes Maude and Jack and Ernie; they'd had fish-eating contests, counting skeletons at the end to determine winners. But he didn't want to see her now. So he was glad to remain behind the scenes, unloading the truck, then opening the boxes and dumping fish onto the slimy counter.

Somewhere in the crowd were Maude and Jack. Jack had to give his speech, in his capacity as honorary captain. But Rob couldn't see them. It was a big crowd. Nine hundred tickets had been sold, and as many more were available at the gate, where a long line had formed.

"Shall we eat now?" he said to Billie.

"Not yet. I want to see the fair." The sky was still light. Around the field, the pines and myrtles had blackened, and color was beginning to fade from the fairgoers, the whole scene shading down to the drained gray of evening.

He didn't think Louise and Hank would actually show up. What might be going on in that house on the edge of the ocean, he could not now imagine.

As for Rob, the fair was what he needed. He was delivered, tossed on shore by waves that might as easily have carried him to the bottom. He and Billie wandered the fairgrounds with swabs of blue cotton candy, consulting their schedule of events. At 6:15 they took their chairs for the Junior Miss Volunteer contest, a lineup of five thirteen-year-olds who were asked to name the three biggest problems facing the world today. He and Billie were among a handful of seated spectators, the rest apparently parents and siblings of the contestants. The chairs wobbled on the rough ground. They chose their favorite, a tall blonde who cited the evils of drugs, abortion, and Satanism. Rob was convinced. He nodded as she spoke, though he knew from past experience that he often agreed with beauty queens as they spoke, and then later (once they were out of sight) had second thoughts. Yet if Satan was threatening this lovely girl, he was against Satan. When she won, he applauded so loud that people must have thought he was kin to her. He felt he *was* kin to her!

"Why are you so happy?" Billie asked when the contestants filed off the stage to make way for the Battle of the Bands.

"Guess," he said.

239

"Because of me?"

"You got it." Because of her, and because of what came with her, the miscellany of beauty queens and bands, the blue cotton candy, the smell of plants and dirt and fish, the general effort everywhere in evidence to mount what small and genuine celebration was within the human capability.

He was caught up in the celebration. Under other circumstances he would not have sat through the Battle of the Bands, six contenders in all; in the past he'd been short with some of these very boys, impatient with the surly way they pumped gas and hung their eyelids low; but now he could see, as they played, how vulnerable they were. The winners took the six-inch trophy without a smile, but once they were off the stage he saw them grinning at each other.

"There's your mother and dad," Billie said. She waved to them. Maude came over to sit with them while Jack made his way to the bandstand.

"He's *nervous,*" Maude said. "He's been trying to memorize this thing all day. I hope he doesn't forget it."

"He'll do fine," Billie said.

Jack was introduced by old Percy the veterinarian, as "Dr. Wyatt, our honorary captain and longtime supporter." The audience was not attentive. There were no more than two dozen people sitting out front. Behind the chairs, people were eating and talking at their tables. Jack stepped up to the microphone, his white hair lifting in the breeze.

"He looks so handsome," Billie said to Maude.

"He does, doesn't he? When he's standing by himself you can't tell how short he is."

"Ladies and gentlemen, I am happy to welcome you tonight to our forty-third annual fair." He paused. "The proceeds of our gathering, including your tickets and your generous contributions, will make possible the purchase of badly needed equipment, namely a new all-terrain vehicle for the rescue squad—that is, if your contributions are as generous as I hope they will be." Billie and Maude laughed. Jack consulted the paper in his right hand and went on.

"I have myself been a member of the Volunteer Fire Department during its entire forty-three-year existence. I've seen it change from a bucket brigade to an up-to-date, well-equipped organization. We have, of course, a professional department now, and we're all grateful to Chief Davis, our outstanding fire chief, and to Sergeants Hendrix and Gibson, and to their staff, Miss Harriet Randle and Amos Hiott. But the Volunteers are by no means outmoded. We continue to serve as needed in our community, and to bring you, every year without fail, this important event in the support of our community, and—"

Jack took a look at the paper in his hand.

"He's forgotten it," Maude said.

"I . . . I suppose that's really all I need to tell you . . ."

"He can't see his notes," she said.

"But the occasion, I think, calls for something more. In all our forty-three years, we have seen changes. We've seen our island grow, we've seen . . . signs of changing times . . . and yet nothing we saw prepared us for the change we see today. Our houses down, our forests gone. And what can this mean for us? I don't know. I'm an old man."

"This wasn't in it," Maude said.

"The devastation . . ." He faltered. He squinted. "We have seen the hand of the Almighty reach down from the heavens, as it is written, 'Alas, alas, for the great city where all who had ships at sea grew rich by wealth! In one hour she has been laid waste.'"

Maude dropped her forehead into her hand.

"But to tell you the truth, my friends"—and here the paper fell from his fingers, fluttered down off the stage—"I am too old to figure all this out. I have tried. I have watched. I was going to tell you tonight that we are on the road to recovery, but I'm not sure of that. I'm not sure of anything anymore. I have not been a good man, and yet I have not been punished. Even this storm, which might have laid me low and robbed me of all that I hold dear, has left me unscathed, while better men than I have lost their all . . ."

Maude was shaking Rob's arm. "Get him down," she said. "Go after him."

Jack was rambling on. "And my wife . . . Maude . . . from the day I proposed to her—do you remember, Maude? You had on a yellow dress, do you remember? We were wading in the surf, and you carried your shoes in your hand."

Rob started to go, but Billie held him back. "Wait," she said. Jack had come to the front of the stage and was looking down at Maude.

"I didn't really think you'd say yes," Jack said. "I didn't think I had a prayer. You were so tall and beautiful, why should you settle for me? It was the luckiest day of my life. July 13, 1945— and when you said yes, do you remember what happened?"

Maude sat with her hand over her mouth.

"I couldn't help it," Jack said. "They were tears of joy." He had moved beyond the range of the microphone, and was talking to her as if there were no one else around. "You were happy for awhile," he said. "I never meant to make you sad."

Then Maude stood up and stepped forward to the edge of the stage. "Listen, I know that," she said. "I know everything you're saying." She held her hand out to him.

"But you were happy for a while, weren't you?" he said.

"I was and I still am. I told you that. You don't listen to me, Jack."

"I've been wanting to ask you, if you had it to do all over again—because we *could* do it all over again, I understand that it's possible. And I've been wondering if you'd be interested in something like that—"

"What are you talking about, Jack?"

"Renewing the marriage vows. They have the whole thing, flowers and music . . . I mean, if you had a chance to do that, would you do it?"

She didn't say anything. She only took his hand in silence,

reaching up to him, her eyes glistening. She helped him down from the stage. He put his arm around her, and they walked away together, she the taller of the two but inclining her head in his direction as she always did to lessen the difference between them. Rob heard her say, "What a lovely idea, Jack."

Several people in the front rows applauded, but the rest hadn't noticed what had happened. A Dixieland band began setting up onstage. Rob watched his parents make their way to the parking field. He was struck by a possibility he had not considered: that his mother loved his father. He had thought her bound to him in complicated ways—by the net of habit and children and the intricate history of wrongs harbored and half forgiven—when really the tie was only love. Something so simple had not occurred to him till now.

"You want to ride the Ferris wheel?" Billie said. "Are you all right?"

He pulled her down into his lap. "We didn't tell them," he said. "I meant to, but they left before I had a chance."

"It's all right."

"You said a man shouldn't get married without telling his mother."

"If you go through with it," she said, "then we can tell them."

"I'm a man of my word. Besides that, once you get a license you can't back out."

"Yes you can," she said. "I'm not that dumb."

"Do *you* want to ride the Ferris wheel," he said, "or are you just trying to think of ways to entertain me?"

"I'm scared of rides."

"On that thing? That baby Ferris wheel? They don't even make those anymore. Look, the only people riding are under nine years old. I'll hold your hand."

He gave two dollars to a mournful-looking teenager who locked them into their seat. They swung forward. At the top they were only thirty feet above ground, but Billie's hand gripped his so hard it hurt.

"You have to relax," he said. "Think relaxing thoughts. And

you have to open your eyes. That's the whole point, not the ride but the view. Lean back. No, open both eyes."

"It's pretty," she said.

From the top of the wheel they saw the whole fair, and beyond its limits to the fire station and the ocean. She did relax, and even took to rocking the boat when they stopped at the top to let on new passengers.

"Will we have flowers?" Billie said. "And a singer? I don't know if I really want a singer, what do you think? Also, Rob, I only have one dress and I don't think I can get married in it, it's a funny color. And will we have a honeymoon?"

He had not thought past the ring and the license. He rubbed his forehead.

"Anything's fine," he said. "Anything you want."

She leaned back in their little boat and looked toward the horizon. In silence they rotated above the fair. The field below was roped off with a yellow plastic line, and at the ticket gate people were still crowding to get something. In the aftermath of disaster, people were eager to contribute; they jostled each other in the line, waved across the field to friends. Couples formed foursomes, and the foursomes joined to make up tables together. One couple stood apart from the rest, just inside the gate. . . . It was the Camdens.

Louise hung on Hank's arm as if she were an invalid. He supported her, but they seemed unsure which direction to take, what they were supposed to do next. He led her to a table and seated her, then took his tickets over to the shack for food. She sat alone at the table, looking into the crowd but with eyes that did not engage the scene, as if she were looking into emptiness. Her table was at the edge of the field, just inside the yellow rope. Behind her rose the myrtle thicket. It was dark, and starting to get chilly.

"Oh, look—the boats," Billie said. She leaned forward over the lap-bar, watching the shrimp trawlers head out to sea, a parade of small lights dropping one by one out of sight over the horizon.

Rob sat back, unable to keep Louise in view. The Ferris wheel rose and fell. From the top he could see her, and during the fall, but he lost her on the climb. He wanted to keep watch over her until Hank came back. How fragile she looked, how unlike herself. She was dressed in festive clothes, a bright red top and a green flowered sarong . . . and he recalled that sometimes the fair night fell on her wedding anniversary. Despite the clothing, she looked defeated and worn. She never changed her position in the chair; she never looked up at the Ferris wheel, where she might have seen him turning, his eyes fixed on her through every downward swing.

"What do you see?" Billie said.

"Nothing."

"Nothing! Then you're blind. Look at the boats, and the bridges, the TV towers. Look, there's a little plane. I wish they had this fair once a week instead of once a year."

"It's only good if it's rare," Rob said. They crested the top and started down. He saw Hank set a plate of food in front of Louise, then sit down beside her.

"End of the ride," Rob called to the attendant, who was talking to the new Junior Miss Volunteer and didn't immediately respond. "Hey, you can let us off now," Rob called, but the wheel cranked him around again.

"What's the hurry?" Billie said.

"I don't know," he said. It wasn't that he wanted to see Louise. But he wanted to get onto solid ground. "I'm airsick," he said.

Billie put two fingers to her mouth and let out a whistle that the attendant couldn't ignore; he pulled himself away from the beauty queen long enough to stop the wheel.

"Maybe you need food. You haven't eaten all day," Billie said. He had been at the fairgrounds since morning, and hadn't thought of eating. His stomach did feel hollow. "Let's go eat with Albert," she said. "I saw him head around the back of the fry shack with a plate. I think he's eating alone."

They found him sitting on a cooler behind the shack. Rob
pulled up two more coolers, and sneaked two full plates from
inside. Billie balanced her plate on her knees. He liked the way
she ate her fish—carefully, in tiny pieces, checking each piece
first for bones. A cautious girl. Somehow her cautiousness reas-
sured him. She wasn't likely to do anything rash, like marry a
man she wasn't sure she wanted to marry.

"I'm grateful to you, Albert, for helping us with the wedding,"
Billie said.

Albert nodded.

"Do you think he'll go through with it?" she asked, winking.
She was not an expert winker. The wink, designed to establish
irony, failed; Rob understood that she was thoroughly unironical,
and meant, always, what she said.

"Him? Sure," Albert said. "He's a steady man. I *have* seen one
not show up, one time. Big wedding, everything set to go but no
groom. End up with everybody hollering and bride cursing. But
I don't think you have anything to worry about."

Billie dumped her empty plate in the garbage bag. "I'm going
to wander around," she said. "You two can have your last beer
together."

"Ah," said Albert. "That's how it happens, every time. Man
gets married, that's the last you see of him. No more nights down
at the inlet."

Rob grabbed her leg as she tried to step past his cooler. "I
don't want any more nights at the inlet," he said.

"You see? I told you," Albert said.

"Don't go," Rob said. "You'll get lost. Someone will take you.
I think I better go with you."

"You can't go with me. I'm going to the ladies' room. Where
is it?"

"Next to the bandstand," he said. "There's a long line. We
only rented four Port-O-Lets."

"I'll be back."

She stepped out of his awkward clasp and into the crowd.

He watched her go, in her jeans and white T-shirt, her tennis shoes.

"You are one lucky son of a bitch," Albert said.

"She's terrific, isn't she?"

"She is, but that isn't what I mean. You are lucky you didn't lose life and limb."

"Everything's all settled now. But you're right, I'm lucky. You know how you feel when things are bad, really bad, and you think nothing can save you, and then for no reason that you can see, the situation goes your way? That's what it is. And with, as far as I can tell, no harm done. You saw them come in?"

"Looking like the walking wounded."

"But together. Alive."

The last team of fryers was on. They were due in the shack. "Let's go," Albert said.

"Albert, listen—" He wanted to say something serious. He wanted to say his thanks, his hopes . . .

"If I listen to you every time you want listening to, both of us could be unemployed and shiftless instead of just one."

They took their positions behind the deep-fat fryers. Two ladies dipped fish in batter and loaded them on aluminum trays, and Albert slid them into the vats, four minutes each, while Rob removed them with tongs and put them onto plates. Teenage girls slapped on slaw and hush puppies and served the plates out over the counter to the ticket-holders. He could see through the opening above the counter, out to the crowd.

"Billie must have gotten lost," he said, trying to catch sight of her.

"She seems like a girl who can take care of herself."

"I have heard her say so," he said, "and I believe it's true."

They fried till their arms hurt. Rob had small blisters on his hands where pops of fat had hit his skin, grease on his shirt and in his hair. Sweat dripped from Albert's eyelashes. Hordes of people had already eaten and gone home, but Rob was still serving seconds and thirds, mostly to oversize teenagers. But by and by the line dwindled. Roughly coincident with the last few customers came the last few fish.

"That's it," Albert said, and tossed his tongs into the dishpan. "I don't ever want to see another flounder."

"I don't see Billie anywhere," Rob said. He got a trash bag and started collecting the plates that people had brought back to the counter, still peering through the front of the shack for Billie. The grounds were emptying. There were only a few tables of people still eating. Down by the bandstand, a handful of people were dancing together as a group to the last of the Dixieland . . . and at a corner table, two women in close conversation, leaning toward each other, one with her arm around the smaller one's shoulders.

He stopped in his tracks. The garbage bag hit a table leg and spilled its contents of fish heads and bones onto the shack floor.

He ought to have foreseen it, the chance that they would get together; he ought to have prevented it. Too late. The faces were solemn. Louise spoke, her eyes on Billie; then Billie spoke, her eyes on the plate in front of her.

"What's wrong with you?" Albert said. "You done dumped fish all over the place." He looked at Rob, then he looked to where Rob was looking. His eyes widened. He whistled.

"If I was you, I'd break that up fast," he said.

"What can I do? I can't go out there. You go."

"Are you crazy? It's not my women getting their information straight."

"Just go sit down with them, that's all you have to do. They'll quit if you show up."

"I won't. You got to do it yourself."

But Rob was already shoving him out the side door, pointing him in the right direction. "I'll owe you my life," he said.

"How about if you owe me a hundred dollars. I'll do it for a hundred dollars."

"This is serious," Rob said.

Albert meandered out among the tables, taking his time, pretending to be picking up saltshakers. When he got to their table, he spoke, and they looked up. Rob couldn't hear what he said or what they said. He muttered to himself, "Sit down," but Albert still stood, chatting. The women had backed off from each other, Louise leaning in her chair, Billie sitting upright. If Albert moved on, they would return to their talk. Finally, he pulled out a chair and sat with them. Rob breathed easier. He had no idea what Louise might say to Billie; but almost anything that she might say could be disastrous.

"Steady, Albert," he said. "Just sit steady, hold in there." Albert was talking, and then Billie interrupted. She said only a few words. Albert got up, collected some more saltshakers, and came back to the shack.

"Didn't work," he said. "Maybe you better consider a bus ticket to the next town."

"What happened?"

"She said—Billie said—would I mind giving them a few minutes' privacy."

"Oh, Jesus."

"How did you get yourself into this anyhow?" he said. "Told a mess of lies?"

"I didn't tell a mess of lies."

"How about two? Two would be enough."

"Maybe, I don't know." Rob was still watching them. Now Billie was leaning toward Louise, and Louise was listening. He put his hand over his eyes.

"Maybe they're talking about the weather," Albert said. "But it don't look like it. I'd have stayed except she didn't make any bones about it, nothing I could do but get up and go."

They waited in the shack. After another five minutes, Hank came back to the table, bringing Louise her jacket. She rose, and he helped her put it on. They left. Billie didn't move. She sat in her chair, looking at the plastic plates. She stacked three or four of them in front of her on the table, and stacked the plastic forks in a nest atop the plates. She watched the Ferris wheel make its last slow turn, and the band move its speakers and amps offstage and into a van, and the fish truck pull away, and the last of the teenage couples straggle in from the beach. Rob went to get her.

"Everything okay?" he said.

"Sure."

"Ready to go?"

She nodded.

All he could do was trust Louise. Billie seemed all right. In fact, she seemed better than all right. She took his hand. In the car on the way home she sat close to him, her thigh against his.

"It was a good fair," he said. "We raised a lot of money."

"It was a good fair."

"Are you crazy about me?"

"Yes, I am," she said.

When they got to the house, he followed her around, bothering her. He watched her brush her teeth. "Am I the man of your dreams?" he said.

"Yes, you are."

"But I need a shower, don't I? I smell like a flounder."

In the shower, he scrubbed himself. He washed his hair, scrubbed his fingernails, his feet. When he got out, he wrapped himself in a towel and went to fix Speedo's supper. He filled the bowl and opened the back door, but Speedo wasn't out there. Rob whistled. "Is the dog with you?" he called to Billie in the living room, where he could hear the television was on.

"His supper's ready," he said, coming around the corner with the bowl in his hand. The living room was empty.

"Billie?"

She wasn't in her room. She wasn't in his room. He ran outside in his towel. The truck was gone.

He managed to get his pants on and find his keys. Shirtless and shoeless, he leapt into the car. He drove fast, knowing if he could catch up with her, he could explain. Even if Louise had told her everything, he thought he could explain it so that she would understand, it didn't mean what she thought it meant.

But he had to catch her first. She would have driven down Tanglewood to Palm, then straight for the bridge. Twice he saw a pickup ahead and gunned it till he was riding the tailpipe and could see it was not Billie's truck. He blew his horn and passed, up to seventy now and closing the gap on the next pair of taillights. But he got all the way to the inlet without finding her. Across the bridge the road split in a triple intersection, and those roads then branched in all directions; he had no idea which she might have taken. He stopped in the middle of the highway, on the approach to the bridge. A car came up behind him and honked, but he heard only something very distant and dim; the car passed him. He rested his head on the steering wheel.

There was nothing he could do. Except one thing, which would not help him find her, but he did it anyway, making a U-turn, hardly seeing the road.

CHAPTER 17

e had thought he would never set foot in this house again. It looked altogether different from the house it had once been, the house of the parties, the house of Louise. He saw no lights. But both cars were in the driveway. He was a fool to come here, but in his panic and rage he didn't think of that. He was a fool anyway, already. He went up the new steps and rang the bell.

"Louise!"

He shivered on the back porch, still without shirt or shoes. The neighborhood was dark. He knocked and called her again, he howled and beat on the door. A light came on outside the basement rec room.

"What's going on?" Ernie said from ground level, but Rob only pounded on the door again.

"Louise! Let me in!"

Hank opened the door. He took one look at Rob and tried to close it, but Rob's foot was already in. The metal strip along the bottom of the door sliced his bare ankle, but he followed with his knee and swung the door wide.

"This is too much," Hank said. "You've gone too far."

"I have to talk to her." He sidestepped Hank and made it into the hall.

"You can't talk to her, and you can't come in."

"I promise, all I want to do is ask her something. Where is she?" He started moving back down the hallway.

252

"She doesn't want to talk to you," Hank said. "She doesn't want to see you."

Ernie was behind Hank. "What is this? What's the problem?"

"Louise," Rob called, brushing away Hank's hand on his shoulder. He kept moving, looking through doors. The rooms were dark. The kitchen was empty, the dining room empty. Before he got to the next door, Hank grabbed his arm but Rob pulled free and stumbled into the living room, on his knees. One dim lamp was lit, and in the chair next to it, she was sitting, her eyes on him. He got to his feet and dodged Hank's swing. He moved behind a sofa, panting.

"I'm calling the police," Hank said.

"No, don't," she said, frowning.

"I want you to tell me what you told her," Rob cried. "What did you say?"

"Well—I . . . I just told her the truth." Her voice was unsure and afraid. She didn't want to talk in front of Hank, but Rob didn't care. He was hardly aware of Hank's presence, or of Ernie's.

"Why, Louise, why?" It seemed to him that the house was spinning. "You made a promise to me," he cried. "You said no one would know."

"You don't understand." In the dim light she looked like a ghost of the real Louise. Her eyes were hollow, her lips uncolored. Hank and Ernie stood in the doorway. Rob put his hands on the back of the sofa to steady himself. He shook his head hard.

"But why? Why tell her? It wasn't for revenge, to hurt me," he said. "I know that."

"No."

"Or to hurt her."

"Of course not."

"Then *what*? What was it for?"

"But it wasn't for anything," she said. "I wasn't thinking clearly, she caught me off guard. I thought I could at least be honest with her. That was all. I could at least do that for her."

"You thought it was a *favor* to her? You knew—you had to know—that she would leave."

"Leave? Oh, no." She stood up. "I had no idea she would leave. I thought I—I thought she was just, you know, getting things straight. She seemed very—understanding. She—"

"Jesus, Louise, she's a *child*!"

Hank moved toward him.

"Wait, wait—" Rob backed away from him, looking at her. "You told her, really, *everything*?"

For the first time, she averted her eyes. She looked at the floor. "No. I only told her what she asked."

"But what did she ask?"

Louise looked at Hank, then toward the porch and the darkness. "She asked me if I loved you. I said yes."

Hank closed his eyes. Louise sank back in the chair. Hank turned away toward the window, leaving Rob's path to the door clear. He took it, heading for the still-open back door and the night air, bumping past Ernie on the way.

Louise called out to him, "I never thought she would go, Rob. I'm sorry. What can I do?"

He heard Hank say, "Louise. It's all right. He's gone."

He made it down the stairs, out of breath and making a low wailing noise against his will. Ernie was two steps behind him. In the sand Ernie caught up with him and spun him around by the shoulder. "Rob, what is—"

"Nothing to do with you," Rob said. Ernie wouldn't get it, Ernie in love with Rhonda and heading into life among the scrub jays. "You shouldn't have come up."

"What is it?"

"Billie's gone," he said.

"And that?" Ernie gestured toward the Camdens' house.

"That was the worst thing I've ever done."

Ernie didn't ask any more questions. "I'll drive you home," he said. Rob didn't object. They rode in silence, and when they got back and Ernie came into the house with him, he didn't object then, either. He seemed half conscious, aware only of one thing in the house—Billie's absence.

"I'm going to sleep here," Ernie said. "Where should I—"

"My room," Rob said. When Ernie had gone to bed, he sat at the kitchen table. It was clear to him now. Of all that Louise might have said, she had said, without knowing, the one thing to send Billie running. He could hear Billie's words: *Not that many people have been good to me.*

He thought he had been lonesome before, but it was nothing like this, back in the house that was empty of her. He was like a man who has been robbed of all that he owns, and can only sit and look around at the emptiness where his things used to be. He could not have predicted this grief, which was so big and dense that after awhile—after sitting at the table with his head in his hands for an hour—he jumped up as if to escape it; but everywhere he could think of to go was still a place where Billie was not. Everywhere, she was gone.

But what were those drops of blood across the kitchen floor? His head spun; he dropped to his knees to examine the trail, which seemed fresh, the spots still bright; and then he realized they were his own, from his cut foot. When he raised his head again, he saw the note on the refrigerator door, under the magnets.

He couldn't read it from where he sat, and he didn't immediately get up to take a closer look. He pretended for a while that it was a grocery list, or one of Billie's cryptic memos. But maybe it said, "I had to run down to the drugstore, back in twenty minutes." He bolted from the chair and grabbed the note.

"This is more complicated than we thought," she had written. And then, in her cramped handwriting, "Love, Billie." The little sharp letters (he remembered how she always frowned while she wrote, and the frown seemed to find its way into the writing) hurt his eyes. He should have crossed the bridge and taken one of the diverging roads, he might have picked the right one. He searched the house for the paper with Carlo's address and phone number, but it wasn't there. And then, at last, the wild swings between hope and despair stopped suddenly. What remained was neither. He lay down on the sofa, not wanting to see her bed, and fell toward the deep sleep that follows frenzy, realizing on the way that the dog—his starved-for-affection golden nigger fisherman dog—had gone with her.

For a week he stayed home, on the chance that she might call, but knowing she would not—knowing it for certain, as well as he knew any fact, the alphabet, the date of his birth. Then he drove the roads as Carlo had, looking for the pickup, but he did not know, as Carlo had known, the kinds of places she would be likely to choose. He tried the navy, well aware that Poe was not Carlo's last name, and that he would get nowhere. These were things that he did because they had to be done. After a week, there were no more of them.

Ernie watched him; Ernie was waiting for him to recover.

"Don't you have to go back to Gainesville?" Rob said. Ernie had been carefully avoiding the subject of Rhonda.

"I'm going," Ernie said. "In a couple of days."

Rob did his best to shape up, so that Ernie could go. For two days he made a show of eating food and opening his mail and watching television, pretending interest in all three. It worked, and Ernie left on Saturday morning. "I wrote down my address and number by your phone," he said, straddling the Harley. "And you're coming down next month, right? You'll be there?"

"I'll be there," Rob said.

2.

Pain can be overcome; cure is possible. There are measures one can take to hasten recovery, or at least to become functional again. But at the moment he could hardly move to and from the refrigerator, because of those magnets on the door. When he took them down he could feel the small release of force under his fingers. He needed to remove all souvenirs of Billie, and then engage his thoughts in something that had nothing to do with her.

And maybe that was the purpose of business and work. As Louise's house had occupied her, work is the thing we do to busy our brains and keep our hearts out of trouble. In the carport he found his long-handled compound-action loppers and his new shovel. He circled the yard, unable to start right in; instead, he went back to the old fig tree. He lopped twigs and then branches, pleased by the soft give of fig wood as the jaws closed against it; and the branches fell at his feet. Once again, it was hard to stop, and maybe he went too far. The tree lost its shape, and when he stepped back he could see that he had cropped it down to something meaningless. He went back to the fence and the vines, meaning to dig them all up, posts and vines and ferns. But all he could do was drive the blade once into the soft dirt next to the wooden root of a wisteria, up to its shiny hilt; and then he stood there, foot on the blade like a farmer distracted by some cloud or thought. He left the shovel standing on its own and went back inside.

Some pain cannot be tricked or cut away, but must be borne.

He put Speedo's bowl on the top shelf of the kitchen cabinet and closed the door.

He had once read somewhere that grief lasts a year. That could not be true; some grief is momentary and some lifelong. Maybe one year was the average. He thought he could get through a year, if it would just *start.* But time seemed stuck. Around him life went on, he saw it going on, saw his neighbors come and go, and the birds come and go (geese coming, swallows going), but all this movement seemed oddly false, as if the action in a play were to continue onstage long after the drama has drawn to a close; it was there, but it was no longer crucial.

After the second week, a refuse-collection contractor made the last of his pickups on the Isle of Palms, clearing the roads of the junked refrigerators and sodden sofas, muddy carpeting, ruined insulation, melted Sheetrock. From one end of Palm Avenue to the other, the shoulders were now clear, and back in the neighborhoods could be heard the sound of the big machines making their final sweep. Even though clear signs of the storm were still visible and would, in some cases, remain visible for years—one hundred years before the forest would be restored, if it did not in the meantime go up in flames, the drying pines making a giant tinderbox—nevertheless a visitor could come to the city and possibly never notice anything out of the ordinary.

He tended the yard, watered her vines, kept the bird feeders full. Huong asked him to sue an insurance company, and in exchange let Rob set up a phone and a typewriter in what used to be a bait shed next door. So he was a lawyer again, taking what business came in off the street. Insurance claims, some workmen's comp. He represented the convicted murderer James Swan before the parole board, and failed to gain his release; Swan's name would come up again in six months, but his chances didn't look good. The victim was a respected businessman, a loan officer manager, and the killing was not done in the passion of a moment but was premeditated over a period of weeks following the foreclosure of a loan and the eviction of Swan, his wife and his son from their twelve-thousand-dollar house.

Still, Rob was working on it. Albert was paying him, and for the other case as well, which was more complicated. Laws regarding the commitment of the mentally ill are purposefully vague. He had to get psychiatric evaluations of Mrs. Swan, for which doctors had to be paid. But there was a chance for release. The evaluations were good. One doctor went so far as to say there was nothing wrong with the patient. In fact, Maude had been to visit her, and was of the same opinion. Once Maude was enlisted in the cause, things looked up; no case could be hopeless if Maude was working on it.

Some days, however, there was nothing for Rob to do. He kept his office door propped open, sat behind his desk and looked out into the sparkling inlet. Anna brought him a seafood lunch in a paper bag. Albert stopped by after the end of a school day and complained about lazy high-school kids. Maude came, with reports on her plans for Ernie's wedding. But all his visitors stayed a bit too long, sneaking sidelong glances at him, asking once too often if he needed anything, wanting to know how he spent his time. He appreciated their concern, and wanted to allay their fears. He answered their questions and volunteered details that sounded healthy (his food, his work, his sleeping habits) and tried to look cheerful, especially with his mother, who had an eagle eye. But he must have looked worse than he thought. She came by to see him almost every day.

He wanted to explain what he had learned, which seemed important: when you reach the low point in your life, it is not as bad as you might have imagined, because it is the bottom and there is no danger of further decline. The worst that can happen has happened. There was a reassuring flatness under his feet, everywhere he went: in the city streets and the island roads, in the broad gray beach, part of which he could see through his door, beyond the parking lot and the inlet. His horizons were limited; he didn't seek any other worlds beyond this one. If he sought anything at all, it was the occasional moment—still rare but somehow easier to come by now, since he had left off striving—when he could tell that his few visitors and his handful of clients were in good shape themselves. He welcomed them, when they came.

And one afternoon, Louise came. She knocked on the open door and stuck her head inside, backlit by the bright sun. At first he didn't know who it was. She was wearing old clothes, jeans and a sweatshirt, her hair pulled back in a rubber band. He could hardly believe she had come to see him. He fell over himself trying to pull up a chair for her, apologizing for the smell of minnows and brine that still lingered in the room. She smiled, nodded, assessing surroundings as usual.

"Pretty bad, huh?" he said.

"It's good. Maybe it could use a window, but otherwise—it's good. You're open for business?"

"You need a lawyer?"

"No. I just came to say hello."

"You look good," he said.

"Thank you. You look terrible."

"So they say. Fortunately, people don't choose their attorneys on the basis of good looks."

"I mean, you look thin and tired."

"I'm all right."

For a minute he feared she was going to suggest some sort of rehabilitative program for him. He still knew her well enough to read her signals, and she was touching her chin the way she had when she gave him the vitamins and the cookbook. But she said nothing, and he was grateful.

She stayed ten minutes. She looked beautiful again, healthy and calm but quieter than usual, as if she had been both strengthened and weakened. He felt like a hospital patient being visited by an old friend: he was glad of her visit, but his illness was a gap between them. She was well, he was not. At least he was pretty sure she was well, in her jeans and sandals, her hair its own color; she hadn't gone off on any tangents.

"Do you want to know anything?" she said.

"Ah," he said, unable to respond, briefly under the impression that she meant the big things, the answers to the mysteries of the universe, and panicking because he did not want to know them anymore.

"He took me back," she said. "I'm okay now. I came to tell you that."

He looked out the open door toward the blue sliver of water in the distance.

"You can see the ocean from here," she said, leaning forward in her chair.

"Do you need anything?" he said.

"No. Do you? Is there something I can do for you?"

He searched his brain; she wanted an assignment, but he could think of nothing. "Nothing except come see me again," he said. "Would that be all right?"

"It would be, yes."

She set her wooden pocketbook on her knees, her hands folded on top of it. "So you work every day? And then you go home?"

"That's about it." Here he could elaborate, give her some details that would make his existence sound regular and okay. "I'll lock up in a little while and walk home along the beach, and when I get home I'm going to grill a hamburger, read some files, go to bed. That's what I do."

She nodded and stood, pushing her hair back from her eyes. He stood, and she held her hand out, in a gesture that was not quite a handshake, the palm slightly upturned, and he took it. Then she was gone.

He was true to his word. At five o'clock, he locked his door and began the walk home. He knew he looked odd, a man in a coat and tie walking at the water's edge, leaving shoeprints in the sand, but he wore the lawyerly costume every day in order to feel like a lawyer. On the beach new dunes were accumulating. Shorebirds ran along with the waves, but he didn't stop to try to tell exactly what they were.

At home he shook the sand out of his shoes and socks. In the orange light of sunset he lit his charcoal fire and watched it flame up, then sat in his chair to wait while the briquettes burned themselves down to embers. He sat in the last of the autumn sun, looking out into the neighborhood. He had the feeling that something had once been meant for him, and he'd missed it, had somehow slipped off the track of it. But who can tell what was meant? He was here now.

He expected nothing in the way of reward or penalty, and so saw nothing in the small, expectant movements about him (the wind slow tonight but now and then rippling suddenly colder, ruffling the oleander, setting the vines and ferns aquiver). He saw no portents. He was thinking of nothing, sitting out behind the house, his back to the door. Nothing when a car stopped in the street and a door slammed; when a dog whined, and the sun sank away. He only sat, hunched. Anyone watching would have seen a man who appeared to be deaf and blind, waiting for a fire to burn out.

While behind him the girl stood in the grass, waiting. He didn't know for a long time that she was there, her backpack slung over one shoulder, and the dog sitting at her side.

It was like her to wait—she was not eager to surprise him, she was hesitant. But when he turned and saw her, standing solemn and thin with her eyes fixed on him, he could tell she was there for good.

Louise denied responsibility. "I found her," she told him later, "but that's all. I didn't even suggest that she come back; it was her idea. Don't thank me." From the phone number in her appointment book, she had tracked down Carlo, and together they'd hunted for Billie using Carlo's method of combing the county; they found her at a playground, children hanging on her skirt. They brought her home. They let her out in front of the house and watched her go in.

"And then what?"

Side by side (he bought a new chair; she likes to sit with him and hear the tale again, how the girl came back that day) they lounge, the dog between them, the sky white and cold.

"Then, finding the house empty, she wandered out into the yard, and stood there, thinking, Oh, his head is balder than I thought it was."

"No, tell it right."

"She stood there wondering if the license was still good."

"Right. And then what."

"Then he looked around and saw her."

"And what did he think?"

"He thought—" He looks at her legs outstretched, heels of her tennis shoes in the grass, toes up. "He thought it was you," he says.

To say more (girl of my dreams, love of my life) would not be enough. She is not his reward, she is pure gift, and no more meant for him than the marsh or the birds lifting from it and stretching thin to a line in the sky. But he may see these things awhile; he may see her.

"And it *was* me," she says. "It is me."